Auraria

AURARIA
TAB STEPHENS

atmosphere press

© 2024 Tab Stephens

Published by Atmosphere Press

Cover design by Kevin Stone

No part of this book may be reproduced without permission from the author except in brief quotations and in reviews. This is a work of fiction, and any resemblance to real places, persons, or events is entirely coincidental.

Atmospherepress.com

To Tommy and Sharon Wimberley,
who fed my need for fantasy and sci-fi books
through countless trips to Abilene and Fort Worth
in the late 1970s and early 1980s.

N
TUNDRA
ELVES
LEILANI
MONSTERS
AURARIA
GOLDEN
VORLAND
FOLSOM
LLANOS
DALELANDS
TARONTO
VIVERNA
CRATER LAKE
POLIS
NORTHERN
OSMAN EMPIRE

PROLOGUE

Logan, the Crown Prince of the Kingdom of Llanos, was smiling. All his careful planning and months of work had resulted in today: the day that his niece, Princess Elisa, would die.

Elisa was the last major obstacle that blocked Logan's ascension to the crown. Her demise would spell doom for the political faction that supported his brother, Prince Miller. Miller, who would be unable to prevent the death of his own daughter, should soon see his supporters desert him. Those same supporters would then have no choice but to submit to Logan.

Logan had arranged for Elisa to undergo a trial by combat to provide a public spectacle. While another noble had brought the charges of treason against Princess Elisa, Logan would be seen as the mastermind who accomplished Elisa's death. In the future, no one would have the courage to resist him.

If Logan was lucky, Elisa would break down in public and ask him to spare her life. However, such a display of despair was unlikely. She was made of sterner stuff than the rest of their family, except Logan himself, of course. If only she had seen the wisdom of capitulating to him. Oh, well; any last defiance would serve as high drama for the crowd.

Logan chose to walk to the coliseum where the trial by combat would be held. He wanted to feel the energy and excitement of the citizens of his capital city, Taronto. He was not disappointed. As appropriate, no one dared meet his eyes, but he could still sense bits of admiration mixed with healthy doses of fear. His subjects knew their place. He would rule them strictly and wisely when he became king.

Logan soon arrived at his seat. In a stadium box below him, Princess Elisa sat restrained for all to see. Her magic powers were bound, and heavily armed guards both watched her and kept an eye out for any who might aid her. Elisa was powerless.

With difficulty because of her restraints, Elisa turned to face Logan. Her steady gaze and calm demeanor belied her condition. "Welcome, Uncle. What a lovely day we are having."

Logan suppressed the rage he felt inside. Elisa was talented at getting under his skin, but he refused to show his anger. "You say the day is lovely? Only one of us will see it that way."

Princess Elisa smirked. "Agreed." She turned away from the crown prince, dismissing further conversation with him.

Logan felt his anger grow, and he barely kept it in check. He could not afford to take the bait Elisa had tempted him with. The little witch was planning something, but nothing she could do would prevent her demise.

The coliseum was ready, and the city bellman moved into position. The show was ready to begin.

CHAPTER 1

The coliseum was overflowing with spectators. The gladiatorial fights had awakened the appetites of the bloodthirsty crowd. Now it was time for the main event: the trial by combat for Princess Elisa. Princess Elisa stood accused of treason against the Kingdom of Llanos. If the trial found her guilty, her life would end tonight.

The city bellman made his announcement to the crowd. Magic amplified his voice so all could hear. "Oyez, oyez, oyez! This trial by combat is now in session. The accused is Lady Elisa, Princess of Llanos and daughter of Second Prince Miller. Lady Elisa stands accused of aiding the witch Sarai, her aunt, in the destruction of the Council of Mages earlier this year. The Council sought to bring Sarai to justice for her crimes. The Council succeeded in killing Sarai, but many brave mages fell in battle to the witch's dark magics and evil treacheries.

"The accuser is the virtuous and forthright Count John, whose eldest son fell in battle against the witch. Count John did see Lady Elisa aid the witch Sarai with his own two eyes!

"For the safety of the citizens of our great city Taronto, Crown Prince Logan has decreed this trial by combat. Lady Elisa is known to all as a wielder of powerful magics, the same as Sarai, and she is strong enough to sway a trial by court away from the righteous hand of justice. Fear not, good citizens. Lady Elisa's magical powers have been bound. She cannot weave mischief today."

The city bellman was not trying to hide his bias toward the accuser, Count John, nor his hatred of Princess Elisa. The country of Llanos was ruled by King Friedrich, who had three legitimate children: Sarai, Logan, and Miller. Sarai had been excluded from the chain of succession during her teenage years. This left Logan and Miller as bitter rivals for the throne as the heads of their own factions.

The nobility knew the real reason for Sarai's death—she had supported Miller for the throne, and Logan had her killed. Nothing could be proven, of course, which left Logan blameless.

Sarai had proven much more powerful than expected. She died, but she took nearly every senior mage within the city with her when the Council of Mages' building imploded six months ago.

This current farce of a trial was Logan's latest effort to undermine Miller. Most of the city's commoners liked Princess Elisa, and her death would weaken support for Miller. That said, commoners filled the coliseum. A death match between nobles was rare entertainment.

A drum roll began. "Now entering the arena, the champion of the accused, Dame Lily, a recently minted knight and a follower of the Earth Goddess."

Most of the crowd was surprised into silence. Prince Miller, Elisa's father, had a very strong stable of fighters under his command. Choosing this unknown fighter, and a woman at that, to represent his daughter? Was Prince Miller already conceding the fight?

Dame Lily approached the middle of the field, bent down on one knee, and placed her palms on the ground in the prayer form used by Earth Goddess followers.

The drum roll started a second time. "Now entering the arena, the champion of the accuser, a man who needs no introduction, Lord Orlando."

The crowd gasped as Orlando entered the arena. They had expected Count John to have a powerful champion, but the fighter known as "Mr. Invincible"? Orlando was the top-ranked duelist in the world, as well as a high priest of the War God. His record was 103–0. He had never lost a professional fight. Miller must have gotten word that Logan had secured Orlando as the champion. Miller was just cutting his losses. Elisa and her champion would both die today.

Orlando was a flamboyant fighter and loved to play to the crowd. He would toy with his opponent for several minutes to give the crowd a good show. Then he would destroy her with a flourish.

Now that the champions had been announced, the crowd was given ten minutes to make bets with their favorite bookmaker. There were no takers at 30:1 odds. The bookies had to increase the odds to 100:1 before there were sufficient people willing to bet on Dame Lily. Most of the bets for Lord Orlando focused not on if he would win but how: the number of strikes he would need to disarm Lily or the amount of time he would need to exhaust her. All the bets for Lily came from spectators sitting in one section of the stands. These were the people who knew her personally, having fought and trained with her in the past.

During the time for placing bets, Dame Lily continued to pray in silence, readying herself for battle. Lord Orlando taunted her mercilessly, describing what he planned to do to Lily both during the battle and after, once he had claimed his victory. He promised her a slow and painful death unless she surrendered and submitted to him. Then she could live as his servant. The unruly crowd had come to see blood, and they cheered each of his insults. Orlando finally ceased his act a minute before combat started. He cast his enhancement magic and personal combat spells.

The betting period expired, and the mages around the edge of the field signaled that the barrier wards were in place and working. Since this trial involved two magical knights, the wards were needed to keep the spectators safe. It would also allow Orlando to use his more powerful magic, which was always a crowd-pleaser. For the combatants, it would ensure that neither received outside help, putting Dame Lily at an even further disadvantage. Such was the wisdom of the crowd.

The city bellman called the two champions to attention. "This trial by combat will be decided when one of the combatants surrenders, is incapacitated, or dies. If Dame Lily wins, then Princess Elisa will be deemed innocent, and she will decide the fate of her accuser. If Lord Orlando wins, then Princess Elisa will be put to death this evening for crimes against the crown. Let the trial begin!"

Lord Orlando immediately closed in on Dame Lily and unleashed a blistering set of attacks. He was armed with a greatsword and mercilessly struck her extremities. His speed and grace with the massive weapon were well known, and he did not disappoint the crowd. In the face of these attacks, Lily was fully defensive. She was armed with a sword and shield, and she used both to ward off the attacks. The onslaught forced Lily to give ground until her back touched the wall. Orlando stopped the attack, and he returned to the middle of the field. He called out to the crowd, and they responded with cheers. He was enjoying himself, and he wanted the crowd to have fun as well. Lily slowly followed him back to the center of the field. Her previously pristine armor was now dented, and splashes of blood dulled the surface.

In the stands, the accused and accuser's boxes were near each other. Count John was a mediocre fighter, and he saw Lord Orlando as having the clear upper hand. John decided to taunt Lady Elisa. She was a great beauty. It would be a shame to see her life end too soon. "Lady Elisa, your champion fares poorly, and she will soon be defeated. I am a merciful man, and I am willing to intercede with the Crown Prince on your behalf. I will ask him to spare your life if you are willing to become my slave. We will have to permanently bind your magic, but you will get to live and enjoy my attentions."

Elisa turned to face John. She was calm and composed. "Such a kind offer, sir. I would be willing to accept if you also accept my counteroffer. If my champion wins, I will not put you to death. I will take your eyes, for they make you see things that do not exist. I was never at the Council's building, you see. I will also take your tongue, for it only tells lies. What say you, sir? Do you accept?"

If Elisa's plan was to send John into a fit of rage, she succeeded. He could barely talk for all the fury radiating from him. "I will accept your offer, you witch. I will show you no mercy!"

Elisa turned to Crown Prince Logan, whose box was above them both. "Dear Uncle, is our agreement acceptable to you?"

"If you wish such a life, then I will grant it. Death would be kinder."

"Thank you, Uncle. Oh, I see the action is about to resume," replied Elisa.

Back on the field, Orlando faced Lily. "Are you ready, little girl?" taunted Orlando. Without waiting for an answer, Orlando savagely attacked again. The result was the same. Lily withstood his attacks, but she was unable to attack him in return.

Orlando returned to the middle of the ring for a second time. He had brought many weapons with him onto the field. They were in a rack on his starting side of the arena. He placed the greatsword on the rack, then selected a longsword and dagger. To the inexperienced spectators, his change appeared part of his act. The knowledgeable observers saw it differently. He had twice attacked Lily using all the skill, strength, and speed he was known for. She and her equipment had suffered, but not nearly as much as they would have expected. He normally removed limbs with such attacks. She suffered dents in her armor and minor wounds to herself. Orlando had not achieved the success he expected, so he was changing tactics.

Orlando's third set of attacks on Lily exchanged brute strength for speed and precision. He aimed for the joints in her armor, trying to penetrate the weak links and disable her limbs. The speed of his attacks was so swift they were difficult to see. Lily was clearly outclassed, and she only blocked one attack in four. The rest landed on Lily as Orlando intended. However, they seemed to have little effect on her. Against these lighter weapons, Lily stood her ground. Orlando barraged Lily for more than a minute, finally jumping back several feet when his sword shattered. His face was covered by his helmet, so his expression was unobservable. He stood staring at the immovable fighter in front of him. His body posture changed. He finally began to take the fight seriously.

Over the next few minutes, he attacked Lily with a series of weapons—a mace, a spear, and a battle axe. Each failed to land a solid hit against Lily. Even the crowd now understood that despite all the attacks, Orlando was unable to seriously wound the unknown female knight.

Orlando was getting desperate. It was time to unleash his greatest weapon. He grabbed his mighty greataxe, a weapon he had once used to split an ogre in two. He readied himself, called loudly on his god for aid, and then sprang toward Lily. Powerful lightning coursed through the axe as he brought it down upon his opponent. His follow-through split the earth in half, sending shockwaves in all directions. The impact had briefly blinded him, but his sight soon returned. He looked at the ground for his handiwork.

He was puzzled by what he saw. There was no broken body and shattered armor. Instead, chunks of rock littered the ground as if his blow had destroyed a statue rather than a person. Oddly, the vibrations in the earth had not stilled. Standing was becoming increasingly difficult.

Orlando heard a voice behind him. "Looking for me?" Orlando spun to face Lily. The unwieldy weapon and the shaking ground proved his undoing. He lost his footing and fell on his back.

Lily stood five meters away. The ground under her feet was still. Everywhere else on the field, the ground buckled and bowed. The surface of the field had become an angry sea.

Orlando, even with his greatly enhanced strength and agility, was unable to stand. The ground grabbed at him, holding him. He would break one arm free only to have his legs tightly restrained. Wave after wave of ground attacked him, draining his endurance. Finally, his struggles grew weaker, and he succumbed to the earth's deadly embrace. His body disappeared beneath the surface.

The crowd was silent, save for one man who screamed, "No! It was not supposed to happen like this. You promised he could not lose!"

Count John was losing his mind to fear, and those near him carefully ignored his screams at the Crown Prince.

Lily waved her hand, and the lifeless body of Orlando returned to the surface. She removed her helmet and turned to face Crown Prince Logan. In a clear voice, Lily declared, "The trial is over. Princess Elisa is innocent. Release her!"

Logan stared at Dame Lily. His anger was legendary, and his ego immense. The impudence of a mere knight to order him. His stare grew more intense as moments turned into seconds.

On the field, Lily slowly turned in place, calling out to the crowd, yelling, "Release her! Release her!" and the crowd took up the chant. Within seconds, the chant was deafening.

Finally, Logan nodded, and the magical bindings holding Elisa were released. Ignoring the Crown Prince, Elisa called out to the crowd, "People of Taronto. This matter is now resolved. Thank you for your support." She left the coliseum without saying another word.

Princess Elisa and Dame Lily walked side by side through the streets of Taronto. Lily was still covered in debris from the battle. Elisa's fine clothing was stained red from when she had tended to Lily's wounds. Crowds parted before them, so they walked unimpeded. Word of their victory had preceded them.

Their well-wishers were subdued, and their distractors were silent.

The coliseum lay on the edge of the Government District. The women's path took them through the gate into the Commoners District and finally through another gate into the Merchants District. Their destination was the Taronto Water Gardens, their temporary home since the sacking of Sarai's estate months before.

The Water Gardens was a unique location within the city of Taronto. Several parks covered the outside grounds, while a mansion contained both spas and hot spring baths. A number of rooms were available for guests, with the most spacious of these containing private baths. The Water Gardens had been in continuous operation since its founding by an elf hundreds of years ago. The king at the time gave the location as a reward, creating sovereign elven land within the city. The facility was now open to the public since the elves became reclusive within their own nation. Nevertheless, a person of elvish descent managed the facility, with the current proprietor being the female half-elf Galene.

Galene met Elisa and Lily at the door of the mansion. Concern clouded her beautiful features. She accompanied the pair to their room, then shut and barred the door from the inside. She spoke a few words in a beautiful language, and a brief shimmering covered the walls. "The wards are up. We are secure now," announced Galene.

Lily collapsed to the floor, supported only by Elisa. The fight and the stoic walk home had consumed the last of Lily's endurance. With Galene's help, Elisa moved Lily to the bathroom and began to remove her armor and clothing.

Galene and Elisa were both talented healers, but their skills were put to the test. The physical wounds were easy enough to fix. The issue was the number and severity of poisons that Orlando had deployed on his weapons. Elisa had expected this treachery, and she had prepared both pre- and post-fight treatments for Lily. An hour passed before both healers were confident that Lily was no longer in harm's way. They cleaned and fed her, then put her to bed. She needed sleep to recover.

Once Lily was safely asleep, Elisa finally permitted herself to feel the emotions that were tightly wound inside her. Rage at her enemies and disappointment in her family lost to the fear of almost losing her best friend. Elisa's small body shook with these emotions and tears. Galene hugged and comforted her while Elisa purged herself of these negative emotions. Eventually, the tears dried, and her calmness returned.

Elisa went to refresh herself while Galene made them tea. The two women sat in the living room, far enough away from Lily to not disturb her but close enough to respond if they were needed. Elisa calmly retold the story of the fight to Galene. Now that Sarai was gone, Elisa was left with only two people she could trust: Lily and Galene.

Elisa rose and hugged Galene. "Thank you. Without your kindness, neither Lily nor I would have survived these last few months. You put yourself at risk by sheltering us."

"Your aunt was my friend. I honor her memory by aiding her star apprentices in the few ways that I can. As for danger, woe unto the humans who threaten elves and elvish property." Galene took a sip of tea. "Have you decided what you will do?"

"Today's victory will buy us a small amount of breathing room. Even Logan will have trouble finding another sycophant to attack us after today. I want to give Father one more chance. His prediction of the trial was faulty. Had I used his champion rather than Lily, then my head would have parted from my shoulders. He seeks to appease Logan too much, and I fear his habit will worsen if I leave. My brother gives him good counsel, but Father sometimes does not hear.

"Unless I can get stronger support from Father, my options for staying in Llanos are limited. I don't want to leave, but I fear it will become necessary. As for my options outside the country, only the marriage offer from Prince Ryne of Vorland is tempting. I met him five years ago at my coming-of-age party. He interviewed me for his nephew, who could not make the trip. Ryne is much older, but he is smart and handsome and the only interesting man that I met. Unfortunately for me, he was already married then. He has gone through much since we last met.

"If I cannot sway Father to take a more aggressive position against Logan, then I may take Ryne up on his offer. My next contact will be tomorrow evening. I'll make my decision then."

"Sleep well tonight, Princess. In the words of my people, 'May your choice lead you to joy.'"

CHAPTER 2

A small, blonde-haired woman entered the private hot spring from her hotel room. Tall stone walls surrounded the bath, separating her from the rest of the visitors but allowing her a view of the night sky. The noises of the city were absent; the wind carried the sounds of nature from the nearby park.

Having cleaned herself, the woman slowly lowered herself into the water, enjoying the warmth as it flowed over her skin. Princess Elisa of Llanos sighed. Whereas yesterday was filled with danger and fear, today was filled with frustration. Her conversation with her father, Prince Miller, had yielded mixed results.

In private, Miller had admitted he had not taken the threat to Elisa's life seriously enough. He had promised to increase security for all their family members, including her. Elisa had pushed her father to take a more aggressive stance against his brother, Prince Logan. Miller had refused, as he feared King Friedrich, his father, would see the change as a threat to his legacy. King Friedrich refused to view Crown Prince Logan in a negative light. This allowed Logan's bad behaviors to go unpunished.

"Come join me, Lily," Elisa coaxed.

"On my way, Princess," replied Lily. She was a tall, powerfully built, extremely fit young woman. Short, unruly brown hair covered her head. Her looks were plain and made more so by her proximity to the gorgeous princess. Clad only in a thin robe, she circled the tub, looking for dangers, both magical and mundane. "I told you to wait until I finished my inspection."

"I checked the area twice and reinforced the wards. Some of us are just faster than others," teased Elisa.

"Let's see how long it takes you to remove full armor, Princess," grumbled Lily. She exhaled a deep sigh, then removed her robe and entered the tub. For a warrior of her stature, Lily had remarkably few scars. That was Elisa's doing. After each injury, Elisa carefully healed her best friend. Once, Lily had tried to explain that men thought scars were interesting, as they often asked to see hers. Elisa had died laughing and explained the scars were not what held the men's interest. Lily had blushed deeply when she realized what Elisa meant. Lily then ceased to complain about the healing treatments.

Her teasing done, Elisa continued in a more subdued and serious tone, "That is why you are my best friend. You know me, and yet you still love me." She slid over to sit next to Lily. The two women enjoyed a few minutes of tranquility.

Elisa began to contemplate leaving Llanos and the changes it would incur. She was now twenty years old and had been an adult since she turned fifteen. Had she been a typical royal daughter, she would have married a foreign prince years ago and produced heirs for him. Instead, her Aunt Sarai had recognized Elisa's potential to be more than just a political bride. Elisa had been admitted at age six as an acolyte to the temple of the Earth Goddess. Sarai had wanted to send her directly to the College of Mages, but Miller refused. Such a move would have overshadowed Elisa's brothers. The temple had been a compromise. A princess who could cast fertility and healing magics would make a fine prize indeed.

By age nine, Elisa's magic power and knowledge had approached that of the head priest. The clergy had resented the princess prodigy. Fearing that Elisa's growth would falter, Sarai had sought a rival for her niece and recruited another prodigy. The six-year-old Lily had been an orphan with a massive mana pool and remarkable drive. The temple had been unable to refuse admittance to Lily since Sarai recommended her, but the child had not shared the benefit of Elisa's status. Where Elisa only attended the temple during her lessons and training, Lily had lived there. The other trainees could not take their anger out on Elisa, so they had punished Lily instead. Before he passed, Lily's father had been a royal guard, and he had taught his daughter to stand up for herself. However, the determination of a young girl was no substitute for size and numbers. The other trainees had ganged up on Lily to abuse her.

Elisa had been one of the few students to befriend Lily. Elisa had been upset by the way the other students treated Lily, and she had offered Lily the protection of her name. Lily had refused. The young orphan had intended to overcome the older students by using her own strength. Elisa had been inspired by the younger girl, and they had begun training their magic together. A year later, the two had become close friends, and Lily had been able to handle her detractors by herself.

In addition to her magical strength, Lily had shown promise as a warrior. Elisa then had an epiphany. Elisa had been approaching the age where she would need guards loyal to her, rather than relying on her father's protection. Lily had been excited by the possibility, but her options were almost nonexistent. Female warriors were rare, and the Knights' Academy was unwilling to accept female applicants.

Elisa had been undeterred. In the first successful business negotiation of her young life, Elisa had made a deal with the Varangian Guard, the mercenary group that protected the Merchants Guild and its Trade Hub. The Guard was based in Taronto, and it constantly trained its members to increase their skills. This training led to injuries, so the Guard had to hire healers as well. Elisa's deal: in exchange for admitting and training Lily, Elisa and Lily would work as healers for the Guard's headquarters.

Prince Miller had been adamantly against the deal. A princess of the kingdom should never consort with common soldiers, much less mercenaries. Elisa had argued that their family might need a quick source of talented warriors, and she would be able to make those contacts while training. The second successful negotiation of Elisa's life had been forcing her father to accept her deal. Thus, the ten-year-old Elisa and the seven-year-old Lily had been made junior members of the Varangian Guard. Elisa had split her free time between the temple and the Guard. She also had to continue developing the skills of a noble lady and royal princess. It had been agreed upon that Lily would live at the temple and train in both locations. Finally, the Guard would have to pay a retainer to the temple for the use of their healers. This had made the head priest happy as well.

The next two years had passed swiftly for the girls. Initially, they had been treated as a novelty, more like mascots than members of the Guard. This had changed as they interacted with more Guard members and their reputations grew. Both Elisa and Lily had taken their responsibilities seriously. Their magical talents were first-rate, and their presence during practice sessions had allowed the instructors to push their pupils past weapon drills and into aggressive simulated combat.

Elisa's status as a royal princess had been an open secret among the Guard leadership. While nominally treating her as a member, they had taken her security seriously. Concerned that her status would be a distraction, Elisa had suggested that they use her as the VIP for advanced bodyguard training. This had proved useful for both the Guard and Elisa. The Guard had received free advertising for their services—who wouldn't trust bodyguards elite enough for a royal princess? In turn, the princess had been free to move through the city, an unheard-of luxury for a noble female her age.

Where Elisa had received the royal treatment she deserved, Lily had been treated like any other recruit. Since the Guard normally only admitted experienced warriors, their indoctrination had been particularly harsh on the young, inexperienced girl. Weapon training, physical fitness, and group combat had filled her time when she was not the on-call healer. To the surprise of many, Lily had thrived in the Guard's environment. She had found her people.

Elisa's magical skills had continued to develop, and her negotiation skills had grown as well. The Varangian Guard leadership had grown aware of Elisa's unique ability to gauge people. She could sense truth from lies and uncover hidden intentions. If she invested mana in her senses, her skill grew immensely, allowing her to see magically hidden bonds and spells as well. This latter effect came at a cost. Her eyes would glow with a light of their own, making her use of magic obvious. The Guard leadership had begun adding Elisa to contract negotiations. She had gained experience dealing with a wide range of people. The Guard had benefited from the additional assurance their clients were dealing honestly.

Since the Varangian Guard and the Merchants Guild were so closely tied, the Guild had learned of Elisa's skills and had accepted her as a merchant apprentice, and soon Elisa had found herself mediating negotiations for both groups.

Lily's skills had grown as well. She had focused more on combat magics, quick spells that required large amounts of mana. Her physical abilities had continued to grow. Puberty had yet to dawn, but she had already grown taller than Elisa. The princess was going to be tiny like her Aunt Sarai. In contrast, Lily took after her late father. Sarai had teased that Lily would soon tower over Elisa like a mighty oak sheltering a delicate flower. This had annoyed Elisa greatly.

During this time, trouble had been brewing for Elisa. The noble girls of Taronto were expected to socialize with each other frequently. Elisa had fulfilled her required attendances, but she had preferred the rough environment of the Trade Hub over the refined parties of the future debutantes. Many of these noble girls had been jealous of Elisa for one reason or another: her rank, her beauty, and her freedom. They had nicknamed Elisa the "Errant Princess" and told lies about her in her absence. Still, Elisa was a royal princess, so they had dared not take their vicious fun too far.

When Elisa had been twelve and Lily nine, their lives had changed dramatically. A scandal had torn through Taronto, and Elisa was dragged into the drama. A baron loyal to Prince Logan had tried to cheat a Merchants Guild member. The member had been a foreigner from the Dalelands. Within their own country, nobles had great leeway in how they dealt with commoners. In this case, the Merchants Guild was independent of all countries, and the Dalelands would not take kindly to their merchants being mistreated.

As Crown Prince, Logan had the authority to settle the dispute, but if he had decided in favor of his baron, the leaders of the Dalelands would have been offended. However, the prince had to protect his vassal to ensure the continuing loyalty of his followers. Logan had needed a scapegoat to provide a favorable decision and also be responsible for the fallout from the aftermath.

Logan's niece, Princess Elisa, had seemed perfect for Logan's scapegoat. She was a high-ranking noble, which gave her the power to render decisions despite her young age. Even better, she had been apprenticed to the Merchants Guild, so she directly belonged to the mediating third party. The final and best part had been that any decision she reached would be attributed to her father, Prince Miller. Logan would be absolved of any blame.

Logan had been very happy with his choice, and he had moved quickly to install Elisa as the arbiter. Unfortunately, the prince had not consulted with those advisors of his who were most familiar with the young princess. Soon, Logan would bitterly regret his choice.

While Elisa's magical skill was well known among the nobility, her cleverness and negotiating skills had not been.

She had spent the previous two years observing and interacting with master merchants from across the continent. Whereas the average Llanos noble considered dealing with such commoners to be distasteful, the princess had eagerly learned. The Merchants Guild leaders had recognized her skills despite her age, and they had helped refine her abilities.

Logan's second mistake had been not understanding Elisa's sense of justice. During her inquiry, she had uncovered a web of deceit that included the baron, a group of smugglers, and shipments of tainted food that could have sickened or killed hundreds of people. The whole scheme might have gone unnoticed had the baron just dealt honestly.

Elisa had convened a public hearing to present the findings of her investigation. The princess had done this after careful consideration. Sarai had warned Elisa that she would face Logan's wrath if she did not suppress the discovery. Elisa had decided to release the information anyway. The corruption of the baron and the barely avoided disaster of the tainted food had been too important to silence.

The hearing had been well attended due to the novelty of a child presiding. Elisa had praised Logan's foresight for rooting out corruption in the kingdom, then proceeded to detail all the crimes the baron and the smugglers committed. Prince Logan had sat calmly during the meeting as he accepted Elisa's findings. He had been in public, so he had kept his rage carefully contained. The prince had been outmaneuvered by a twelve-year-old girl. Her praise of him had kept him from striking back at her. With respect to the baron, the prince's hands had been tied. The baron had lost his head the same day.

Elisa's conduct during the hearing had gained her both new admirers and new enemies. Elisa had been praised by the Merchants Guild for her honest and thorough investigation. The citizens of Taronto had respected her for the concern she showed for the common people. The nobles of the city had seen it differently. While still a child, Elisa had exposed the secrets of the noble class. She was dangerous; Elisa seemed a royal in the mold of her aunt.

A week after Elisa had reported her findings, she and Lily had both been promoted to priestesses, then summarily removed from the temple school. The parents of other noble children attending the school had pressured the head priest to remove the two girls. The nobles had not wanted their precious children to be exposed to such radical individuals.

The expulsion had left Lily without a place to live. She had earned her place within the Varangian Guard, but the barracks were not set up for a nine-year-old girl. Sarai had come to the rescue. She had invited Lily to live with her, and Lily had gratefully accepted. Elisa had become jealous, and she convinced Sarai to accept her as well. The princess had moved in a few days later.

Home life had been strained for Elisa before this. She had notified her father before she released the report. Miller had objected, correctly predicting the report's effect on her own reputation. Miller had conflicted feelings about Elisa. He had been proud of her strength and independence, but he had feared her inflexible sense of justice would cause her harm. Father and daughter had agreed a change of scenery would be good for her.

The next three years had been wonderful for Elisa and Lily. They had continued their work for the Varangian Guard and the Merchants Guild, and Sarai had instructed them in new types of magic. Sarai had expected both girls to split the household chores equally. Lily's home life had improved, her chores limited to caring for the three of them, while Elisa's home life had worsened. She no longer had maids to meet all her needs.

Sarai had considered Elisa's education as a noble female to be complete. Elisa would still have to attend required royal functions, but she would not have to deal with the young noblewomen who mocked her behind her back. Once Elisa had started living with Sarai, the petty rumors increased. Elisa had not cared. She had finally found a home that made her happy.

Life with Sarai had never been boring. They had often traveled incognito on little "trips," as Sarai had called them. These "trips" always had a purpose, had often been dangerous, and had led the girls to amass many skills. The legality of several of these "trips" had been questionable at best, but since they were never caught, who cared?

Miller had continued to grow concerned about Elisa's marriage prospects. She should have been engaged years earlier. Prince Miller had received complaints about Elisa's lack of decorum, but these had contrasted with the compliments he received for her work with the Merchants Guild and Trade Hub. She was carving her own path through life, much like his sister Sarai had done before.

King Friedrich and Crown Prince Logan had not been amused. A royal princess was a negotiation tool, allowing countries to forge new bonds or strengthen existing ones. Elisa's skills and knowledge made her quite the catch, but potential grooms had been wary of her. Elisa was rumored to be uncontrollable and free-spirited.

Logan needed to remove the princess from Taronto permanently. He and several of his vassals had found their business opportunities limited by her helping run the Trade Hub. Marrying Elisa to a foreign ally was the best option. It would both leverage Elisa's social position and remove her as a thorn in the prince's side. The question had been how to find someone who would accept such a troublesome princess.

To solve the issue, the Llanos royal family had held a Bridal Faire during the week of Elisa's fifteenth birthday. The event had been publicized a year in advance, and prospective noble brides and grooms from all over the continent had traveled to Taronto to participate. The Trade Hub had run the Faire, with Elisa taking the lead as chair of the event.

The Bridal Faire had been a rousing success, and the Trade Hub had agreed to run the event every three years. Noble families had been happy to forge new bonds across national borders. Merchants had been happy, as the Faire had provided a central location for them to show their wares meant to make wedding days special. King Friedrich had been happy, as the event brought a massive influx of new revenue. Only Crown Prince Logan had been unhappy. Over thirty potential grooms had turned down their chance to marry Elisa.

There had been one bright spot for Logan. Much of the success of the event had been attributed to Elisa's leadership, so she had been moved into management of the Trade Hub and away from the rank-and-file work of the negotiation mediators.

Another three years had passed, with Elisa turning eighteen and Lily fifteen. Lily was then an adult and a full member of the Varangian Guard. Prince Miller had granted her knight status as guardian for Princess Elisa, so she became Dame Lily.

Puberty and hard work had transformed Lily into a tall and powerfully built young woman. Since her path had not been through the Knights' Academy, her skills had remained a mystery to the public at large. Elisa had tried to talk her into competing in tournaments, but Lily had declined. She did not want personal glory. Her Guard colleagues had acknowledged her strength, and she had been able to stay with her best friend, Elisa.

Where Lily had kept her talents hidden from the public, Elisa's fame had continued to spread. She had led the following triannual Bridal Faire to even greater success. Elisa had been lauded far and wide as the organizer of the event.

Crown Prince Logan had been furious. Elisa was gaining popularity equal to his own. His anger had grown when he realized that the princess did not participate, citing her responsibility in running the event. The entire purpose of the Bridal Faire was to get the princess married. In Logan's mind,

Elisa was maneuvering to keep herself in Taronto. She was revealing herself as a threat to his path to the throne.

Logan was a man capable of spontaneous, violent outbursts. Fortunately for him, he had advisors capable of planning for the long game. Elisa was protected by Sarai—therefore, Sarai needed to be removed before Elisa could be addressed.

Logan's plan had come to fruition eighteen months later. Through his agents, he had secured strong allies within the Llanos Council of Mages. Money, favors, and threats had been exchanged to guarantee these allies, but at last, Logan had been ready to make his move. His plan had been to have the Council permanently seal Sarai's magic, making her unable to protect herself and Elisa.

Sarai had appeared before the Council twice a year to provide a report of her activities. She had been considered a member of the group, but her royal status had prevented her from taking a leadership role within the Council. Her power had made her dangerous, so she had been subject to review by the Council.

The morning before her appearance, Sarai had told Elisa and Lily that she was expecting trouble and that she feared Logan was involved. Elisa and Lily had both agreed to go with her, but Sarai had refused. Elisa's safety was important, and Sarai would not involve her. Elisa had pushed back hard but ultimately relented. The trio had known the dangers of political games. Placing both Sarai and Elisa in the same attackable location would play into Logan's hands.

Preparing for the worst, the trio had collected many of Sarai's most important books and treasures and placed them in an extra-dimensional space accessed by a magic bag. Sarai had entrusted the item to Elisa, then sent Elisa and Lily to stay with her friend Galene at the Taronto Water Gardens. The Gardens served as the Elvish embassy. Even Logan would not be so bold as to attack Elven sovereignty.

That afternoon, Sarai had met with the full Council of Mages. Twenty-two of the twenty-four senior members had been in attendance. The other two had been traveling. As Sarai had expected, the meeting was a trap. The leader had brought false charges against her, and he had demanded immediate action, citing the clear and present danger Sarai represented. The normal course of action would have been a thorough investigation and trial, but this had been a kangaroo court.

The leader had demanded that Sarai surrender, but she had refused. Barriers had been raised around the council room, locking Sarai into a battle against twenty-two foes. A handful of attendants outside the barrier had been witnesses to what had transpired.

The leader had again threatened Sarai. "Sarai, surrender now and face our justice. We will let you live."

Sarai had remained calm and composed as she surveyed the room. Had she faced two or three members, she might have had options. Instead, she had faced the combined might of the Council of Mages. Logan's hatred for her had known no bounds. Sarai had accepted that she would not get out of the room alive. Then her choice had been to take her enemies with her. It had become the time to make her final stand.

"Surrender so that you can seal my magic, rendering me helpless? That does not sound like much of a life," stated Sarai.

"You are trapped, witch. Surely you aren't so arrogant that you think you can survive against all of us. You are out of options."

Sarai had answered with laughter. "You misunderstand. I'm not trapped in here with all of you. You are trapped in here with me."

Her bold and confident statement had made the mages pause. Sarai had commanded the attendants to run, and they had felt the compulsion even through the barriers. They had run for their lives as the battle behind them had begun and had barely made it outside before a powerful surge of magic erupted behind them. A spherical detonation had rocked the building, imploding the inside of the building and all its contents. Only crumbling walls outside the blast had survived.

The implosion was the largest single disintegration that had been witnessed in modern times. A senior, accomplished mage could disintegrate an object the size of a turkey. Sarai had unleashed a spell unthinkable by modern magicians.

The loss of Sarai had been tragic for both Elisa and Lily. She had been their friend, mentor, and protector. When Sarai had left that day, she had said her normal goodbye. Sarai had expected to return that evening—worst-case planning had been something the trio normally did. Elisa had Sarai's books and materials, but many of them were magically locked. Had Sarai truly feared death, she would have told Elisa how to unlock those items. For the confrontation to escalate like it had, something unexpected must have occurred. Elisa had been at a loss to explain what had happened.

Logan's plan had led to Sarai's demise, but the cost had been bitter. The loss of the Council had been a massive blow to Llanos's safety, as the group of mages had acted as a deterrent to foreign powers who considered attacking Llanos.

The backlash from the Council's demise had bought Elisa and Lily six months to plan. They had used their time wisely. Elisa had strengthened her contacts with the foreign countries of the Trade Hub. The weaker countries did not dare defy Llanos, but several of the stronger ones had been willing to give Elisa sanctuary if she needed it. For Lily, the Varangian Guard was willing to spirit the women out of the country at a moment's notice. Elisa and Lily's scenario planned for several possibilities and generated contingencies for them all.

Two days before the trial by combat, Logan had finally made his move. Count John had made his accusation, and Elisa had been arrested. Prince Miller had been caught off guard, and he had attempted to intervene, but Prince Logan had stopped him.

Logan had wanted a public spectacle to ruin Elisa's reputation in addition to ending her life. Logan had decreed the trial by combat, knowing that Orlando was a much stronger fighter than anyone Miller could field. Logan would finally have his revenge against the niece his sister had given her life to protect.

Lily had been expecting Orlando to be her opponent, and she had planned accordingly. In a straight fight, she had not been strong enough to beat him. Fortunately for her, his success and sense of superiority had turned him into a showman. Logan's hatred of Elisa had played into this as well. Logan had instructed Orlando to ensure that Lily suffered slowly in front of Elisa.

Lily had taken the fight very seriously. She had expected poisons, so she took counteragents before the fight began. From the moment she had entered the arena, she had begun feeding mana into the ground to make the arena hers. She had used extreme levels of body-enhancing magic to withstand the brutal attacks by Orlando. Even with all Lily's preparation and careful execution, Orlando could have won the fight had he taken her more seriously from the start.

Orlando had already lost the fight by the time he had chosen his greataxe. Lily's command of the arena's surface had been complete. She had allowed Orlando to make his attacks before drowning him in the dirt. Lily had been sending her own message, and it was heard loud and clear. Lily had not won by a fluke or mistake. Orlando had given his best at the end of the fight, and she had crushed him utterly.

Elisa completed her musings. She and Lily needed to decide. They began talking through their options.

Staying in Llanos was no longer possible. While Count John had been the scapegoat for that, the loss of the trial by combat was another blow to Logan's pride. Logan would continue to threaten both of their lives.

Elisa despised the thought of leaving Taronto. She had built a life for herself within the Trade Hub, much as Lily had done with the Varangian Guard. Sarai had given her life so that Elisa and Lily could continue to live as they wished. Leaving Taronto meant admitting defeat to their mutual enemy, Prince Logan. However, it was clear that their lives depended on getting away from Logan and his allies.

They considered running off together to a foreign land far from Taronto. They had the skills to survive and prosper. While an attractive option, distance alone would not prevent Logan's revenge.

Elisa and Lily needed their own allies at a safe distance from Taronto. They had three options, with the last being a surprise. Prince Ryne of Vorland had offered marriage rather than just refuge.

Elisa had last seen Ryne at the first Bridal Faire. Prince Ryne had upset some of the nobles with his informal ways, but she appreciated his straightforward and honest manner.

Four months after meeting Ryne, Elisa had learned that his dukedom had been invaded by monsters while he had been away. His city of Auraria had been lost to the invaders. His wife, children, and retainers were all dead. The Kingdom of Vorland had been able to keep the monsters from spreading further, but no headway could be made to recover the territory.

News of a resurgent Prince Ryne had reached Elisa two years ago. The broken leader had reforged himself over the intervening three years, growing personally stronger and assembling an odd group of powerful followers. He even counted a significant number of non-humans among his fold. The nobles of both Llanos and Vorland considered such associations highly inappropriate and even blasphemous. But no one could argue with Ryne's results. His small but capable group of adventurers began to win battles against the monstrous army.

Prince Ryne had continued to progress and had retaken his city of Auraria a year ago. His offer of marriage had arrived shortly after Sarai's death. Elisa's family had pushed her to accept the offer, but she had refused. Taronto was her center of power. The allies she had made through the Merchants Guild were here. Giving up all her work to become a political bride? The thought repulsed her. Only because she had amassed her own power, separate from her family, allowed her to refuse. Fortunately for her, Elisa did not need her father's support. She politely declined the offer of marriage, citing her need to remain in Llanos.

Last week, Mizu, Ryne's agent in Taronto, had contacted Elisa. The situation in Auraria had stabilized, and Prince Ryne was ready to receive her. Ryne wanted to announce their betrothal the following day. The timing and forcefulness of the offer was…curious. In retrospect, Prince Ryne was providing her a lifeline. The updated offer had occurred before Logan moved against her. Had Elisa taken the offer last week, this whole debacle might have been avoided, but she had delayed her response. Had Ryne known of the dangers that Elisa and Lily had been destined to face in Taronto?

Unlike the other two offers of refuge, Ryne's offer explicitly mentioned Lily in addition to Elisa. Delivered before the trial, Ryne's offer had complimented Lily before her fame had become established in Taronto. Some of her work for the Varangian Guard had benefited Vorlandish merchants, and the appreciation of those merchants had reached Ryne's ears.

This sealed the deal for Elisa. Lily was Elisa's chosen family, and Ryne understood that. Lily agreed, but only after teasing Elisa that she said the prince's name with a dreamy look in her eyes.

Elisa and Lily exited the bath, dressed, and started making plans. Hopefully their new life in Vorland would be calmer than the one they had shared in Llanos.

<hr />

Two days after Elisa's acceptance, the Kingdom of Llanos announced Princess Elisa's betrothal to Prince Ryne of Vorland.

As neighboring countries, they were often at odds with each other, resulting in many skirmishes over the years. The kings of both countries hoped this marriage would make the peace permanent.

Surprisingly, a week after accepting Ryne's offer, Elisa and Lily found themselves imminently leaving Taronto and heading for Ryne's city of Auraria. This was highly unusual for royal betrothals—they normally took months or even years to plan. A new royal marriage allowed for reaffirming current alliances and forging new ones. New trade treaties and military support agreements were commonly negotiated during the betrothal planning. None of this took place for Princess Elisa's betrothal. Prince Logan was using his power as Crown Prince to remove Elisa from Llanos as soon as possible.

Logan made his hatred of Elisa clear in two additional ways. The first was the composition of the princess's escort. A princess had to be guarded and supported on her trip to her future husband. Normally, the king would provide strong security by dispatching a squad of royal guards. The princess would then use her household staff for her personal needs. Logan disrupted this process. Arguing that the loss of the Council of Mages placed Llanos at high risk, Logan successfully kept the royal guards in Taronto. Prince Miller provided the guards, but even then, Logan was successful. The leader of the chosen escort guards was a young knight loyal to Miller, and the complement only contained ten competent fighters. The escort should have been many times larger, as the princess would travel through dangerous locations. However, a larger number of guards, more experienced leaders, and more capable soldiers were not permitted.

To add insult to injury, Logan forced a compromise on the personal support staff: half were from Elisa's household, and the other half were chosen by those loyal to Logan. On the surface, this did not seem to be a great issue except for the inclusion of Lady Philippa as a lady-in-waiting. Philippa was a known detractor of the princess. She was chosen to cause mischief within the group. However, as the first daughter of a count, she could not be summarily dismissed. Beyond Philippa, the maids and attendants selected by Logan also could not be trusted. They might be spies or worse.

The second way Logan interfered was through the princess's dowry—the payment that the bride's family pays to the groom's family at the time of marriage. The dowry for a royal princess should have been paid from the royal treasury. Logan successfully argued with King Friedrich to prevent the release of funds, his reasoning being that Llanos needed to keep the money to rebuild the Council of Mages through an aggressive and expensive hiring campaign. Freelance mages, the best talent available, were difficult and costly to recruit.

Prince Miller offered to pay the dowry, but Elisa refused. She argued that Miller would need his money in the future and said that she would take care of the dowry herself. When pressed for details, Elisa refused to answer.

Prince Logan caught wind of Elisa's decision, and he assumed she meant she would use Sarai's wealth to pay the dowry. The kingdom had seized Sarai's estate soon after her death, but no great riches were found in her residence. Logan concluded that Elisa must be hiding the wealth somewhere, and she would take it with her when she left Taronto.

Prince Logan and a squad of royal guards confronted Princess Elisa and Dame Lily just before they left the city. Logan demanded that they surrender any and all magic items. Such items were the property of Llanos and were not to leave the country, he insisted. A royal mage conducted the search, and only a single item was found: an extra-dimensional pouch. Logan seized the magical pouch. He surmised that it must contain the wealth that Elisa had hidden. The prince was unable to open the bag. Elisa explained that it was enchanted against thievery. The bag would not open for two full months—the time that the trip was expected to take. Forcing the magic bag open would destroy it.

Elisa asked for the pouch's return, as it contained a great deal of riches. Logan refused, claiming that such wealth was the property of Llanos. Lily offered to intervene, but Elisa stopped her. A confrontation here might lead to the spilling of royal blood. Elisa relinquished her claim to the magical pouch, and the princess's escort left the city.

After a week of travel, Princess Elisa's escort group stopped for the night at a waystation along the main road. The waystation was already occupied by a merchant caravan from Taronto headed toward the Polis city-states. The caravan had suffered damage to one of their wagons, and they had spent the last two days repairing it, but they were now ready to depart in the morning. After some discussions, the two groups decided to travel together for mutual protection. They were headed in the same direction for the next week. The escort's leader, Sir Aden, did not like the idea initially but was convinced once Lily mentioned she knew several of the men who were guarding the caravan.

Meeting the caravan was not a coincidence. Elisa and Lily had arranged for a group of trusted people from the Merchants Guild and the Varangian Guard to meet them once they were clear of the city. Whether Lady Philippa or Logan's other spies believed it was a chance meeting did not matter, as they had no grounds to refuse the princess. For some of their remaining time in Llanos, Elisa and Lily would be surrounded by allies.

Seeing Lily with her fellow Guard members made Elisa both sad and envious. The part of her that cared for Lily was sad—she was taking her friend away from her extended family, the Varangian Guard. Elisa wanted to be happy for Lily that she had such friendships, but the princess admitted, at least to herself, that she was envious of Lily. A royal princess could trust very few people with her innermost secrets—Lily was all that Elisa had left. Her merchant contacts were business relationships—trusted, but not friends.

Elisa, fighting the bitter taste of envy, continued to watch Lily. Lily was an introvert who hid her emotions from others.

She was the perfect guard and protector in public. But here, surrounded by her Guard friends next to a campfire, Lily was alive. These were her people—the surrogate older brothers and uncles who had raised her since she was seven. These men respected her as both a friend and a colleague. Lily was safe in being herself around them. She told bad jokes and got groans in response. Her Guard friends understood her sarcastic sense of humor and replied in kind.

The night before the two groups parted ways, one of the merchants handed Elisa two magical pouches. These were the items that Prince Logan had tried to find. One contained the books and papers of Sarai, while the other contained the newfound wealth that Elisa and Lily had made during the trial by combat. During the trial, the only spectators who had bet on Lily to win were her friends from the Guild and Guard. Through their friends, Elisa had done the same with her wealth. If Lily had lost, both women would have died, so Elisa had gambled it all.

The trial had made both women, along with their colleagues, quite wealthy that day. Some of the money had been used to buy useful magic items that the women now owned. The rest had been kept for their travels and destination.

As for the pouch Logan seized, well, it did contain riches, at least as defined by two priestesses of the Earth Goddess. The fertilizer was rich with nutrients that would grow many fine plants. The bag was set to explode when the thief-deterrent magic expired. This form of fertilizer distribution magic was well-known within the agricultural community. Leaving the bag inside an enclosed space, such as an office or home, was a bad idea. Unfortunately for Prince Logan, this form of magic was unknown among his servants.

Chapter 3

The man moved swiftly over the broken terrain. He smelled smoke from the direction of Viverna, a village near the Vorlandish border. He was still several kilometers away, so the smell was not from cooking fires. As a scout for the Vorland army, he needed intelligence quickly so his captain could respond to the potential threat. With a sense of foreboding, he accelerated his pace.

The army company based out of the city of Wincheesh was tasked with escorting a foreign noble through Vorland. The captain had provided a few details at the briefing that morning—no significant danger was expected, the escort was more of an honor guard, and the noble would be arriving the day after tomorrow at Viverna. The company expected to arrive in the village by dinnertime. The scout had taken a shortcut through the countryside to arrive at the village first and alert the local garrison.

A herd of deer scattered at the scout's passing, but he was already over the next hill before the deer began to move. Running as fast as he could, the scout reconnected to the main road at a vantage point above the village. Viverna lay one kilometer away to the southwest, and the village was on fire.

The scout touched his forehead and routed magical energy to his eyes. He enabled sight-enhancing magic to survey the scene before him. It was worse than he had thought. A large group of monsters had swarmed the village from the northwest. Goblins and wolves composed the smaller, quicker troops—several scores of them. A quarter of them were already in the village. The goblins moved in small packs, like puddles of putrid green color, spreading fire and destruction in their wake. In contrast, the wolves moved in tightly organized packs, efficiently killing villagers who struggled to get away.

Farther back from the village, a pack of ogres—nine, no, ten of them—was visible. These creatures were twice as tall as a large man. Unlike the poorly equipped goblins, the ogres were both heavily armed and armored. Even worse, they moved in a rough formation, and they would likely fight as a team. The identity of their leader was obvious. At the end of the group was a giant, his head and chest clearly visible above the trees around him. His bellowing voice shouted orders to his troops. The scout could hear him clearly, even this far away. The village was not facing a simple attack by a stampede of monsters. It was facing annihilation from the horde.

The scout cupped his hands to his mouth and infused the air in his lungs with magic. As he spoke, the air carried his words to his captain far away. Such magic was seldom available at the company level. "Scout William reporting. Viverna under attack; a hundred-plus goblins and wolves, ten ogres, one BF giant. Heavy damage. Using stealth into village for further assessment. Over." A gust of wind carried William's words to his captain.

Moments later, a second breeze brought the reply. "Captain Refren replying. Company proceeding with haste. Estimate one hour to village. Foreign noble is princess. If present, save at all costs. Out."

The foreign dignitary was a princess traveling in their country. Death or injury to such a person could easily start a war. Protect the princess—his direct orders aligned with his hidden ones.

His orders clear, William cast a series of battle spells. His senses expanded, and his agility increased dramatically. The sun was still high in the sky, so shadow magic would be of little use, but the smoke and confusion would aid his stealth. He pulled a well-used longbow and readied his arrows. He might need his secret weapon, but he did not want to show it needlessly to prying eyes. He moved quickly to the village, using the terrain and trees to hide him.

He began encountering scattered goblins and wolves at the village's edge. Wolves were consuming fallen prey while the goblins began to loot and then set fire to the houses. William felt the anger burning inside him, but he kept his mind calm and focused. Attacking the monsters now risked alerting them to his presence. William decided it was worth the chance. He needed a clear path out of the village if he had to retreat. That would be his reason for engagement if he was questioned later. Not the small, lifeless body he saw the wolves fighting over.

William needed to deliver one-shot kills quickly and consistently lest he be overwhelmed by the monsters. A headshot was the best option, but performing this feat on dozens of monsters would require accuracy that a normal archer could not achieve. The arrows left behind would threaten to expose his hidden identity, but he had to take the chance. The battle would be over before the army company arrived. He would have to rely on his magic to keep him veiled.

Weapon ready, William got to work. The bowstring sang ten times in the next ten seconds. Ten fallen foes littered the ground.

William steadily moved toward the village center where the church of the Earth Goddess stood. Any survivors still in the village were likely within its stone walls. A few more monsters crossed his path and were dispatched. William could hear the ogres and the giant approaching. They seemed to be headed to the church as well.

Taking cover behind a damaged building, William surveyed the church. More than a score of wolf and goblin bodies covered the ground before the main entrance. A lone knight in heavy armor with a shield and a sword stood on the steps. Blood covered the knight's armor. The person looked exhausted. A semicircle of a half dozen wolves was arrayed before the knight, patiently waiting to attack.

William could hear more monsters moving toward the church; the ogres and giant would arrive soon. Time was precious. William moved forward, firing arrows as he ran.

Dame Lily stood on the church steps. A pack of six wolves approached her slowly, watching and waiting for her to drop her guard. A dozen of the monsters lay dead around her, a temporary wall of flesh, hide, and bone to protect her flanks. Nearly a score of goblins covered the ground farther from Lily. They had thought distance would give them protection as they filled her with arrows. The goblins were dead wrong—emphasis on *dead*. Dame Lily was a holy knight dedicated to the Earth Goddess. She was deadly with both sword and spell. However, she had protected the church entrance for the last half hour. Her mana, her magical power, was nearly exhausted, and her body ached with fatigue.

Lily debated casting healing magic, but she decided against it. Unlike her previous foes, this pack of wolves would attack her as a group while she was distracted.

The stalemate did not last long. Both Lily and the wolves could hear more monsters heading toward the church. Lily's prospects were grim. The lead wolf lunged at Lily, who brought her shield up to intercept. The large creature slammed into her, but she held her ground. However, bracing against the attack pulled Lily's sword arm out of position and allowed a second wolf to bite and latch onto her. The second wolf thrashed violently, forcing Lily off balance. Sensing victory, the lead wolf launched itself at her head.

Lightning and thunder filled the area immediately around

Lily. Both wolves were thrown back, stunned. Lily resumed her guard position and moved to dispatch each wolf. Two quick sword swings resulted in two more dead wolves. But what of the other four? Now shifting her focus to living foes, she was surprised the rest of the pack had not taken advantage of her fall.

To Lily's amazement, the rest of the pack was dead, a single arrow lodged in an eye of each of the wolves. The source of the arrows was sprinting toward Lily. Covered head to toe in green clothing, the small figure carried a bow with an arrow at the ready. A blue armband signified the Vorlandish army. Lily had to stop herself from attacking the archer. As a neighboring country, Vorland was often at odds with her country of Llanos. However, Lily was escorting Princess Elisa of Llanos to meet her future husband, Prince Ryne of Vorland. At least, that was the public reason for the trip.

While the archer might not have been her enemy, Lily did not drop her guard. She would watch the archer closely. The risk to the princess was too high.

The archer arrived at the church steps and positioned themself on the top of the stairs near the doors. "Protect me while I'll cover you," the archer requested. Their voice was higher pitched than Lily had been expecting. Given their size, perhaps the archer was a woman or a young boy.

Lily was uncomfortable having her back to a potential enemy. However, she had no more time for thought as the next pack of wolves and goblins arrived.

Dame Lily had trained extensively in group combat with the Varangian Guard, but having close support from an archer was new to her. Even if the archer was friendly, one misstep by Lily could result in an arrow through her back. The archer seemed aware of this as well. The shots were well-aimed, and none of the arrows were anywhere close to Lily. For her part, Lily tried to keep her sideways movements small and focused. She used her shield against goblin arrows while the threat of her sword kept the wolves out of melee range. In short order, this wave of foes was dispatched.

"We have a few moments before the next set of enemies arrive," the archer stated while pulling three potion vials from a pouch at their waist. The archer handed two to Lily, then drank the last one themself to prove the potions were safe.

Trusting her instincts, Lily drank both of the gifted potions. She was surprised by the taste—it was not like the vile concoctions she normally used. Her pain lessened, her wounds began to close, and her mana began to recover. While not enough for a full recovery, Lily was much improved. Her surprise at the potions' effectiveness must have shown on her face.

The archer laughed, saying, "Good stuff, huh?" The archer suddenly grew serious. "Is the princess here, and is she safe?"

Lily flinched. Why would a foreign soldier know about Elisa?

"I'm part of Vorland's escort for the princess," the archer replied in response to Lily's distress.

"Yes, she is safe inside the church with the rest of our security detail. Many of the villagers are inside as well. We considered fleeing the village, but the church appeared to be the best option," Lily answered.

The archer visibly relaxed. "Praise the Goddess," they said.

Lily found this response comforting.

"I need to report this to my captain." The archer cast a messenger spell, using the wind to carry words back to the army captain. They stood close enough to Lily for her to overhear the conversation.

"Scout William reporting. Princess confirmed in village—currently safe but village under heavy attack. Two defenders left. Need reinforcements ASAP. Over."

A few moments later, the response came. "Captain Refren replying. Protect the princess at all costs. Failure is not an option. En route to relieve you. Estimate fifty minutes. Out."

"The Vorlandish escort company is headed here as quickly

as they can, but the two of us will need to hold this position," the archer stated grimly.

Lily agreed with their assessment.

The archer continued, "The bulk of the monsters, and the strongest of them, will converge on us soon. Attacking them will be foolhardy—"

"I will hold this position with or without you. None shall pass!" Lily passionately interrupted.

The archer's face broke into a fierce grin. "Foolhardy and the stuff of legends."

Dame Lily felt a massive wave of confidence. She would almost certainly die here today, but she would die with zero regrets. Lily thrust her arm out to the archer. They grabbed each other's forearms in the greeting of warriors. "I'm Lily."

"I'm William," was the reply.

Ah, so a young boy, thought Lily.

William surveyed the area. "This respite is too long. We should have seen the next wave of monsters by now. They are likely massing for a single large push." William's tone was thoughtful and calm as he relayed the dreadful news. "We are not going to survive without help. I have items and spells that will help us, but I need to keep their origins secret, even from my captain," he continued.

William made an odd gesture with his left hand. His well-worn bow disappeared. Reversing the gesture produced a different bow. This one looked more like a living tree branch than a polished, curved stick of wood. Lily raised one eyebrow in response.

William looked at Lily's battered sword. Her magic had taken a toll on the blade. With his free hand, William flicked his wrist again. A scabbarded longsword appeared in his palm. "Please take this. Just give it back when we are done. It is a loan from a certain prince."

Lily unsheathed the longsword. She felt an odd sensation. The hilt was changing to fit her hand. The blade shone with an icy gleam, and the air around Lily became cold and refreshing. Lily's eyes grew to the size of saucers. She had seen magical swords before, but she had never held one. The touch was invigorating.

"Finally, I can offer magic that will help us fight together. It is called Battle Awareness. Do you consent?" His gaze was steady as he sought her answer.

"We've just met, and you are already asking for consent? Most guys at least buy me dinner first," Lily answered with a grin.

William had clearly not expected her response, and his calm demeanor broke. He snort-laughed, then rolled his eyes.

Lily, with a grin, said, "Yes, let's do this!"

William once again held Lily's forearm in a warrior's embrace. He whispered a spell in a foreign language familiar to Lily. The sound of the language was beautiful and clear—it was Elvish! Lily's exhaustion disappeared, her senses sharpened, and her mana became stronger. She closed her eyes and could hear the nervous heartbeats of the villagers inside the church and the rage of the monsters approaching. Her spatial awareness expanded. The spell complete, William let go of her arm and backed away. Even with her eyes closed, Lily knew precisely where he was. Lily opened her eyes. This magic was incredible.

Combat was imminent, but Lily wanted to offer one last prayer to the Earth Goddess. As she began her prayer, William joined her. His words were different, but the two prayers meshed well. As their prayers ended, a red, glowing tendril of light linked the two. They looked at each other in confusion. Neither had expected the light.

Suddenly, the tendril of light pulsed brightly. For a brief moment, Lily knew the totality of William: mind, body, and soul. Her mind struggled to comprehend what was happening. Images—some were memories while others were clearly dreams—flooded her mind. The images flashed by too quickly to follow. The next moment, the light vanished, and Lily's mind returned to normal. She staggered forward from the release of the mental pressure. William caught her...no, he had staggered forward as well. They had bumped into each other and remained standing, like two drunks leaning against each other. A look of utter shock covered William's face. Lily was sure it was a mirror of her own. They needed several seconds to recover.

What was that? Lily heard William say, but his lips had not moved. Lily was concerned but hesitated to ask.

"That was...odd. The prayer seemed normal," he continued. Noticing Lily was staring intently at his face, he asked, "What?"

Can you hear my thoughts? Lily thought.

William's eyes got very big. *Yes,* was his stunned reply.

Does your spell include telepathy? Lily asked.

No, this is very...unexpected, William answered.

Telepathy magic existed but was extremely rare. The spell required great familiarity between the participants, such as blood kin. Even lifelong friends would find telepathy difficult to achieve. Near-total strangers would find it virtually impossible. Nevertheless, a strong magical bond had been forged between William and Lily. Lily could feel the panic in William's mind. He truly did not understand what was happening. As her own stress level began to rise, she felt him clamp down on his emotions with an amazingly strong will. His mind was clear, and he was focused on the immediate problem—the battle with the monsters.

Dame Lily and William were out of time. The monsters began their attack. The final battle for Viverna began.

The monsters' plan was simple: throw wave after wave of goblins and wolves at Lily and William until the pair drowned in a sea of foes. The lead wave of monsters was pushed forward by the wave behind, so there were no long pauses when each side could catch their breath. The ogres and the giant began throwing housing debris at the church, as timbers and chimney stones were plentiful in the demolished town. However, their attacks were futile. Dedicated to the Earth Goddess, the building was well-constructed and fortified with strong magic. The obvious weakness was the front doors to the church. The ogres and giant switched to attacking Lily and William in between the waves of smaller monsters.

During the first minutes of the battle, the magical bond was far more of a hindrance than a help to Lily and William. Had they previously trained together, they might have been unimpeded, but they had literally just met, so they struggled. The bond between the two was evolving in unexpected ways, and their coordination suffered.

At the beginning of the second wave, a lucky wolf scored a bite on Lily's sword arm. The pain she felt was less than expected, but it caused William to miss his shot. William felt an unexpected pain in his arm as well, and a small wound appeared. The bond was causing damage to be shared by both, with each receiving a portion of the wound. While the sharing might allow Lily to not die if she received a fatal injury, an attack that caused Lily to become unconscious might affect William the same, preventing him from rescuing the downed knight. Lily and William were now bound by a common fate, and it forced the archer to fight more defensively than he otherwise would have.

So now we share pain and injury...I wonder if the reverse is true, William thought. He cast a quick and simple healing magic—a minor personal heal. The magic was less effective than normal, but Lily gained the benefit as well.

Lily, I'm going to split my time between healing and archery. Try to keep the monsters' attention. I'll make sure you remain battle-ready.

William's thoughts remained calm and composed, and Lily decided to continue trusting their shared fate in his hands.

Will do, she replied.

The second evolution of the magical linking was in the way their telepathy worked. At first, it seemed only strong thoughts—similar to talking loudly—were exchanged between the two. But as time passed, less effort was needed. Their minds merged the mental link into a shared mental space.

Their combined thoughts became muddled, and mental focus became difficult due to the distraction of the other's thoughts. William switched to thinking in Elvish, but that did not help enough. Mental-strengthening magic, useful against charms, proved useless against the mental link. This concerned William greatly as he was quite resilient against mental magics. The bond was already working inside his mind, so external protections did not work.

The final evolution made the mental distraction even worse. They began to share each other's senses. Seeing the world through another person's eyes sounds great, but not when one's brain must process two different images at once.

Lily now shared William's senses of smell and hearing, which were much sharper than her own. He had to be good at ignoring the putrid odors from the creatures near him to retain as much focus as he did. The foul smells made her want to retch. As for hearing, the sounds of battle were now much more intense and intruded on her focus.

William did not escape the increased distraction either. Lily had spent the last several years training her tremorsense—detecting moving creatures through vibrations in the earth. Unlike sound, which is received by the ears, tremorsense is received through the feet or other body parts in contact with the ground. Where a normal Earth priest could use tremorsense to identify a basic location—and in fact, William knew which spell to use for that—Lily's mastery allowed for pinpoint accuracy of her foes. Lily was used to the strange sensations being transmitted via her feet. To William, it felt like he was stepping on large numbers of sharp rocks.

All three evolutions held much promise if they could be mastered, but on the battlefield against a superior force, a distraction could prove fatal.

After almost being overwhelmed by the last wave of monsters, in a fit of desperation, William used his stealth magic in a novel way. Stealth magic was normally used to hide by confusing an opponent's senses. William instead built a mental wall to isolate his thoughts from Lily. This quieted their shared mental space, allowing them to focus again.

Fifteen minutes had passed in the battle. Most of the goblins were dead, and only a dozen wolves were left. While there had been a massive loss of monstrous troops, the plan to exhaust Lily and William was on pace. The ogres began to close in on the pair.

The ogres were each four meters tall and protected by crude, heavy armor. A couple of the ogres wielded clubs, but the remainder carried more advanced weaponry, such as massive swords and axes. The ogres' size would prevent more than three from attacking the pair at a time, but the blows from their weapons were terrifying. Single-shot or single-blow kills would no longer be possible. Each ogre would require multiple hits to kill.

In an act of desperation, William took a gamble. As the battle progressed, each of his quick healing magics became more effective. The shared bond no longer seemed to be splitting the healing between the pair. He wanted to see if his personal body-enhancing magic would follow suit.

William communicated his idea to Lily. She agreed. Lily needed to protect him for the next ten seconds. Lily changed her stance against the remaining wolves to fully defensive. By no longer attacking, several wolves were able to slam and bite at Lily at once. The combined weight of the creatures shoved her back several meters and threatened to knock her off her feet. Only through a surge of incredible effort did Lily keep the wolves from overwhelming William and herself.

Lily felt a tingle of excitement in her spine as William finished his spell. Her movements were quicker and more refined.

The movements of the monsters seemed to slow in comparison. William's body-enhancing magic had affected her as well.

Not to be outdone, Lily asked William to cover her. He flipped over her head at the precise moment that she fell back. The two had switched positions, with William in a melee stance and Lily behind him. The wolves immediately launched themselves against William, swarming the lightly armored archer. Even with his enhanced agility, William could not avoid the mob and protect Lily at the same time. The wolves' coordination was truly impressive. One wolf bit and attached itself to his bow while another lunged at his neck. One from each flank bit and grabbed his arms. But none of the wolves understood the fierce smile on his face. William disappeared under a pile of wolves. The last pair prepared to launch themselves over the wolf pile to attack Lily.

A moment later, an explosion rocked the front of the church, detonating away from the doors. Lily stood unscathed, and William was wolf-free. An area twenty meters from the doors was wiped clean of foes, living and dead alike. William was panting heavily, and the mana cost of the spell had been extremely high, but he had made a pause in the fighting. Lily got her ten seconds of protection.

Lily used her time to cast her best body-enhancing magic. The magic effects spread to William as well. He could feel his strength expanding and his skin hardening. "Whoa. Thank you!" he uttered in surprise. Stacking the effects of multiple body-enhancing magics should have been nearly impossible, but the two of them, together, did it with ease.

Lily and William shared a brief moment of hope. They were still horribly outnumbered, and the strongest of the monsters had yet to enter melee combat. Worst still, the ogres were displaying a high degree of combat coordination. These were not mindless creatures—they fought with purpose and direction. Even if Lily and William survived the ogres and lesser monsters, they would still face an insurmountable foe, the giant.

The hope the pair felt was not born from a certainty that they would win. Their future remained bleak. Instead, the confidence came from understanding that neither of them would abandon the other. The red tendril of light had exposed their souls to each other. Whatever the outcome of the battle, they would stand by each other to the very end.

A moment later, the giant threw a massive tree trunk at the doors of the church. The knight had to face it head-on lest the doors be breached. Lily intercepted the projectile with her body and shield, but the impact slammed her into the ground. The shared bond kept Lily from dying, but now both she and William were heavily injured. William began casting healing magic as Lily struggled to resume her guard position. The ogres poured into the church courtyard, their movement unimpeded by the corpses of the lesser monsters. The battle of attrition continued unabated.

CHAPTER 4

Captain Refren and the First Mounted Infantry Company of the Duchy of Wincheesh in the Kingdom of Vorland arrived at the edge of Viverna. The sounds of battle could be heard coming from the village center, and a massive giant was seen fighting something near the church. The company quickly dismounted, formed ranks, and began a quick march into the village. Captain Refren wanted to secure the princess as soon as he could, but moving too quickly risked encirclement by the monsters. They moved in standard formation: an outer screen of sword-and-shield fighters protected the company's pikeman.

The company's route followed William's path of destruction. The scattered goblins and wolves, each dead from an arrow through the eye, were initially a novelty but soon became a feature of the decimated village. Only the captain and the company's veteran soldiers seemed to notice. The rest of the company was focused on the battle unfolding before them.

Captain Refren stopped the company at the edge of the church grounds. A nightmare scene lay in front of the soldiers. The corpses of goblins, wolves, and ogres littered the area. Blood and gore seemed to cover every exposed surface. Three figures were still moving—a massive ten-meter-tall giant, a heavily armored knight with a glowing white sword, and an archer in Vorland's army colors.

At first glance, the giant's heavy, crude armor was largely

untouched—the thick metal could repel the attacks of even the strongest human warrior. The joints in the armor were a different story. It looked like the giant had fallen into a cactus patch—needle-like sticks filled every joint—neck, shoulder, elbow, and knee. The giant bellowed in pain with every movement. The archer circled the giant, adding more arrows to the joints.

When the company arrived, the giant had been facing away from them. As it swung its massive club where the archer had been but moments before, the giant turned, its face now visible. Both eyes were a ruined mess, and tears of red streaked the giant's cheeks. Its ears shared a similar fate. The sides of the creature's dark helmet were stained crimson. The archer's arrows had been delivered with inhuman accuracy.

The knight with the glowing sword was the star of this show. He was darting around the feet of the giant, attacking the ankles and legs, and narrowly avoiding the crushing impact as the giant stomped its feet. The glowing sword carved furrows in the giant's legs, painting both ankles and feet with the giant's blood. It was an awe-inspiring sight, and the soldiers stood entranced.

Captain Refren rallied his soldiers and moved them back to a safe distance. The chaos of the battlefield was extreme, and it was unclear how the company could assist. Still, he readied the pikeman at the front of the group. At a moment's notice, the captain could move his troops forward to engage the giant.

Something about the movements of the knight and archer did not make sense to Refren. It took him a moment, but then he realized the knight and archer were moving in perfect coordination, but neither had spoken a word.

Their next maneuver together took his breath away. Circling around the giant from opposing sides, the two met just behind the giant's right leg. The archer had stowed his bow and placed his hands before his body, interweaving his fingers in the form of a basket. The archer bent his knees in preparation for the knight. The knight approached at a full run, placed a foot in the archer's hands, and was launched high into the air by the archer's quick upward motion. The knight flew through the air and scored a deep gash in the back of the giant's already damaged left knee. The knight's landing was a bit rough, but he rolled out of danger and returned to running with barely a stutter.

The pair repeated their maneuver on the giant's right knee. The giant's joints were so damaged that its legs collapsed underneath it. The ground shook from the impact. The giant bellowed in pain as he thrashed his arms, desperately trying to destroy the knight.

Over the din of battle, the knight yelled, "ARE YOU VORLAND'S ARMY?"

Captain Refren yelled back, "YES, WE ARE."

"YOU MIGHT WANT TO MOVE BACK A BIT FURTHER. THIS IS MY FIRST GIANT, SO I'M NOT SURE WHERE IT IS GOING TO LAND!"

The captain ordered his troops to move back another thirty meters. While Refren noticed something odd about the knight's voice, the wisdom of the request was solid.

The knight and archer performed the aerial feat a third time, launching the knight at the now-reachable giant's neck. The sword flared with magic as it sliced. The giant made several guttural sounds and placed its hands on its neck to stop the bleeding, but to no avail. Fresh blood sprayed across the church grounds, painting the gruesome scene bright red. The massive creature's body began to convulse.

The knight flew through the air one final time, now landing on the giant's shoulder. With its head tilted forward, the giant exposed the back of its neck. Yelling "TIMBER!" the knight slashed the magical sword. The giant's head bounced several times as it rolled along the ground, finally stopping just outside the churchyard's gates.

A few seconds later, the giant's body toppled forward.

The knight remained on the shoulder, finally jumping off just before the tremendous impact shook the ground. After a graceful landing, the knight flicked his sword clean, sheathed the blade, and began walking toward Captain Refren.

Refren moved to meet the knight. Covered in the blood and gore of the giant and the other fallen foes, the knight looked like the avatar of a dark god. The captain's look of concern must have shown on his face, as the knight stopped suddenly, looked down at his body, and uttered a high-pitched exclamation. "Sweet Goddess!"

"Please forgive me, Captain, but my master would be very unhappy with me if I introduced myself in a state such as this. I just need a moment!" Without waiting for a reply, the knight moved back several steps, turned away from the army troops, and placed his gauntlets and helmet on the ground beside him. He raised a hand to the sky and uttered a single word. A sudden downpour of water fell from the sky, but only on the knight and his immediate surroundings. After a dozen seconds, the water stopped as quickly as it began. Much cleaner than before, the knight picked up his gear and turned to face the troops.

After making eye contact with the knight, Captain Refren had a sudden realization. The knight was female, not male. The tone of her voice and her movements in battle now made sense to him. The signs of her gender were subtle. Even with her helmet off, her armor hid the shape of the body beneath.

The captain's mission briefing had mentioned that the Llanos princess was guarded by a female knight named Dame Lily. The briefing had few details on her: besides serving the princess, Lily had served as a combat healer for the Varangian Guard.

The Vorland military tracked potentially dangerous individuals and groups inside the country and then assigned threat levels based on destructive potential. A normal combat healer would be considered threat level "low." Dame Lily's fight with

Orlando upgraded her to "moderate." However, after witnessing her prowess in battle, Refren planned to report back to HQ that her level should be upgraded to "extreme."

The smiling female knight bowed slightly to the captain. "Thank you for waiting. I did not want to make a bad first impression!" Once no longer obscured by the helmet, her voice was clear and pleasant. "I am Lily, a knight of Llanos and priestess of the Earth Goddess. Pleased to make your acquaintance."

There was an audible collective gasp behind the captain as the rest of the troops realized the gender of the knight. Refren turned his head and glared. His men went silent. He turned back to Lily. "I am Captain Refren of the First Mounted Infantry Company. Welcome to Vorland, Dame Lily. Rest assured, meeting you has been...memorable." He gestured to the giant's head, lying several meters away.

Lily responded with a mildly sheepish grin. "I need to check on the church."

"Understood. My troops will handle the mop-up actions. I need to give them orders, then I will be right behind you."

The captain turned to his lieutenant and gave instructions to secure the village. The company quickly and efficiently began executing its orders. By the time Refren finished, Lily was on the church steps next to the scout, William. Gathering a small group of guards around him, Captain Refren moved carefully through the churchyard to meet the pair.

The scout broke a piece of fruit in half, and he shared it with the knight.

"Oh, wow, this is so good!" exclaimed Lily.

William's voice was too quiet for Refren to hear, but Lily responded by shoving him and laughing. "What do you mean, 'that still only counts as one'? Look at the size of my giant!"

William responded.

With fake outrage, Lily declared, "Well, of course size matters!"

Refren halted and surveyed his nearby troops. Without

exception, each soldier had stopped what they were doing and was now trying desperately to contain their laughter. The tension and fear left over from the battle were wiped away in an instant. Dame Lily was a monster, but she also seemed friendly and somewhat naïve. As he continued his walk, the captain thought to himself, *Don't worry, Lily. You have made quite the first impression.* As they continued to move, one of the soldiers started cheering. He was soon joined by the entire company.

A few moments later, Refren arrived at the church. William addressed the captain, "Captain Refren, your orders were received and executed. The church has not been breached. Requesting permission to stand down." The scout's eyes no longer seemed to focus. He was well past his limit for exhaustion.

"Permission granted, William. Excellent job," replied Refren. "Dame Lily, my troops have secured the perimeter. You are safe to open the doors. I understand we are escorting a VIP of your nation. May we meet privately to discuss?"

Lily turned to the doors and hammered a series of knocks with her fist. A few moments later, the doors opened. The soldier inside recognized Lily and exclaimed, "Praise the Goddess!" Others inside the church echoed his words.

Princess Elisa was among the first to greet Lily at the doors. Elisa had spent the battle caring for the injured and worrying about Lily. Elisa knew she was in public and surrounded by strangers. Launching into the arms of her best friend was not acceptable princess behavior. She still considered doing it. Fortunately, the fiercely proud smile on Lily's face told Elisa that her knight was okay.

Princess Elisa shared introductions with Captain Refren, then asked him to speak with the recovering Sir Aden while she tended to Dame Lily. Refren was a man who could read the room—the princess needed a few minutes to confirm that her guardian was okay. Refren moved to the cot where Aden was resting.

Elisa began to lead Lily to the back of the church, but she

stopped dead in her tracks. Elisa trusted her intuition. There was an odd magic in the air, and she felt a tingle down her back. The princess scanned the area, looking for the source.

"Princess Elisa, I have a cut on my arm that I would like you to inspect," said Lily. Elisa turned to her knight. Lily was the type of person who would bleed out before she inconvenienced a noble. Lily was asking her to ignore the magic. Elisa did so, and the pair moved into the office at the back of the church.

"Lily, I am almost out of mana, and I used the last of healing potions to save the villagers. I'm sorry I don't have—" the princess began to apologize.

"Here," interrupted Lily. She held two pieces of an odd fruit in her hand. She grabbed one piece and threw it in her mouth. Her jaw moved as she bit into the fruit. She closed her eyes as a look of bliss spread across her features.

Lily opened her eyes to see a very puzzled princess. "Open your mouth," commanded Lily, and Elisa obeyed. Lily placed the remaining piece of fruit in between Elisa's parted lips. Elisa was confused, but she trusted Lily, so she bit into the fruit.

Lily giggled as she watched the expression on Elisa's face. Elisa's eyes grew huge as the delicious flavors spread through her mouth. Elisa's eyes closed in delight as she felt the magical energy spread through her body, replenishing a large portion of her mana.

Elisa now had the energy to cast a warding spell so their conversation would not be overheard. As soon as the spell was complete, Lily explained that they should be careful with their words. Their conversation was not private, as William would likely hear Lily's thoughts. Lily gave Elisa a quick recount of the battle, along with a brief explanation of the magical bond.

Elisa stayed quiet as she cured Lily's wounds. The two women were brief, as they did not want the others to become suspicious.

With Lily's wounds now healed, the two women invited

Refren and Aden back to the office, along with the village priest and the mayor. The group discussed the battle and the aftermath, and much praise was heaped on Dame Lily. Oddly, the role of the Vorlandish scout in the battle was not discussed. It was almost as if he had not been present. Refren's soldiers would provide security for the night, and the group would reconvene in the morning after the princess's group had time to rest.

Before Captain Refren left, Princess Elisa asked him to call for the scout named William. Elisa heard reports that the young man was injured in battle, and she wished to make sure he was okay. Refren did so, and soon the archer clad in green was bowing before the princess. The princess's eyes were glowing as she asked him to remove his cloak so Lily could inspect and heal his injuries.

William paused for a moment before he complied with the princess's order. Her eyes narrowed for a moment, as if they had witnessed a surprise.

"William, Lily now calls you a comrade-in-arms. Is this true?"

"Yes, Your Highness, I had the good fortune to witness Dame Lily's amazing battle, helping here and there where I could."

"I thank you for aiding my guardian. Lily, how are his injuries?"

Try to act injured, William, scolded Lily. *Your magic has piqued Elisa's interest, and she is not going to let you get away.*

Can I at least get some food and sleep first? I'm exhausted, "new friend."

Lily almost giggled in response, but she caught herself. "Nothing life-threatening, Princess, but I feel he should stay under observation with our group," answered Lily.

"Make it so," said the princess. "Both of you eat, then get some rest."

The next couple of hours were a blur for Lily and William.

After giving her report of the battle and facing a litany of questions, Lily was finally helped out of her armor. The village priest was kind enough to cast cleansing magic on the pair. While not the same as a good bath, at least the stench of battle was gone. One of the villagers brought them food, which they ate ravenously. After that, they were guided toward adjacent cots.

William, thank you. Without you, I would have fallen at the doors of the church, and the princess and everyone else died soon after.

The archer could feel her heartfelt gratitude and respect through their bond. *Dame Lily, you were amazing. I'm glad I got to fight at your side, and I'll do it again, anytime. Well, maybe after some sleep.* Soft, wonderful laughter filled Lily's mind. Its feminine nature startled the knight, making her wonder again who William really was.

William sensed Lily's wonder, and he panicked. His mental defenses slammed back into place. *Lily, I'm so sorry. I don't understand the nature of the magic affecting us. I...I'll be back later. I'll see you in the morning. I need to seek guidance from my masters.*

Before Lily could respond, William fled the church and disappeared into the night.

William awoke slowly the next morning, having had just a few hours of sleep. He had arrived back at the church just before dawn. The princess had left instructions with the guards to allow him to pass, and he quickly fell asleep in a cot next to Lily.

His mind was still foggy, a half-remembered dream on the edge of his consciousness. In the dream, William had approached a tall, well-built, handsome knight. The knight had complimented William on his bravery and valor. William could feel the butterflies in his stomach and the hot flush of embarrassment on his cheeks. His heart had been racing. *Should I take this chance to confess my love?* Dream-William had thought to himself.

Shocked fully awake, William sat up on his cot. A few feet away, Lily was talking with a tall, well-built, handsome knight—Sir Aden! Lily's cheeks were bright red.

Gah! William mentally exclaimed.

Lily froze in shock. She slowly rotated her head to make eye contact with William. *Can you still hear me?*

Yes, William replied. His mental barrier shook under Lily's internal exclamation. Lily was far more descriptive and colorful than William. While the mental bond had been essential during the battle, having it active all the time was a frightening option for the female knight. She did not want to share her idle thoughts, particularly the ones that she was currently having about Sir Aden.

While this was occurring, William felt eyes on him. He glanced to his left, and a gorgeous blonde woman was carefully studying both Lily and him. Small in stature and perfect in proportions, the woman had a mischievous smile. It was Princess Elisa, whom he had met last night.

The princess rescued Lily from her awkward pause. "Good, our new friend here is awake. William, I have questions for you and Lily. Please come with me. Sir Aden, please confer with Captain Refren on the village status and security. We should be finished in twenty minutes. Report to me in the church office."

"At once, Your Highness." Sir Aden left.

Lily and William followed the princess into a small office at the back of the church. On the way, she asked an acolyte to bring them breakfast.

Lily and William had woken up starving. Elisa had already eaten, so she updated William on what happened before the battle while the two ate.

The princess's group had arrived in Viverna just minutes before the monsters' surprise attack. The number and speed of the goblins and wolves had pushed the princess's security detail into a running defensive battle. Sir Aden had made an on-the-fly decision to seek refuge at the church rather than shelter at the village inn. As the princess's personal guard, Lily had grabbed Elisa and princess-carried her while Sir Aden and the group's fighters made a defense screen. The trip to the church had been costly. Three of the ten escort fighters had been killed, and Sir Aden had been gravely wounded.

The town guards had been protecting the church when the princess arrived. The guards had held the door, giving Lily and Elisa time to heal the wounded. As more monsters had begun to appear, Lily had taken a position in front of the church doors. The town guards had become badly damaged and exhausted, so Lily had guarded the doors by herself until William had arrived. William could hear the pride in Elisa's voice when she told of Lily's accomplishment.

The village had been fortunate that the attack occurred in the evening. The village farmers had already returned for dinner, so none of them had been caught in the open. The villagers were a hardy folk and able to handle small raids by bandits or monsters, but this horde had been far beyond the size of previous incursions. The loss of life in the village was significant, but likely would have been catastrophic without Lily and William.

Lily had spent significant amounts of her magic healing the guards, so she had begun her defense with her mana partially depleted. Even with healing, the rest of the guards had been in poor shape, so they had been set as the last line of defense for Elisa within the church. Sir Aden had been at death's door and received personal care from the princess.

While the battle raged outside, Elisa had cared for the most injured in the church. The death toll would have been much higher without her. "With her blonde hair, lovely face, and kind behavior, the villagers thought an angel had descended from Heaven to care for them," Lily said between bites of food.

In response to Elisa's annoyed look, Lily continued, "Hey, I'm just telling you what the village priest said. I think he is a fan of yours now, by the way." Lily smirked at her friend.

"Are we talking about hero worship? I think you have me beat. Just watch how the army soldiers treat you..." Elisa wore a mischievous smile. Lily lowered her head and resumed eating while Elisa continued to fill William in. "Except for the tragic loss of the three fighters, our group survived. The rest of the party was able to secure my carriage and the wagons at the inn's stable, and the horses were protected. The stable did see sporadic fighting, but our comrades were able to handle their own defense." The princess finished her recap and waited for the pair to finish eating.

During their meal, Lily and William kept looking at each other. Yesterday, they had met in the heat of battle and had fallen asleep soon after. This was the first time they could study what the other looked like. While William's clothing was the same, Lily was not in her heavy armor.

To William's eyes, Lily was a tall, powerfully built, and extremely fit woman. Lily was an adult but had only left childhood behind recently. Her short brown hair was unruly, and she half-heartedly tried to tame it when she noticed William's gaze. Her features were plain, particularly next to the gorgeous princess, but she had an honest face that drew his attention. William was guarding his thoughts, but Lily still felt his appreciation toward her. Her cheeks began to turn pink.

Princess Elisa stood with a grin, pulled a hairbrush from her pocket, and walked behind Lily. The princess began brushing Lily's hair, which caused the knight's cheeks to turn deep red. "Don't mind us," the princess said to William.

William turned his eyes back to his plate, but he could not hide a gentle smile. Lily heard William think, *They are such good friends and so adorable together,* and felt William emote a warm, happy feeling. Lily's embarrassment hit epic levels. Elisa's laughter only made it worse.

The princess returned to her seat, allowing Lily to recover. Lily was annoyed with losing her composure, and she defiantly turned to examine William. William turned to face her in response.

Lily saw a small, athletic man, more than a head shorter than herself. His facial features were soft and almost feminine, like a boy still waiting on puberty. None of his other features were distinctive. He was kind of...forgettable.

Sorry? William thought guardedly at Lily.

Lily gulped and broke eye contact in shock. *Please forgive me!* she replied.

Lily felt William's emotions as he answered, *No worries.* He remained calm and composed.

Once they were finished with breakfast, the princess served tea for all three of them. William was surprised, but Lily just accepted it.

Princess Elisa ritually chanted a barrier around them. Casting this way took more time, but it made the barrier stronger and consumed less mana. The three could now talk freely without outside influence and observation. William appeared uncomfortable under the princess's gaze. He kept his eyes on his tea and his mind as empty as he could.

"My name is Elisa. This is just a conversation among friends. Rank and position mean nothing for now. Is this okay with you?" the princess asked.

"Yes, Your Highness," William replied, his voice cracking.

"Just Elisa. We are close friends. Close friends who don't withhold secrets from each other. Do you understand?" the princess asked.

"Just do it," Lily said with a sigh. Apparently, this was a frequent occurrence between herself and the princess.

"Yes, Elisa," William said.

Elisa chanted another spell, and her eyes began to shine. Looking at William, her eyebrows went up in shock, but she quickly recovered. "William, you are much more than you seem. Where did you go last night, and who are your masters? Oh, when did you don a magical elven chain worth a king's ransom? I thought I saw it last night, but it was gone when you removed your cloak."

Lily was surprised by this, and she looked carefully at William's garments. It seemed to be a simple leather shirt that a scout would wear. But during the battle yesterday, he had taken blows that should have split him in two, body-enhancing magic notwithstanding. Lily had been too busy at the time to give it much thought.

William met Elisa's gaze. He smiled, then dropped his I-am-uncomfortable-in-front-of-royalty act. She was using at least truth magic, and perhaps something more. "Since we are all close friends here, let me reintroduce myself. I am William, and I am employed by Prince Ryne, the Duke of Auraria. I was assigned to the army company as part of your honor guard. Secretly, the prince sent me to ensure your safety. The captain of the army company is not aware of my actual mission. The captain is loyal to Prince Nevan, whose territory we are in."

"Is the captain or the company a threat?" asked Elisa.

"I sense no ill will from anyone in the company. However, the attack on the village was no accident. We should remain vigilant until we reach Auraria."

"Thank you for your honesty. As you know, close friends are careful to keep each other's secrets. Don't you agree, Lily?"

"Of course, Elisa," Lily agreed.

William said, "As for my armor, it was a gift when I left my village. Last night, I removed it before I took off my cloak. I was asked to provide my identity to only those who need it, and displaying my armor would have been bad for my cover." He turned to Lily. "I can equip and unequip my armor in an instant." He raised his clothing so that Elisa and Lily could see the finely made armor he was wearing.

"Humans cannot use elf-made items." Elisa made this a statement; she was not asking a question.

"You are correct, Elisa. I am not human."

"Yet you appear to be. I sense strong magic around you, but it deflects my attempts to understand it. I think I sensed you using it last night to remove the memories of you from the battle. You said you are employed by Ryne, implying you are not his vassal. Who are you?" asked Elisa.

"I am an elf. I am on loan to Ryne. My mother is Willow."

Elisa and Lily exchanged surprised looks. There was a lot to unpack from William's statement.

Few humans had detailed knowledge of the Elven nation. Sarai had spent time there, which was incredibly rare. She carefully guarded her experiences, so Elisa and Lily knew few details. But one name stood out—Willow, the feared Witch Queen of the elves. William also dropped Ryne's title, which was startling in itself. A commoner or lower noble would never do such a thing.

Elisa confirmed, "Willow loaned you to Ryne, and he sent you to protect us?"

"Willow and Ryne think highly of you." William turned to face Lily. "Both of you." He paused for a moment to let his comment sink in. "As for the magic around me, Elisa, you are truly gifted if you can sense it at all. It makes me seem unremarkable and easily forgotten. By noon today, few will remember my part in yesterday's battle, even the people who saw me fight. Their minds will remember Lily's performance, not mine. Two days after I leave, people will struggle to remember I was here. The magic, which Willow named Leave No Trace, allows me to pass freely through human lands and carry out the missions assigned by my mother and Ryne."

"Will Lily and I forget you?"

"No. You two are...different. Your willpower is exceptional. In any case, Ryne has instructed me to aid you in your journey, so I've exempted you from the magic. Furthermore, I bring both my skills and a variety of supplies to aid you in your journey."

Lily suddenly remembered the sword William had loaned her. She began to unbuckle and return it before William stopped her.

"Keep the sword for now. The Vorlandish soldiers saw you using it. It would raise more questions if you were suddenly missing it."

Lily thanked him and patted the sword hilt. She had grown quite fond of the sword and would be happy to keep using it.

"Why did you leave suddenly last night?" the princess asked William.

"The bond that I now share with Lily caught me by surprise. My orders were to aid you from the shadows, taking only direct action—like the battle last evening—when absolutely necessary. Being unable to hide my thoughts and memories from your knight compromised my mission, so I sought new orders from both Ryne and Mother. I ran from the village on the chance that some distance between Lily and me would allow me privacy. This proved to be true."

"What are your new orders?"

"Ryne instructed me to trust you both completely. If you wish, I'm allowed to take more direct action on your behalf rather than remain out of sight. The prince is concerned that there may be more attempts on your life." William faced Lily. "As for Mother, well, she is excited about examining the magic binding us." William shuddered.

Is Queen Willow scary? thought Lily.

No, she just gets a little...intense...when she finds something that interests her.

Lily sensed that William was telling the truth but downplaying it significantly. Her stress level increased.

"Sounds like your mother and I are both excited. We both want to know how the mental link works," Elisa stated. "I sensed strong binding magic on you last night, but I could not untangle it. I cast my strongest severance magic while you were both sleeping this morning, but the binding was completely unaffected. Let's examine you now that you are awake."

Elisa rose from her chair and began to circle William and Lily, carefully studying them from all angles. "Move your chairs closer together." They did so. A couple of minutes later, she said, "Touch fingertips." The moment Lily and William made physical contact, they both were startled and flinched away from each other.

"Touch fingertips again. Don't move away from each other," ordered Elisa. Lily and William repeated the contact and held it this time. "Lily, what's happening?"

"Touching William sends a tingling feeling down my back. It's not painful, just very...intense."

"Okay, you can release from each other." Elisa made non-committal sounds of "hmm," "oh," and "ah" as she continued to study them. After several minutes, Elisa sat back down. "What did you do?" she asked with a laugh. "I've heard of the red thread of fate linking lovers. This more like a rope, or perhaps an anchor chain."

William and Lily recoiled from each other. This only made Elisa laugh harder. Lily became increasingly upset. William was just confused. Elisa requested, "Tell me what happened last evening."

Lily and William told their story. Lily did most of the talking, with William adding details. Elisa was quiet until the part about their prayers. Her eyes grew quite large and then shone more brightly. The pair gave the highlights of the massive battle and soon finished.

Seemingly out of nowhere, Lily turned toward William and said, "Thank you."

At Elisa's puzzled look, William said, "I complimented her summary. Very efficient and accurate."

Eliza grinned. "You did not say that out loud."

"Oh, sorry," replied William sheepishly.

"William, you mentioned your Battle Awareness spell is cooperative magic. It provides an unconscious link between the participants to share their senses. I can see the elements of that spell. However, this mental bond of yours feels more like a really, really overpowered marriage ceremony." Elisa continued before Lily could respond. "William, when you offered your prayer, did you pray to the elven Goddess of Protection?"

"Yes," William replied. His eyes narrowed as he comprehended Elisa's meaning. Lily felt his mental wall strengthen and looked puzzled.

Elisa grinned as she explained. "Another one of Sarai's brief glimpses into elvish culture. Protection is only one of the aspects of the elves' goddess. Other aspects include love, loyalty, and family. The distinction between family and friends is small to an elf.

"So, here is a possibility. Lily, last evening, William found you in dire straits, and the town was about to be destroyed. You are willing to sacrifice your life to save me, but William had been instructed to save us both. He called on his deity for help, and wow, did she deliver. Divine intervention, and now he has a divine life-pledge to his new beloved Lily. A life-long bond for a near-immortal race."

William's face betrayed no emotion. His mental wall was rigid and imposing.

Elisa pouted a bit at William's lack of reaction. "What, no response? Teasing you is not fun. Or perhaps I've just not found your weakness." After a quick grin, Elisa turned to her best friend. "Lily, I'm kidding. William did not pledge his undying love to you. I don't know why you have a mental bond. We will just have to keep researching."

Elisa's explanation did not change Lily's mood. The knight remained upset. Having a stranger hear her innermost thoughts was uncomfortable. Her mind sometimes considered inappropriate things, things she would not even tell her best friend, Elisa. At least she could feel William's mental wall blocking their thoughts from each other. His mental armor would protect them until they could make this nightmare end.

Elisa continued, "I don't think this bond is permanent. It

will likely end on its own. If not, we will visit Queen Willow as soon as possible. But for now, I'm clear that we need to keep you together." Elisa paused. "Let's have a conversation with your captain, William. You will now be a part of our little group. We'll test the extent of your bond later."

William and Lily bowed to Princess Elisa as she dispelled the magical barrier around them.

Outside the office, Captain Refren and Sir Aden were talking.

"Ah, gentlemen, please join us. We need to have a short discussion," Elisa politely commanded. The two officers entered the room and stood at attention before the princess. William and Lily stood to her side. The captain noticed the odd placement of his scout, but he waited to be addressed rather than pointing it out.

"Captain, thank you for lending me William. If he had not come to our aid yesterday, I fear what may have transpired."

"My pleasure, Your Highness," the captain replied.

"Given the threat to my life and my loss of retainers, I would like to keep him by my side. I hope you understand."

"Yes, ma'am. Although he recently joined us, and he is a bit young, I believe he will grow into a fine scout someday."

"Sir Aden, will William's addition be all right with you?"

"Yes, Princess. I would like to test his fighting skills, but I'm sure we can find a place for him."

Elisa looked sharply at William. He gave an almost imperceptible shrug. Refren had seen William fighting the giant yesterday. Today, it was as if William had not been present at all. His magic was working.

"Captain, Commander, thank you both. We will be staying in Viverna for the rest of the day to help the recovery. I want a full assessment of the village ASAP. Lily, you will assist me in tending to the villagers' immediate needs. William, backtrack the monsters' path and return to me at sundown. If you find anything that needs my immediate attention, use your magic to contact us. Dismissed."

Lily felt a headache forming. Elisa was curious about the mental bond, and she wanted to test it. Lily felt like a guinea pig.

William had left the village to determine the source of the monsters, so he was progressively getting farther and farther away from Lily. Lily was helping Elisa heal the last of the villagers. Several more groups had survived by hiding in secure basements, but their nerves and bodies were frayed by the attack. While performing the healing, the princess would ask the same questions between patients: "Where is William?" "Can you still contact him?" "How strong is the connection?" "Can you sense his health and emotional state?" Elisa recorded the answers on a scroll she kept on the desk beside her. For his part, William was quite happy to provide the information, but Lily was tired of being their communicator.

Fortunately, Elisa prioritized village recovery over analyzing the data. But one thing was clear—William was moving at a ridiculously fast rate.

"William did not have a horse last night, and he left on foot this morning. He was a foot scout for mounted infantry..." Lily said.

"That's not normal, is it?"

"No, not even close."

"Well, okay, back to work then."

The two women shook their heads and laughed.

Just before the lunch break, Elisa and Lily finished healing the villagers and switched to using their magic to make a disposal pit for the monsters outside the village. The plan was to dig a deep pit, throw in the remains, use fire and holy magics to purify and reduce the remains, and then cover the pit. The army company was making steady progress in moving the monsters' remains to the site. The pit still needed to be formed.

Lily and Elisa started casting their spells, working in unison. They were both skilled priestesses, and they had done similar work before. Lily sensed something was wrong about a minute into the chanting. Elisa had stopped and was staring at Lily in disbelief.

"What?" Lily asked in confusion.

"Look at the spoil!" Elisa responded, pointing at the two dirt piles from the holes they were digging.

"Uh..." Lily said in confusion. Her pile was much larger than Elisa's.

"Keep digging," ordered the princess.

After a minute, they stopped. The results were the same. Lily's magic was about three times more powerful than Elisa's when it should have been the same. Why? Was the bond making her magic stronger?

Elisa placed a hand on her chin, and her eyes took on a faraway look. Lily knew what this meant. Elisa was very clever, and she was currently thinking of ways to leverage Lily's new strength.

"Where is William? How far away is he?" asked an excited Elisa.

"He is at the edge of the dense forest near the border. Forty kilometers away. He thinks he needs about thirty minutes, and then he can head back."

"Ask him to stop and contact you every few kilometers. We are going to dig more holes at each stop. Tell him why."

"Done. He seems really interested, too," said the long-suffering Dame Lily with a sigh.

Arriving back at the village, William reported to Princess Elisa and gave her his findings. Dame Lily, Sir Aden, and Captain Refren also attended the meeting. Elisa deployed a magical instrument so they could talk in private—it was more convenient than continually casting and dispelling warding spells, and it worked better for larger groups.

The monster army had originated in the forest near the border, forty kilometers away from Viverna. William had found remnants of conscription magic—a type of magic that could compel monsters to gather and then force them to pursue a goal. The size of the group, the distance they had traveled, and the focus the monsters demonstrated in their attack all indicated that a powerful mage or group of mages was involved. William had been unable to identify the culprit.

The timing of the magic had coincided with the princess's security detail crossing the border a couple of days earlier. The princess had made good time in crossing Llanos and reached the border before she had expected to. Rather than asking Captain Refren to meet her at the lightly defended crossing, Elisa had felt she would be safer meeting in Viverna. In retrospect, the decision had been wise but had resulted in loss of life and damage to the village. The alternative could have been the destruction of the princess's entire party.

The culprit had clearly learned of the change in the princess's plans and sent the monsters to the village. William suggested, and Elisa agreed, that they should assume that the princess's security force was under physical surveillance, likely by spies or scouts, since the security detail had deployed significant countermeasures against magical surveillance.

Aden argued that this discovery made leaving the village their top priority. They needed to get the princess to Auraria as soon as possible.

However, Elisa overruled Aden. "I appreciate your concern, but if I leave, it will force Captain Refren's men to leave with us as escorts. This village is in dire condition and needs immediate help. I don't want the Vorlandish people's first experience with their new princess to be atrocious. We will stay in Viverna for a week to help them recover."

Sir Aden did not like her decision, but he understood and accepted it. Captain Refren thoughtfully considered Princess

Elisa. He could think of only one other noble who would risk their own personal safety to aid common folk: the princess's future husband, Prince Ryne.

The meeting ended, and Aden and Refren left to execute the princess's orders.

Elisa, Lily, and William stayed behind to eat dinner and discuss the day's experiments on the magical bond.

Princess Elisa was clearly impatient to discuss their magical findings, so the three ate their dinner quickly. At the onset of their discussion, Lily expressed concern about the appearance of William interacting with Elisa so much. The princess's party was unlikely to raise direct objections, but her two ladies-in-waiting did not hide their displeasure. Having an unknown man so close to the princess was unseemly.

"Lily, I acknowledge your concerns, but I have some new plans I would like to discuss, and William's participation is vital. Besides, Leave No Trace will make our spectators forget him," said Elisa.

"Princess, I agree with your assessment, but I need to explain my magic a bit more. Leave No Trace places a strain on the caster in proportion to the number of people whose memories had to be altered. In the case of the recent battle, the Vorlandish army had a clear focus for their admiration—Lily. Thus, I was able to hide my presence within her shadow. But even with that advantage, the memories of more than a hundred people had to be altered. That placed a significant strain on me. Let's be careful in the future. I don't want to fail you when you need me most."

"I hear you and understand, William. Thank you," replied the princess.

Elisa continued their discussion with a recap of the powerful bond that had formed between Lily and William. The bond was much longer lasting than the battlefield magic that William had cast. The bond allowed for direct mental connections much more easily and robustly than a telepathy spell—Elisa had once shared such a spell with her now-deceased aunt. The downside of the new mental link was that the bond was so efficient it prevented mental privacy, much to Lily's horror. The bond allowed personal magics, such as body enhancement, to be shared. Those magics were also significantly stronger than they had been before the bond. Senses, including enhanced ones, were also shared, as were mental images, at least in the form of dreams. The link was affected by distance. Touching created the strongest effects, but the second-strongest effects persisted for a kilometer.

Elisa proposed that the bond was due to the cooperative nature of William's magic interacting with the Earth Goddess's magic that Lily used. Elisa called the effect "resonance"—she had learned it from Sarai. Neither William nor Lily had heard of it before. "The simplest version—the two types of magic work very well together. The combined interaction is much stronger than the sum of each magic individually." Elisa's proof was that Lily's earth magic was five times stronger than Elisa's when William was nearby.

Elisa became increasingly more passionate and excited as her explanation continued. "And that is why, rather than terminating your bond, we need to add me to it!" she finished.

A mixture of horror and confusion covered Lily's face. To her credit, she did not say a word. However, with a direct line to Lily's thoughts, William was nearly overwhelmed by her unhappiness. William strengthened his mental wall, but it barely dulled Lily's mental tirade.

"Princess, please let us take a step backward. You have focused on the positive aspects of the bond. Mental privacy is not the only negative," said William.

"What do you mean?" asked Elisa.

"There are three concerns that I would like you to consider. First is the shared fate aspect of the bond. An attack on me directly affects Lily; if I suffer damage, then so does she. If we add you to the bond, then I suspect that you will suffer injury as well. Bodyguards are meant to protect their princess, not endanger her."

"That is a very good point, William. I acknowledge that the danger to me will increase. If we were only a group of warriors, I would withdraw my request. However, we are all three trained healers, and we can use our magic to recover and reinforce each other."

Wow, she wants us to spider tank, thought William.

Huh? responded Lily.

It's a long-forgotten term for a party using remote heals from each member to tank incoming damage. I'll explain the details later. We better focus on Elisa's exuberance right now.

Thank you, William. The archer felt Lily's heartfelt emotion through their bond.

"If we are careful, we could mitigate the risk that way," replied William.

"What is your second concern?"

"The unknown effect of adding a third person to the bond. Yesterday, you experimented with digging holes and noticed Lily's greatly improved earth magic. What you did not see is the effect it had on me. Lily was directly siphoning from my mana, even when we were at a great distance from each other. I sensed that I could prevent the loss, and I consciously decided to let her. If we add you and all three of us are casting magic, I'm unsure what the effects will be."

"Another very good point. We will proceed carefully, and we will stop if there are issues we cannot overcome."

"That leads to my third concern. We don't know what is causing the bond nor how to terminate it. Adding another person, particularly a high-value person like yourself, is very risky. Why is joining the bond worth the risk?" asked William.

"Ah, sorry, I'm getting ahead of myself," Elisa replied. "If my estimations are correct, the three of us will be able to form a protective wall around this village in the next week."

William blinked, and his face grew serious as he digested Elisa's words. William was vaguely aware that Lily had switched from internally yelling to mentally pleading, asking him not to entertain such an insane task.

Elisa and William started a highly detailed technical discussion on the feasibility of walling off the village. Elisa showed William her drawings and calculations. He made a few minor suggestions, but he appeared to see the logic in Elisa's proposal. Lily bided her time.

William said, "Elisa, now that I know what you want to do, I have a fourth concern. I'm worried about mana consumption and recovery. Even using ritual casting, which trades lower magic costs for increased casting time, forming your wall will burn through almost all the recovery potions and fruit that I have with me. Ryne has already given me permission to use them as needed, but we will make the rest of the trip low on magical consumables. Are you sure you want to take that risk?"

The look in Elisa's eyes answered William before her words did. She was used to making high-stake gambles when she saw a high-reward goal she wanted to accomplish. "I need to make this wall."

Elisa calmly turned to Lily. The two women were best friends. They knew each other very well. It was now Lily's turn to explain why Elisa's idea was dumb and would never work. Elisa considered Lily's pushback very important—Lily had prevented a number of her harebrained ideas in the past. William merely watched and listened for now—he understood this was no longer his fight.

The knight said, "First, the entire village will watch us construct the wall. That many people could overwhelm William's magic."

"Good point. To lessen the strain on William, we will hide

him among the guards who protect us so that his actual role is not obvious. Next," replied the princess.

"Second, we will be vulnerable to attack as we work."

"You have described William's magic as giving you incredible spatial awareness. With the amount of earth and rock we will be moving, any attackers could be crushed in moments. We also have both the security detail and the army company to protect us. Next."

"Third, we will be exhausted and vulnerable while we sleep. I will not be able to stand watch."

"Great point. We will keep all the magic crystals to power the portable barrier. We should have a ten-day supply. You and I will sleep within the barrier. William will need to make other arrangements."

William nodded in agreement, but he stayed silent.

"Fourth, I'm sorry, but I hate this. I feel so awkward. I...I don't want you to hear my thoughts. They get weird and icky sometimes..." Lily's voice trailed off. She hung her head in shame.

Elisa's tone became soft, and she stepped forward to embrace her friend. "I'm very sorry for asking you to do this, Lily. You give me all you can, and I just ask for more. I got excited about the project, but I haven't explained my real reasons for wanting to help the village.

"Yes, the wall will protect the villagers. That should be enough. But we can't help everyone, so why are we helping Viverna? My real reason is quite selfish. The people of this country don't know me. I want to rebuild my reputation without being subject to the politics and scheming of the Llanos nobility. Back home, I was a burden to my father. Here in Vorland, I have a clean slate. I can take calculated risks and try crazy things to gain the attention and affection of the Vorlandish people.

"Lily, did you hear what the army is saying about you today?" Lily looked alarmed, but Elisa continued, "Please be calm; they are only saying good things. They are in awe of you and your heroics. By tomorrow, the villagers will have emotionally recovered enough to listen to the soldiers' tales of your battle. Your fame will grow. How you ended the threat to this village. How you saved them and gave them hope."

Elisa paused. "I need my moment to shine, but I can't do it without you. I'm sorry you serve such a selfish princess. I wish I could be a better friend to you."

Elisa started crying hard, ugly tears. Lily gently lifted the princess off the ground and hugged her. After a minute, Elisa began to calm down. The two women continued to embrace for a few more minutes.

Elisa began to speak, but her cheeks got red. After a couple of calming breaths, she said, "Lily, I don't want you to know my thoughts either. But since I'm asking you to mentally bond with me, I'll tell you. Lily, I have so many conflicting feelings about you. I'm envious of your strength. You don't need a prince to save you. Hell, you would be the one saving the prince. I admire you, and I wish I was more like you. You are honest, brave, and caring. You should have been one of Llanos's paladins, but you decided to stay by my side. I need your strength to survive. I'm worried that, one day, you are going to wake up and hate me for keeping you all to myself. I want to tell the world how wonderful you are, but I'm afraid they will take you away from me."

Lily was calm now. Elisa had thoughts that were confusing and weird, too.

"Elisa, *I'm* envious of *you*. You are the perfect girl—gorgeous, petite, and feminine. In armor, everyone thinks I'm a guy. I admire you, and I wish I was more like you. You are smart, shrewd, and straightforward. You are the only family I have left. I'm worried that when you marry the prince, then he will be your protector, and you will no longer need me."

"I will always need you."

"I'll always be by your side."

"Sisters before misters?"

"Girls rule; guys drool."

The touching moment had turned into Elisa and Lily joking with each other. They were in their own private little world. The sound of a throat clearing brought them back to reality. They suddenly turned to face the forgotten William.

"Welcome back," William teased. "As for my stray thoughts, I am a guy. I'm going to be in close contact with two women whom I find extremely attractive." Lily started to protest, but William stopped her. "If we are going to do this, let's just agree to forgive each other now for our stray thoughts in the future. If we work hard enough, we will have no time to think, and then maybe I will survive until the end of the week."

As William left the princess and Lily, he checked with the knight. While her outward emotions were supportive and friendly to the princess, her inner feelings remained in turmoil. *Lily, are you sure you want to do this?*

I'm sure that I don't want to do it, but Elisa is very persuasive. Telling her "no" is very difficult for me. She wants the fame that accomplishing an impossible task will give her. She has convinced herself she needs this. Her ego and pride will make this wall happen. We will just deal with the consequences.

The resignation within Lily's thoughts was clear to William. He let his annoyance and anger flow back through the bond. *Elisa takes advantage of you as both her servant and her friend.*

You are correct, William, but it is my choice to support her. I am all she has right now. Mixed feelings of embarrassment and shame flowed back to the scout. William could feel Lily's hesitation.

You don't have to ask for my help, Lily. Ryne asked me to provide it, and you have earned my trust. I'll help the princess for your sake, and I'll keep my thoughts to myself for now. Well, at least as well as I can with the bond present.

Lily laughed at his joke through the bond. She was happy to have her new ally.

CHAPTER 5

The trio ate an early breakfast and then began to execute the princess's plan. First, they had to successfully add Elisa to the bond. Since they did not understand how the bond worked, they decided to follow the same procedure that William and Lily had used previously. William cast his Battle Awareness, then all three followed with prayers to the goddesses—William to his and the women to theirs. They used the ritual version of the prayers since they were no longer in mortal danger. Casting this way took longer but preserved mana.

Two red strands of light appeared, one between William and Lily and the other between William and Elisa. The strand with Lily appeared almost immediately, while the one with Elisa grew slowly over time. "I guess William is a common thread," said Elisa.

Lily snickered, then said more thoughtfully, "William, this feels different than before."

"I agree. Last time, the link and the pulse happened quickly. Maybe because we took our time with the prayers this time?"

The thread of light to Lily peaked in intensity, then disappeared. There was no pulse this time and no overwhelming exchange of memories.

"Oh, did you feel that? I felt the bond become stronger or...more taut?" asked Lily as she tried to describe the odd sensation in words.

"Not to get your hopes up, Lily, but I think this means the

bond fades over time," explained William. He could feel Lily's happiness through the renewed link. She considered this news exciting—she wanted to be done with the shared mental space as soon as possible.

William turned his attention back to the slowly forming thread of light with Elisa. Elisa's eyes were glowing with magic. She was carefully studying how the magic worked.

William strengthened his mental barriers. After the intensity of the experience of "oneness" with Lily two days ago, William feared that the clever and perceptive princess would see right through him. During the previous event, Lily had been overwhelmed by the sharing of memories and only retained a core impression of William. In contrast, William retained the knowledge of Lily's memories. He had seen the purity of her soul and been amazed. Elisa's teasing of a divine life bond had been dangerously close to how William felt. William did not want to share this, or his other deeper secrets, with the women. At least not yet.

Elisa was focused on the strand of red light forming between William and herself. She was aware of the conversation between the other two, but she paid them no heed. The fascinating process happening now claimed all her attention.

Last night, after she and Lily had retired for the night, Elisa had bombarded the knight with detailed questions about her previous experience with William. Lily's answers did not satisfy her. For her cautious and introverted friend to accept William so completely, something deeper than "he is a very loyal and good person" and "I trust him the same way I trust you" must have happened in the moment that the red thread pulsed.

Elisa wanted to be ready. Even knowing that William might see as deeply into her as she saw into him, she was ready to take the risk. As the link continued to build, she used her special sight-enhancing magic. She opened her eyes to the full experience.

After an antagonizing wait, Elisa's thread pulsed. Time slowed to a crawl around her. With an intense focus on the bond, she felt her awareness slingshot out of herself, along the thread, and into William's mind. She felt a mild resistance, but then she was through. Her environment shifted, and she no longer saw a world she knew. She found it hard to describe, but she was not "seeing" William's static memories. She was "in" his world. She barely registered this thought before her location changed.

Elisa was standing in a massive building and surrounded by thousands of people. All of them were human, and they were rapidly moving in several different directions. Their clothing was strange. Even with no obvious knights or guards to direct them, they moved efficiently. Lights, voices, and colors of all kinds surrounded them. An immense picture—it was moving!—displayed a larger-than-life young woman drinking from a strange metallic can. The woman smiled, and then writing flashed on the image, next to a huge version of the can. A second later, the can was replaced with a view of a sparkling ocean. Elisa continued to watch for a few moments before her attention was drawn back to the crowd. Elisa saw a line of children in bright yellow, shiny clothing approaching her. One of them bumped her...no, the child passed *through* her. Elisa did not feel the child, but her location changed again.

She was now in the countryside, on the side of a hill. Healthy green plants and trees surrounded her, and in the valley below, she saw flooded fields full of green sprouts. In the world she knew, these plants only existed far to the south, at the southern edge of the Osman Empire.

Her location changed again, and she was surrounded by the sound of angry dragons. She ducked in fear, but nothing attacked her. She looked around, and she saw men, women, and children. Their attention was focused on the sky above them. No one seemed afraid. Even the children wore smiles. Elisa turned her attention to the sky. There was a group of small metallic dragons flying by at impossible speeds. She could feel the vibrations of their roars in her chest.

Elisa's location changed again, and once again, she was outside and surrounded by many thousands of people. The buildings around her stretched far into the sky. Her senses seemed to deceive her. The dark sky indicated it was night, but the area around her was lit like daytime. Massive moving pictures covered some of the buildings, while lights of all colors shone from the rest. On the impossibly wide street in front of her, odd carriages of all sizes drove by at speeds faster than a running horse. Even with her senses overloaded, she smelled strong alcohol on a man near her. He stumbled, hitting and knocking a teenage boy toward the street. Elisa felt her body react without thought. She launched herself in front of the boy, then used her arms to throw him back into the safety of the crowd. She had just enough time to see the terrified expression of the man in a large white carriage before she fell to the ground and felt no more.

"Elisa…"

"Hmmmm…just a few more minutes, Lily…zzz…"

"Elisa! Wake up!"

Elisa slowly regained consciousness. She needed a moment to get her bearings. Lily's worried expression filled most of her view. She was lying in Lily's arms. "I'm okay, just give me a moment," said Elisa. After the shock of her visions, the knight's embrace felt wonderfully familiar. *So comfy,* she thought as she closed her eyes.

"You jerk! You had me worried, and now you just want to sleep!" vented Lily.

Elisa reopened her eyes. She reached up and touched Lily's cheek. The tips of her fingers felt the moisture of Lily's tears. "I'm sorry," she replied. *Now, just gaze into her eyes, and she will do whatever I want,* thought Eliza.

Lily's expression hardened in an instant.

Uh-oh, thought Eliza. *Hello…can anyone hear me?*

Loud and clear, "Princess," was Lily's answer.

Oh wow, this mind link sure is powerful. I can really feel your sarcasm, Lily. Hehe...oh boy.

Elisa, you are in so much trouble! Lily knew all of Elisa's tickle-sensitive places, and soon the princess was laughing uncontrollably.

William sat nearby and was happy for the distraction. He rebuilt the mental defenses that Elisa had so casually destroyed minutes before. Elisa had just experienced his former life, and she would soon be hounding him for answers. Fortunately, she had not uncovered his secrets from this world...yet. For his own part, William had seen everything that was Elisa. The depth and complexity of her mind was amazing. "Clever" was too tame of a word. She was hungry for power and leadership. She genuinely cared for Lily, but everyone else was a pawn she would sacrifice when needed. Ensuring that she used her powers for good, well, that would soon be Ryne's problem.

Where William felt an intense affection for Lily, Elisa caused him concern. Looking at the two women together made William want to compare them, but that would be a dangerous exercise while the shared mental bond persisted. For now, he tried to keep those thoughts to himself.

***

After recovering from forming the bonds, Elisa, Lily, and William continued to work on the princess's plan. They needed to test the effectiveness of their magic, as well as their ability to work collectively. They noticed immediate issues they would need to overcome.

First was sensory overload. Elisa added her magical sight to the group, which already included Lily's tremorsense and William's acute sense of smell and hearing. The combined amount of information pouring into the shared mental space was simply overwhelming and made conscious thought difficult and spellcasting nearly impossible.

After a few minutes of experimenting, William was able to find a crude but simple solution. By applying specific mental blocks to the sensory information from each woman, he was able to regain control.

Ah, much better, thank you, William, thought the princess.

You are...ah...welcome, Elisa, replied the scout. The strain in his response was obvious.

William, are you okay? asked Lily.

Not yet, but I'm getting better. Blocking the senses completely is not the answer. It feels like I'm building pressure inside my head when I do. I think I need to allow some information through, just not too much.

How can we help? asked Elisa.

Elisa, close your eyes for now to limit your sight. Lily, pull your feet off the ground to limit your tremorsense.

Fortunately, the trio had engaged magical warding to prevent others from seeing their experiments. Otherwise, it would have been a strange sight indeed, with the princess looking around with her eyes closed and Lily sitting in a chair with her feet straight out in front of her.

After a few minutes, William was able to adjust the sensory blocks correctly. His headache receded for now.

I take it that this sensory overload was worse than during your battle, said Elisa.

Yes, this was more extreme, but the battle was still bad. Then again, mortal danger is great for focusing the mind in the moment.

Now that the sensory overload was under control, the extreme ease of telepathy became obvious. Any stray thought that any one of them had was immediately known by the other two. They had been expecting this problem but not the severity of it. Elisa was caught planning her interrogation of William to learn more about his magic and the elves. William's casual glances at Elisa's bottom and Lily's chest made his appreciation for the women's physical attributes very clearly known. Lily daydreamed of protecting both her princess and her new small friend, William. This left all three of them in various states of embarrassment.

William, why don't you take a jog around the village and put a bit of distance between us? I'm curious about something, said Elisa.

The scout welcomed the excuse to leave, and he was gone in a flash. A few minutes later, he was a couple of kilometers outside the village. *How is this?* he sent back to the women.

That's fine. Now, everyone, act normal for the next few minutes. No deep or powerful thoughts. Don't make a conscious effort to send your thoughts. Just notice the scenery around you, instructed Elisa.

Several minutes passed.

Princess, is this long enough? asked William.

It is. Lily and I did not catch any stray thoughts from each other, even though we're holding hands. Neither of us sensed any of your thoughts, William. Same for you?

Correct, almost as if the bond was not active.

Excellent. I think we can make a few deductions. William, you are the problem, teased Elisa.

Ah...sorry?

You are the common thread. You formed the link with Lily previously and then with me today. We should consider them two separate bonds rather than one which covers the three of us. The strength of each bond depends on our distance from you, not from each other. Given the effectiveness of your sensory blocks, which reside within your mind, I suspect that the shared mental space is entirely within you.

Your deductions seem logical, Elisa.

The princess tried to sense if William was surprised by her conclusions, but she felt only calm from his end. She could feel something blocking her access to his mind. These must be the mental barriers or walls that Lily had mentioned. She imagined herself poking at the wall, but it did not change.

Princess, please stop.

Uh? Lily was confused.

Elisa is probing my defenses.

Oh, sorry! exclaimed the princess.

Sorry you were caught, not sorry that you tried, stated William.

True, thought Elisa quietly. She had been caught, and lying would only make things worse. She could not hide her motives and intentions from William and Lily so long as the bonds existed. Elisa had just encountered a limitation that the mental bond imposed on her, and she was not happy about it.

The trio ran a few more experiments, and then they moved to the edge of the village to begin the wall construction. Elisa and Lily would perform the publicly observable ritual chanting while William supported them nearby, disguised as one of the guards. For maximum effect, he had to be within stray-thought range. None of them were excited about that.

They started at the western edge of town near the road. Their plan was to circle the town in a clockwise direction. Even if they were only partially successful, it would provide protection along the monsters' path. The plan was to excavate soil and rock, compress and harden the materials, and then shape the materials into a wall. The hole left behind would become a moat. At eight meters tall and five meters thick, the wall would be sturdy.

Sir Aden and Captain Refren were notified that Princess Elisa was conducting one of her experiments, but they were only given basic details. Captain Refren, not knowing the princess, imagined she was trying to construct a palisade.

The trio began the construction ritual. They worked for an hour—Lily instructed the ladies-in-waiting to use hourglasses to measure the time. At the end of the hour, while Lily and William rested, Elisa inspected and measured their creation. She ran back to the others, checked her calculation, and exclaimed, "Six days! We can do this in six days!"

Constructing the wall was noisy, and the sudden appearance of a two-and-a-half-story-tall stone feature scared several of the traumatized villagers. However, curiosity soon drew a massive crowd. The audience waited quietly for Elisa and Lily to finish, fearful of interrupting the construction of the amazing structure. The formation of a massive and continuous stone wall—it was an awe-inspiring feat of magic.

After her exclamation, the princess turned to face the crowd. "Don't mind us; we're just building you a wall," she teased the crowd. Her tone was informal, and her expression happy.

The tension in the crowd broke. They cheered.

The village elders, whom the princess had summoned, walked out to meet her in front of the large stone structure. The mayor, a large and boisterous man, waited for the cheering to calm. "All right, that is enough gawking; you've all jobs to do. If our new princess is going to provide us such a splendid structure, then the least we can do is make the village inside worthy of such protection."

The villagers cheered again but then departed to do their own work to recover the town.

Princess Elisa addressed the village elders. "Sorry to surprise you with this, but I wasn't sure we could do it."

The mayor spoke for the others. "Your Highness, please don't apologize. This is the best surprise we could have received."

"Glad to hear that. Now, if you and the others have a few minutes, I would like to review my plans with you and get your feedback."

The mayor was confused. "You are asking for our opinions?"

"Of course! It would be a poor gift if we built you a wall that you did not like."

The village elders became excited. They were used to nobles running over them all the time. However, this princess wanted their feedback. The elders grew less timid as they talked and realized the princess was being truthful. She listened to them. She agreed with many of their comments, and when she did not, she explained why. They decided where the openings would be, as well as locations for lookout towers for the village defenders to use. The village elders left the meeting in high spirits.

The sound of construction continued through the day. The villagers found the sound comforting. The princess was working hard to keep them safe.

While the public enjoyed the magic show, the trio struggled to overcome the challenges that arose during construction while also hiding their problems from those same spectators.

As William had feared, the overall mana cost of the construction was staggering. While the resonance effect of the bond made their magic extremely powerful, it burned mana quickly as well. They noticed that reducing the rate of construction made them very mana-efficient, but unfortunately, that was not an option. The trio would need to push themselves to their limits to accomplish the deadline that Elisa had announced.

The magical fruit that William possessed held the solution. Three times per day—for the morning and afternoon breaks as well as for lunch—William produced a tasty fruit for each of them that fully recovered their mana. It was the same fruit that Lily and Elisa had shared after the battle for the village. The fruit took too long to work to be useful in combat, but for ritual casting, it was ideal.

Had William produced the fruit just once, Elisa might not have questioned him, but he would need to repeat this trick over and over for all six days. William would divulge neither the source of the fruit nor how many he had left—just that he had a sufficient quantity for the construction task.

William, how valuable are these mana fruits? Lily asked with a sudden insight.

Lily and Elisa could feel William's strained humor through the link. *If we burn through fifty-four of them to finish Elisa's wall, then the wall's worth almost two sets of my elven chain mail.*

Oh my, thank you for using them on our behalf, William. You, Willow, and Ryne are truly generous, said Elisa, taking the magical sacrifice in stride.

Lily was appalled. To burn such great wealth on the princess's vanity project. How stupid! Lily froze. She had just projected her frustration through the link. She hazarded a look in Elisa's direction, ready to face the princess's wrath. Oddly, Elisa behaved as if nothing had happened.

Lily, you are fine. I was able to prevent your feelings from being shared with Elisa. Since I'm the hub for the mental bonds, it looks like I do have some control over them, William thought at Lily.

So, this link is just the two of us?

Yes, it is. Although, don't assume it will always be. I must intentionally focus to control these conversations.

Thank you, William. I let my emotions get the better of me. Lily let her appreciation flow through the link.

The next issue arose due to the princess's lack of teamwork experience. Lily and William had both trained extensively in small group combat, where each member had an assigned and important role, but Elisa had no similar kind of training.

For example, William had to keep reminding Elisa to sync her casting with his and Lily's. He used the analogy of an orchestra when the musicians were not playing in time with each other—the music quality was poor. The conductor needed to lead the orchestra, and the musicians needed to obey the conductor.

Elisa, you are not the conductor right now. I am. I'm the one who can keep us in sync.

Then do a better job of leading. I'm not using my abilities to their full potential. We are wasting time.

No, Princess, you are overdrawing mana through the link. You are stressing both Lily and me by stealing our mana to feed your magic. Our magic is suffering. At this rate, we won't last the day, much less the week.

Now that she was paying attention, Elisa could sense the stress that the other two were feeling through the link. Without comment, she changed her behavior to match William's request. While her own performance was no longer at full speed, the group's construction rate improved remarkably. Elisa's ego prevented her from admitting that William was correct.

The last major issue of the day was Lily's magical efficiency—the amount of construction she could accomplish for the same amount of mana as someone else. In short order, William realized that Lily's massive mana pool resulted in her magic being inefficient. Unlike normal casters, Lily had never learned to conserve her magic pool when casting. Instead, she focused on strengthening her spells or making them quicker to cast, both of which drew more mana than normal.

Through the bond, William and Elisa were able to share what they felt and how they used their magic. After real-time feedback and training, Lily increased her efficiency significantly. She was a wonderful student, and both Elisa and William praised her. It made the knight very happy.

The day ended with construction still on schedule. The exhausted duo of Elisa and Lily barely had the energy to make their way back to the inn. They cleaned themselves, ate dinner, and soon headed to bed. William separately departed for the countryside.

William.

Yes, Princess?

I want to understand what I saw in your memories this morning, but I can feel your extreme reluctance to talk about them. We are also both exhausted. If I let my questions go for now, do you promise to tell me later, once we know each other better?

Mother considers those memories to be elven secrets, so she will want to meet you first before she gives me permission.

Ah, very interesting. Well, let's put aside that discussion for now. Great work today! Good night, Lily. Good night, William.

Good night.

Good night.

Fortunately for all three, if they had any shared dreams, no memory of those dreams remained the next morning.

Once the trio overcame their major issues, the next five days were a continual but predictable grind. The accumulated exhaustion began to weigh on them, but constant reuse of the same magic made them more efficient, so they did not fall behind schedule.

They began each morning by renewing their bonds. The renewals did not trigger sudden and deep memory exchanges, so the drama and trauma were avoided.

There were several surprises they discovered during the construction. Lily knew several military marching songs and chants from her time in the Varangian Guard. The ritual magic they were casting was a natural fit for the songs. It would have been awkward to sing the songs out loud, but they were perfect for their shared mental space.

Elisa knew an incredible number of jokes from her time with the Merchants Guild. Many of the jokes were quite risqué. It became her habit to taunt Lily and William during breaks. Lily was so easily embarrassed that Elisa was not entertained. William was a different story. He remained calm and collected regardless of her jibes. Elisa was very competitive, so she continued to push harder. By the fourth day, Lily pled with Elisa to stop—it was causing Lily to become quite distracted. Elisa agreed to the ceasefire, but only until the construction was done. Elisa pledged to embarrass William to his very soul once the wall was complete.

The pledge finally got a response from William. *Bring it, Princess*, he taunted.

Please let me out of here. These two are crazy! Lily thought.

William responded with a mental chuckle. Elisa's laughter was wickedly spicy.

William had an incredible depth of both mundane and arcane knowledge.

I thought you were just an army scout? Elisa queried.

The scout motto is "Be prepared," William replied.

Elisa huffed in irritation. Lily giggled at Elisa's frustration. The astute princess had yet to solve the riddle that was William. She wished she could ask about his memories now, not later.

At the end of six days, the wall and moat were complete. The village elders made plans to divert a nearby river to fill the moat, but they would handle that on their own.

The villagers created a feast in the village square for a celebration party that evening. The guests of honor were Princess Elisa and Dame Lily. Only a few of the partygoers even noticed that William was missing.

You have a knack for avoiding attention. You must tell me how you do that, Elisa thought.

Enjoy your party, ladies. You deserve it. I am going to enjoy my sleep, William answered with a drowsy chuckle.

Elisa, remember your promise, thought Lily. *Now that the wall is done, no more renewing the mental bond each morning. We are going to let it run its course.*

Yes, Lily, I remember. Oh, the mayor is about to get the party started. Let's enjoy ourselves this evening.

The mayor offered a series of toasts to begin the meal. The response to each toast was louder and more heartfelt than the previous one.

"To Captain Refren and the brave soldiers of the First Mounted Infantry Company, we bid you thanks for helping us recover our village and for your past and future protection.

"To Sir Aden and the party of the princess, thank you for healing our wounded. Without you, many who celebrate today would not have had the change.

"To Dame Lily, the Hero of Viverna and the Slayer of Giants. Bards will sing of your prowess in battle, which is only exceeded by kind and generous heart."

The army's response to this toast was deafening. Elisa grinned at Lily's conflicting emotions—fierce pride and extreme embarrassment. Pride won out that night.

"Finally, to Princess Elisa. In our darkest hour, you gave us hope...sorry, just a moment." The mayor's deep emotion was obvious to all. He took a moment to compose himself. "Several of the villagers you healed felt that they had been touched by an angel. In six days, you accomplished a miracle. We thank the Earth Goddess for sending you to us in our hour of need. Princess Elisa of Llanos, you have won our hearts. We are proud that you are our guardian angel!"

After the cheers calmed down, the mayor stepped aside so that Princess Elisa could speak. The small, exquisitely beautiful woman addressed the crowd.

"Thank you for your kind words. Thank you all for your support this past week. I wish we would have met under happier circumstances. We honor the fallen who have reached the Goddess before us. We share our sorrows, and we share our happiness. We dedicate this evening to you, our lost family members, friends, and neighbors. We will not let your sacrifice be in vain. We will grow stronger together. To the fallen!" Elisa raised her glass in salute.

"To the fallen!" the crowd replied, then drank.

The princess bowed deeply to the audience and then returned to her seat.

Captain Refren and Sir Aden sat next to each other during the celebration. The captain asked, "Are all the nobles in Llanos as charismatic and personable as the princess?"

"No, she is a rare bird. Vorland is lucky to receive her," replied Sir Aden.

"Agreed. And if she marries Prince Ryne, the two of them will be the joy of every commoner and the fear of every petty noble in the kingdom."

"Sounds like an interesting future," Sir Aden commented, "but why is serving such dynamic leaders exciting and exhausting at the same time?"

"Because they demand the best from you."

"Amen, brother."

The food was mostly finished, and the drinking began in earnest when Lily's dangersense was triggered, and she looked around for the threat. In this case, there were no monsters nearby, but something worse. The princess was barely hiding an impish grin, and she was not as tipsy as she pretended to be. Through the link, Lily sensed that Elisa had formulated a new plan, and that Lily was its focus.

Elisa noticed Lily watching her, and she made an effort to hide her thoughts. Elisa winked at Lily, then turned away. Lily felt a cold chill down her spine.

"Mr. Mayor, please remind me of the common meaning of your village's name," the princess requested.

Elisa, what are you planning?

"My pleasure, Your Highness. In the common tongue, Viverna translates as *wyvern*, the fierce and powerful two-legged dragon. The founder of our village once captured and tamed one of the magnificent beasts, and he used it to protect the village. Our founder was a very literal man, so he named both his wyvern and the village Viverna."

"What an amazing story, Mr. Mayor. So, the first hero of Viverna was a wyvern, a two-legged dragon?" said the princess.

Elisa, what are you doing? asked Lily in a panic.

"Yes, Your Highness, our legends state that Viverna the wyvern protected our church from a horde of monsters, very much like the way Dame Lily protected the same church."

"Really? How fascinating. Both heroes of Viverna—practically creatures of legend! They are so similar in so many ways…"

Please, Elisa, don't do this! Lily mentally pleaded.

Encouraged by the princess's train of thought, as well as a good amount of alcohol, the mayor added, "The Hero of Viverna village, Viverna the Wyvern. For titles, that is a bit of a mouthful, don't you think?"

Captain Refren's voice entered the conversation from Lily's other side. Lily turned to face him, and the smile on his face chilled her to the bone. "Your Highness, Mr. Mayor, are we all having similar thoughts? The Hero of Viverna, Dame Lily, is such a long title. If only there was a way to shorten it..."

"Gentlemen, you must be reading my thoughts! Humm, well, Viverna means *wyvern*..." noted Elisa.

"And a wyvern is a type of dragon..." added the mayor.

"So, the Hero of Viverna is the Dragon Hero," concluded Captain Refren.

Elisa, please stop this! Lily was beyond frantic by now.

"I have to admit that the Dragon Hero Dame Lily has a nice ring to it, but it still seems a bit long," stated the princess.

"Everyone, I think you are embarrassing Dame Lily. It's not very nice to tease a guest of honor. Please stop for Lily's sake," interjected Sir Aden.

LISTEN TO SIR ADEN! HE IS MY HERO! Lily mentally declared.

Unfortunately, everyone ignored Sir Aden. They were having too much fun to stop now.

"Dragon Hero Lily is better," explained Captain Refren.

"But the Dragon Lily would be best!" finished the mayor.

"TO THE DRAGON LILY! CHEERS!" shouted her companions.

Lily's new, unofficial title spread like wildfire through the celebration.

I DON'T WANT A NICKNAME! I JUST WANT TO BE LILY!

None of us get to choose our own nicknames. Our so-called friends do that for us. At least it is a cool name. I'm going back to bed. Please be quieter; it's hard to sleep, requested a sleepy but amused William.

Lily's alcohol consumption increased significantly as she

attempted to hide her embarrassment and ignore the occasional cheer of "Dragon Lily!" Combined with the exhaustion from the last few days, Lily soon fell asleep at the table.

Elisa started to wake Lily so that they could walk back to the inn, but Sir Aden stopped her. As the mayor motioned for the crowd to be quiet, the handsome and gallant Aden gently picked up Lily and princess-carried her away from the party. At that moment, unbeknownst to her, Lily was the envy of every female celebrant. Elisa soon followed, after tossing a smile and a wink to the crowd.

Along the way, Lily woke up briefly and saw Sir Aden's kind face very close to hers. In her exhausted delirium, she figured she must be having a wonderful dream. "Wow, up close, you are even more handsome than I realized."

Aden smiled but did not respond.

Lily cupped his cheek with her hand. "Since this is a dream, I can tell you how I feel. You are wonderful and strong and kind. I wish you were my boyfriend. I wish I had the courage to tell you when I am awake." Her words finished, Lily fell back to sleep.

The group heading to the inn consisted of Elisa, Lily, Aden, their guards, and the two ladies-in-waiting. Unfortunately, Lily was both loud and understandable when she spoke.

"This remains among us. Do you understand?" commanded the princess. There was an edge to her voice that made her intentions clear. The others acceded.

Lily woke with a hangover the next morning. This was not the first time she had suffered ill consequences for her drinking, but she did not make a habit of it. Fortunately, she knew a couple of spells that would lessen the effects. She was well-practiced with these spells, as they had been in high demand during her time in the Varangian Guard. She had cast them many times for hurting soldiers.

Unfortunately, her magic could not change the past. The princess had successfully labeled her with a new nickname and, given the response of the party celebrants last night, she would be stuck with it for a long time.

The mental link was quiet, so Lily seemed to have her mind to herself. Needing a distraction to prevent a fresh bout of embarrassment, Lily savored the wonderful dream she had the previous night about Sir Aden. The room she shared with Elisa was empty, so Lily took her time getting dressed. She wished she could avoid everyone today, but that was not an option. Now that the wall was done, they would be leaving the village today.

Still not quite ready to face the princess, Lily used the back staircase to head for the inn's courtyard. There was a well there for public use. A splash of cold water on her face seemed like a great idea.

Just before she opened the door to go outside, Lily heard a loud, angry voice in the courtyard. Fearing that a fight was about to break out, she quickly ran outside, hand on her sword, looking for the trouble.

Surprisingly, the courtyard was empty, but now she could hear the voice clearly. It was Lady Philippa, one of the ladies-in-waiting. While she was still in her room, the shutters to her windows were open. She was practically screaming in rage.

"DID YOU HEAR THAT SHAMELESS HARLOT PRETENDING TO BE ASLEEP? AFTER SIR ADEN AGREED TO CARRY HER DRUNKEN, OVERSIZED BODY BACK TO THE INN? 'Since this is a dream, I can tell you how I feel. You are wonderful and strong and kind. I wish you were my boyfriend. I wish I had the courage to tell you when I am awake.' SIR ADEN TOOK PITY ON HER, AND SHE TOOK ADVANTAGE OF HIM. HOW COULD HE EVEN SUFFER TO BE NEAR THAT CLUMSY, UGLY COW!?"

"Lady Philippa, please calm down. You are being too loud. Others will hear you!" said another female voice, likely one of the maids.

"How dare you tell me what to do! Do you know who I am? I'm the daughter of a count. I will have you flogged for your disrespect!"

Lady Philippa's voice continued to fill the courtyard, but Lily no longer heard it. She was frozen in place, completely horrified. The embarrassment of her dream being real barely even registered. Her mind twisted Lady Philippa's words in the worst way: *Sir Aden pities me... He thinks I'm a clumsy, ugly cow? Aaaaaaaah!*

The mental bonds were still active among Elisa, Lily, and William. Elisa and William had decided to let Lily sleep in while they readied the escort for its departure. Sir Aden and Captain Refren were handling the security details. The princess, with William as her attendant, was making the rounds of the village to say their goodbyes.

Before Lily woke, Elisa and William discussed if and how to let Lily know that her "dream" was, in fact, reality. The princess decided that she would let Lily know later in the day while they were in the carriage. That would allow Lily to get over any embarrassment before she had to see Sir Aden at dinner that night.

Plans changed suddenly when Lily screamed in the shared mental space.

Lily, what's wrong? Elisa asked but could not get through to her knight. The princess excused herself from her conversation with a village elder and then headed back to the inn. *William, run ahead and see what is wrong.*

Not until I hand off your security. Aden and Refren are nearby. Let's head to them first.

Elisa was frustrated by William's reply, but she could not countermand him. Her safety was the priority, even if her knight's pain tore at the princess's heart. Moreover, Elisa wanted to run to Lily, but the sight of such a spectacle might terrify the villagers. She continued to be a proper princess, moving slowly through the streets of Viverna.

The pair found the commander and captain a couple of minutes later. William took off with inhuman speed.

"Sir Aden, please accompany me back to the inn. We have some last-minute escort arrangements to make."

"At once, Your Highness. Captain, I'll meet with you again after we are done."

Less than a minute into her walk back to the inn, Elisa was contacted by William.

Elisa, I am with Lily. She overheard Lady Philippa lying about what happened last night, and she is quite upset. I'm trying to calm her down now. Please meet us in the private room at the inn.

The walk to the inn took several minutes, and one of the off-duty fighters stopped Elisa and Aden along the way. He had overheard the entire rant back at the inn, realized the problem it presented, and rushed to find Sir Aden. The man was visibly nervous reporting to royalty, but with the princess's encouragement, he gave an accurate recounting of Lady Philippa's tirade. Elisa thanked the fighter and sent him on his way.

The princess turned to face Aden, who had remained quiet during the report. The male knight was struggling to remain calm. His jaw was clenched in anger.

"Sir Aden, let us continue to the inn. When we get there, will you please see to Lily? I'll handle my lady-in-waiting."

"Thank you, Your Highness. Unless you would prefer Lady Philippa to disappear from the village right now. I'm very willing to handle that duty."

"We both know the political ramifications of the death of a count's daughter. They would all fall on your head since you are the one headed back to Llanos once the escort is done. But please know that it gladdens my heart that you are willing to take such action on Lily's behalf."

"My pleasure, Your Highness. I owe my life to both you and Dame Lily."

"Do you know what you want to say to Lily?"

"I do. I had a lot of time last night to think about it."

Elisa's eyes shot up in surprise, and she looked questioningly at Aden.

The handsome knight's face suddenly turned red. "I am very fond of Lily, but I did not know she felt the same." They walked in silence for a few moments before Aden continued, "Unfortunately, I am promised to another. I plan to be truthful to Lily." The sadness in his voice was clear.

A few minutes later, Elisa mentally announced her arrival. *William, Aden and I are almost there. Is it okay if we come in?*

Yes, Elisa, please do.

The princess entered the room first. Lily appeared calm, but Elisa could feel her friend's raw emotions through the mental link. Lily was a mess inside.

"Lily, there is someone here to see you," Elisa said.

Lily looked up and saw Aden standing behind the princess. She panicked, but Aden quickly moved to grab her hands and hold them in his own.

"Dame Lily, please look at me," requested Aden in a calm and soothing voice. Lily kept her gaze firmly on the floor. "Lily, I understand you overheard a horrible person shouting lies about me and about how I feel about you. May I please tell you the truth?"

In a quiet voice, Lily asked, "Is this a dream? I am sure that my dream version of you would say such kind things."

"You have dreams about me?" asked a surprised Aden, his face growing red.

Lily made eye contact with the embarrassed male knight. In an instant, she knew two things. This was very much real life, and she had just admitted something she should not have. Her embarrassment rose. However, neither Lily nor Aden removed their hands from each other's.

Elisa needed to break the tension in the room. She knew just the thing—a common adversary. "For the love of the Goddess, you two are so adorable. Look at you holding hands and being nervous about sharing your feelings."

"Elisa!" exclaimed Lily.

"Your Highness!" echoed Sir Aden.

Lily and Aden had both responded with annoyance at the princess, exactly like Elisa had intended. The awkwardness left the room.

"Looks like my work here is done. Why don't you talk between yourselves? William and I are going to step outside. Let us know if you need anything."

CHAPTER 6

Princess Elisa and William left the inn to discuss what to do with Lady Philippa. She was the daughter of a count loyal to Prince Logan, so they had to treat her cautiously. Elisa knew she had been included in the escort party to be a thorn in Elisa's side. Lady Philippa was performing her duty magnificently. However, her lies about Sir Aden threatened to undermine the party's cohesion. Furthermore, she had ignored a direct command from the princess to not speak about Lily's words last night. Her disruptive presence had to be removed.

Elisa included William in her planning. She needed advice she could trust, and she could not involve Lily this time. Elisa generated a plan, but it was likely to produce drama, so they waited for Lily to finish before proceeding.

Thirty minutes later, Lily reached out to Elisa and William and asked them to return to the inn. Lily had not leaked any strong emotions, so the pair were unsure how the meeting had gone. The door to the inn's common room opened, and Lily was standing next to Aden. They were awkwardly trying to determine how to part—a handshake or a hug.

Hug him! commanded Elisa.

Lily obeyed, and both Lily and Aden seemed happy. As Aden was about to break the embrace, Lily grinned mischievously and gripped him tighter. Aden responded and escalated. A friendly embrace turned into a bear-hug competition. Their armor creaked, and they winced as each tried to force the other to submit. They were evenly matched and immensely strong.

"No magic!" cried Elisa. She had sensed Lily was about to escalate. Lily grumbled but complied.

The others in the common room were cheering for their favorite, with the split between fighters being even. After several minutes, the contest ended without a clear winner. Both contestants were smiling.

Sir Aden saluted Lily and bowed to the princess, then went outside to finish preparations for their departure. Elisa and William followed Lily back into the meeting room.

Lily was quiet and a bit sad. Elisa and William waited patiently.

After a short pause, Lily explained, *I wanted a boyfriend who might become a husband. Instead, I made a new close friend, but only a friend. He did not reject me. He could not accept me in the first place. Before the escort mission started, he promised to honor his father's wishes. His father is a baron in the east of Llanos. Their northern neighbor is another baron. The barons were bitter rivals in their youth, but old age has mellowed them. The northern baron's daughter will be of age in two months. The barons have conspired to have their children marry to settle their differences.*

*Aden told me he did not sleep last night. He wrestled with whether to marry the girl back home or to cast her aside and pursue me. In the end, he felt he had to honor his promise. If he broke his promise, then he felt he would not be worthy of me. It was such a heartfelt explanation that I feel sorry for him. At least if he rejected me, I could be mad at him. U*GH! Lily facepalmed and sighed. She looked up at Elisa with a small, sad smile.

Elisa thought, *Lily, I'm proud of you. Let's talk more as we travel. For now, I want you to confirm with everyone that we are ready to get underway. And please ask Lady Philippa to report to me here.*

Lily looked puzzled.

William explained, *Elisa is going to deal with the person who hurt her best friend.*

Lily wore a genuine smile as she left the room.

Lady Philippa was annoyed when she entered the meeting room. The errant princess sat at the table. Her only guard was a young boy in forest garb. A strong wind could have knocked him down. Philippa moved to sit at the table.

"I did not give you leave to sit," the princess stated in a direct voice.

Lady Philippa narrowed her eyes as she stared at Elisa. "Excuse me?" was her antagonistic response.

"This meeting is to address your behavior during this trip. Your presence in the party has become a distraction and a danger. You will remain in Viverna until Sir Aden and the remainder of the escort pass through on their return trip," the princess explained.

Lady Philippa exploded with barely contained anger. How dare this royal embarrassment talk to her like this? Philippa was the first daughter of a count of Llanos. Elisa was the disgraced and ridiculed third child of a duke. In the eyes of Llanos society, the women were almost of equal rank. Granted, Elisa's father was currently in the line of succession, but if the rumors were true about the king's health, that would soon be changing.

Lady Philippa had been ordered by her father to attend and escort Princess Elisa. Philippa initially rejected the command but relented when she discovered her reward. If she were successful in her mission, she would be engaged to the first prince's second son. After the death of the old king, she would become a princess.

The trip had been an absolute nightmare. Princess Elisa and her escort were far too comfortable with commoners, sometimes even treating them as equals. The only eye candy on the journey was Sir Aden, and he had fallen for the so-called Hero of Viverna, that clumsy, ugly cow, Lily. The attack on the village had been terrifying, but the recovery had been worse. Helping these filthy commoners repair the hovels was beneath her.

Her mission was simply to confirm that Elisa had been transferred to Prince Ryne and then report back to her father. Staying behind in Viverna would prevent her from fulfilling her mission and might jeopardize her engagement. "How DARE YOU—" she began to scream.

Lady Philippa stopped mid-scream. A wave of terror filled her heart, and she froze in place. She slowly turned her eyes and stared at the guard she had mistaken for a young boy. He had not moved nor spoken, but he was suddenly radiating overwhelming murderous intent.

Lady Philippa's knees buckled, and she fell to the floor. Her bladder let go, leaving a wet spot on the floor around her. She was barely aware of anything that happened. Her focus was on the intense figure of the guard.

The man lowered the hood of his cloak. Lady Philippa struggled to remember why he looked so familiar. Slowly it dawned on her. She had heard a story of a terrifying creature that killed without mercy. A man of such evil that all feared his presence. Slowly, the story returned to her. "You...you are the Shadow Prince...please have mercy on me," she cried.

If the rumors were to be believed, the Shadow Prince was the current reincarnation of the Demon Lord, a being so vast and powerful that none could stand against him. Now standing in his presence, Lady Philippa knew the rumors were true.

The Shadow Prince's mouth split into a cruel and thoroughly evil smile. "I give you a choice: you will either listen and follow the princess's instructions, or I will deal with you... personally."

"Please, Princess Elisa, forgive me. I promise I will obey you. Please save me from him!"

Princess Elisa continued, "As I was saying, you will remain in Viverna. You will make yourself useful and continue to aid in the village's recovery. The head priest and the mayor will be watching over you. I pray they have only nice things to say about you on Sir Aden's return. We will leave enough money for your continued room and board at the inn. If you need anything else, talk to the mayor. Now, clean up the floor and leave."

Lady Philippa did so, trying desperately to avoid the Shadow Prince's gaze.

Well, that was unexpected, Elisa stated after Philippa left. *I was not the focus of the intimidation, and I nearly wet myself.*

Thanks for soundproofing the room with your spell. These encounters are awkward at best, and this one was much worse than normal. This kind of intimidation relies on the target's worst fears. I am never quite sure how it will go, William replied.

Lily had been silent up to this point. She had been waiting in the common room for her friends, and she had experienced the encounter through the mental link. She got a case of the giggles. *The Shadow Prince? The boogeyman of the continent? The creature that parents use to scare their children into behaving? The new Demon Lord. BWAHAHAHA! Oh my Goddess, that is awesome!* Lily paused for a breath.

William thought, *My warding magic is great when I need people to forget me, but sometimes I need to leave a lasting impression. I can do that through the intimidation effect. They won't remember me, but they will remember something out of their worst nightmares. To make the effect more powerful, Ryne employed a group of bards to circulate new stories about a man of overwhelming evil based on long-told tales. Your lady-in-waiting must have heard these stories. I must admit, the whole "Shadow Prince" name is new to me. Apparently, you are not the only one to have gained a new nickname, Lily.* William's annoyance was clear through the link.

You are always full of surprises, William. Seriously, who are you? asked the princess.

I'm just a simple young man trying to make his way in the world. I had an...interesting childhood. But that is a topic for later. We need to start traveling again.

The trio left the inn and joined the escort. They resumed their journey to Auraria.

The trip from Taronto of Llanos to Auraria of Vorland normally took two months. The village of Viverna was five weeks' travel from Taronto. Princess Elisa's group had three weeks of travel remaining.

The company had begun the journey with twenty people but was now down to fifteen. They had lost three guards during the battle of Viverna, William was added, and Lady Philippa was removed. Elisa left two guards behind for Philippa, but she refused to leave one of the maids. Philippa was about to get a rude awakening about how non-nobles lived.

For the next ten days, the group would be traveling through Prince Nevan's land. Nevan was the second prince of Vorland, and he was a close ally of his brother, Prince Ryne. Captain Refren and his Mounted Infantry Company owed their allegiance to Nevan. The army escort would be useful while moving through the open countryside. This was their land, and they patrolled it regularly.

The combined group reached the border between Nevan's and Ryne's territories on schedule. Even with the large group to discourage potential enemies, the trip was still eventful.

The first surprise was personal and handled quietly. On the third day of the trip, William woke up feeling under the weather. He felt weary, and his stomach was cramping. Wondering if he had eaten bad food the night before, he cast purification magic, but it did not help. Oddly, his chest hurt for no apparent reason. He had never suffered this particular set of symptoms before, so it took him a while to understand what was happening. The mental link between himself, Princess Elisa, and Dame Lily continued to diminish each day, but it was still active enough to share emotions and physical feelings.

The combined group was camping at a waystation along the main road. The facilities were primitive, so Elisa and Lily slept in the princess's carriage. Dawn was almost an hour away, so the camp was still and quiet. If he wanted to take care of this discreetly, he needed to move quickly.

William had been trained in a wide range of skills, and he had access to an amazing variety of spells. However, the spells and techniques he sought now were not ones he had used before. He conjured a small light in his tent, then produced a thick book from his extradimensional space. The book was a gift from his mother, Willow, and it contained knowledge she had gained throughout her long life. *Willow's Book of Wisdom* was the title.

He found the chapter he needed. It began, "*I always figured we would talk about this subject in person, but I guess you have an immediate need?*" As a book meant only for his personal use, William's mother always started each chapter with a pun, a taunt, or a joke. Sometimes there would be a warning, but that was only for the immensely dangerous stuff—elemental summoning, for example. Given his present discomfort, William ignored her jibe and continued to read. As always, the chapter contained detailed descriptions, explanations, and illustrations. Willow was an exceptional teacher and mentor, but she was also his mom, so she was still annoying even when she was helpful.

Ten minutes later, William possessed more knowledge of "female issues" than he had ever desired. It was a low bar—he wished he knew nothing. During the time he was reading, the abdominal pain had grown more acute. As his discomfort increased, he began the hard part—convincing the women with whom he shared the mental link.

Good morning, Princess. Good morning, Lily, William began.

No, it is not, was the mentally grumbled reply from both women.

Not feeling well? I understand, William continued.

No, you don't! Lily's reply was very hostile.

Right now, I do understand.

The women were silent.

Oh, sorry, Elisa replied finally.

My mother left me instructions on what to do. Please let me help you both.

Silence.

I don't have to do anything strange. Lily will punish me if I do anything creepy or weird.

Still silence.

William was getting desperate. He needed to start scouting the area soon, and the pain would hinder his abilities. *Please, ladies. Let me help you. I don't have the correct body parts to handle these odd sensations and feelings. I admit I'm not tough enough to be a girl.*

William could sense Elisa thinking. *Okay, but on one condition. You will promise to grant a request I give you in the future. You will not complain, and you will not balk. I won't ask anything against your morals or ethics. Do you agree?*

Ah. William realized he was now negotiating with Princess Elisa. William had to admit she was both clever and forward-thinking.

Flattery is nice, but agreement is better, Elisa said. She had not fallen for William's feint.

All right, Princess, I agree.

Excellent. Now, please show us the latest example of how William knows something he should not know.

William ignored the sarcasm, then approached and entered the carriage. Shadows covered him in darkness. He released the shadows once the door was closed. The light was dim inside.

Elisa and Lily were both in their bedclothes. His visit

would be considered scandalous if anyone discovered him. The clothing itself was quite modest, but in both Llanos and Vorland, a large amount of an unmarried princess's worth was tied to her chastity. William needed to act quickly and then escape.

William explained the technique and the corresponding spell. Like many elven spells, this one focused on pain mitigation while not harming the body's normal processes. Since this was not an emergency, this spell seemed the best to use.

Lily's eyes narrowed dangerously when William described the physical contact between the caster and the patient. *You want to put your hands where?* she asked.

One on your stomach and one on the lower back.

You will do it to me first. If I approve, then I will allow you to treat Elisa. If I sense any perversion or inappropriate behavior, I will sever your manhood on the spot.

I understand. Normally, William would have been nervous. The pain through the mental link had driven any naughty thoughts far away.

Lily exposed her midriff and lower back. She glared daggers as William approached. He tried to ignore her and gently placed his hands on Lily. Lily quickly inhaled in panic. William stopped, but he did not remove his hands.

Are you okay, Lily? asked Elisa.

Yes, I'm fine. This just feels odd. I'm not used to a man touching me like this. Go ahead, continue.

William's hands were small and slightly rough. They felt warm and comforting against her skin. *This spell will take a bit longer, as I have only now learned the chant.* Pleasant Elvish words filled Lily's mind. She felt herself calming down and a warmth filling her body. After a minute, William finished and removed his hands. Lily felt a twinge of regret that the treatment was over. Assessing her body, Lily still felt the sensations of her menses, but her pain was gone. However, she could still feel the discomfort coming from Elisa.

Through the shared link, Elisa had experienced Lily's successful treatment. She gave her permission and exposed her skin as well. Given Lily's earlier threat, William did not move until Lily also granted permission.

William repeated the procedure on Elisa with equal success. He then covered himself in shadow and left the carriage.

The women went back to sleep as William began his scouting.

An hour after sunup, the combined group was ready to travel. Princess Elisa was enjoying the morning, and her mood had turned mischievous. *Lily, are you aware of any techniques as effective as William's?*

No, I'm not. The more skilled healers have spells to address women's health during pregnancy and childbirth, but even those are for emergencies due to their side effects. I've never heard of such subtle and wonderful magic.

Neither have I. William, how do you know such things?

William cleared his throat. He was reluctant to discuss this topic, but both women seemed to be in good spirits, and he wanted to keep them that way. *The magic comes from my mother. Elven women are extremely long-lived, and they are capable of pregnancy through almost all of it. Given what I experienced today, I suspect the motive for crafting such magic was driven by the expectation of facing hundreds of years of such discomfort.*

Oh my Goddess, how old is your mother?

One thousand and seventeen.

How old does she appear? questioned Elisa.

Please don't make me answer. You will not like the answer, pleaded William.

Tell me! demanded Elisa.

Unless there is a disease or some curse magic, an elf's body stops physically aging at around twenty years old.

For the next couple of minutes, the shared mental space was filled with colorful and spicy language.

Once the outrage lessened, William continued. *Now you*

know why the elves seldom engage with the outside world. Jealousy and anger from humans led the elves to withdraw inside their borders. Visitors are rare and always special.

Sorry, William, I was just going to tease you that you could become rich using your technique in a major capital like Taronto. Women would kill to have you aid them.

William snorted. Mother warned against that. "Men should not use these spells, but if they do, they should only use them on women they trust and respect. You will provide her a comfort no one else can give. She will be your friend for life, but her lover will attempt to slay you in a most gruesome fashion. True story."

William seemed to focus on the last part of the warning. Elisa and Lily focused on the first part. In any case, the first unexpected development of note in this part of their journey was successfully concluded.

CHAPTER 7

The second development was an event both planned and public. The attention-hungry princess wanted more fame for herself and Lily, but her latest strategy required more spectators. Fortunately, the city of Folsom was ideal for her needs.

The combined group arrived in Folsom on the seventh day of the resumed trip. While smaller than the namesake city of the Wincheesh Duchy, Folsom was a bustling trade hub and the city nearest to Auraria.

The combined group reached their accommodations just before lunch. The Vorland military maintained a large barracks complex in the city. Princess Elisa accepted Captain Refren's invitation to stay in the complex. While an inn would have been more relaxing, the added security of the barracks was comforting.

After securing their rooms, the princess's party joined Captain Refren and his soldiers on the large practice field outside. The soldiers were standing in a large circle. The mood was relaxed, and Sergeant Carter was addressing his troops.

"Troopers, we have a bit of time this afternoon for training. I know you love training."

The soldiers responded with good-natured grumbling. "What did I just hear? Where is the enthusiasm?" taunted Sergeant Carter.

The soldiers responded with a half-hearted cheer, but they were all grinning. This was standard banter between the soldiers and their much-respected Sergeant Carter.

"I am disappointed, troopers! I planned a special surprise for you, and this is thanks I get?" yelled Sergeant Carter.

"Hoorah!" the soldiers responded in perfect unison.

"That's better, but I don't think our guests heard you!" Sergeant Carter gestured to the princess's group.

"Hoorah! Hoorah! Hoorah!"

"Much better. Captain, the troopers are yours." Sergeant Carter stepped aside, and Captain Refren stepped forward.

"Troopers, our esteemed Llanos comrades, Sir Aden and Dame Lily, have agreed to train with us today. They will each participate in mock battles against anyone willing to step forward." As Refren was talking, Aden and Lily stepped into the nearby practice rings. "Remember, we are sparring here today, so no permanent damage."

Sergeant Carter added, "But what are a few bruised bodies and egos among friends? Humm, I like that line. Has a nice ring to it, hehe."

The soldiers were genuinely excited. Against their own knights, the soldiers would often hold back lest a bruised noble's pride force them on KP duty for a month. But if any of them could land a solid hit on one of the Llanos knights, they would have bragging rights for the rest of the year.

A rack of wooden practice swords was placed next to each of the practice rings. Aden grabbed a sword, then began to warm up his body as he waited for the soldiers to queue in front of him. A collective gasp from the crowd caused him to pause. Everyone was focused on Lily.

Rather than borrow a practice sword, Lily was kneeling in the dirt with her right hand touching the ground. Loose sand swirled around her arm. With a look of extreme concentration, she slowly stood up. Her hand was now gripping a handle of polished stone. As she continued to rise, a blade of stone rose from the earth. Her spell complete, she took a few practice swings. "Mind if I use this?" she asked Captain Refren.

Captain Refren motioned to Sergeant Carter, who walked forward to inspect the weapon. He nearly fell forward from the weight of the odd sword. "The weapon is properly dull and absurdly heavy. Dame Lily, if you wish to handicap yourself thus, please be my guest."

A few minutes later, the mock combat began. Well, at least it began for Sir Aden. His queue was a dozen deep with both experienced veterans and excited new recruits. He took each challenger in turn, with each battle lasting a maximum of three minutes. He allowed the challengers to pace themselves. With the younger fighters, he offered tips and feedback when they paused between attacks. He took brief breaks every half hour, but otherwise fought throughout the afternoon without pause.

Dame Lily's queue was empty for the first hour. She stood there stoically, but inside she began to despair. *Don't they like me?* she asked Elisa and William.

Making your own sword from dirt was probably a bit much, teased William.

For the love of the Goddess, this feels like a children's ball where the boys are too afraid to ask the pretty girl to dance, huffed Elisa. She walked over and spoke quietly to Sergeant Carter. He nodded, then walked over to Lily. The two talked for a few moments. Lily was smiling and much happier.

Sergeant Carter stepped in front of Lily's practice ring. "Troopers, you have such bad manners. Dame Lily has been waiting patiently, but no one steps forward."

"Neither have you, Sergeant," responded a heckler from the crowd.

"So true, trooper, so true. I mean, this young, beautiful knight slew a giant in front of our own eyes. Who would not be intimidated?"

Lily's cheeks reddened at the sergeant's words.

"Still, we would be poor hosts if we denied our guest a bit of sparring. Therefore, Dame Lily has consented to allow

group combat against her. That's right, you chickens, you are allowed to coordinate your attacks against the flower of the Llanos military. And what is the First Mounted Infantry Company of Vorland known for? Mass attacks!"
Several groups of soldiers began to coordinate and form the queue.

Before the first battle, additional rules were created. The groups had to start at the edge of the circle in a one-fighter-deep line—this kept the entire company from rushing her at once. Still, a group as large as a dozen could engage her. The fights were limited to ten minutes. Lily was allowed to use magic, but only body-enhancing magic. Her area of effect and ranged attack magics were not allowed.

The first fight was a group of four young males. Individually, they had been intimidated, but together, they were fearless. They had seen the weight of Lily's sword and expected her swings to be slow and predictable. They charged her all at once at the start of the match. The match ended thirty seconds later when the last challenger left the ring. The first three had left the ring by flying through the air from Lily's shield bash. The last one she had to chase. The spectators pulled back a healthy distance from the ring.

"That was awesome! I was running towards her, then boom! I was flying backwards. Do you see how high I flew?" exclaimed one of the men.

"Wow, trooper, you are both young and stupid," Sergeant Carter taunted. "Everyone, what did we learn? Say it with me—shields are weapons, too!"

The first fight had broken the ice, and Sergeant Carter was a perfect emcee. Lily was still immensely powerful, but she no longer seemed unapproachable. Each consecutive group of fighters became more coordinated and focused, and they started to challenge Lily.

The last fight was destined to be Lily's favorite. She had been steadily battling for over two hours. She was tired and hungry, but she was having so much fun. The last group was composed of the twelve women of the First Mounted Infantry Company. They had watched and analyzed every previous fight. Their leader was a veteran with two decades of experience. They were focused and ready for this fight.

Elisa, I'm spent. If I fight completely defensively, I might be able to run out the clock. But no guarantees even then.

Lily, I'm sorry to ask, but this must be a capstone event against your sisters-in-arms. I want the bards to sing about this battle.

What are you thinking, Princess? asked Lily cautiously.

Thank you for asking...

Lily winced at Elisa's plan, but she agreed it would be interesting. William was stoic about his part. After all, the princess had called in her favor—he agreed to do as Elisa asked without complaining.

As the contestants prepared for the final contest, Princess Elisa of Llanos stepped into the ring. She was a tiny, beautiful woman with a commanding voice. "Soldiers of Vorland, thank you for a splendid day. Your leaders told me you were brave, and you have proven that today. Your coordination and skill honor the wolf that is your emblem. But you face one of Llanos's finest warriors. You may have heard that Dame Lily has the soul of a dragon, and if we challenge her enough, perhaps we will feel her roar."

What are you doing, Elisa? Please stop it! pleaded Lily.

Hush, you, I'm just playing to the crowd. Proceed as we discussed.

The long-suffering female knight let out a long sigh within the shared mental space, but she kept her public face stoic.

Elisa dramatically pointed a finger at Lily. "Dragon Lily, I will use my magic to aid these lovely warriors. Together, we will defeat you. Do you accept this challenge?"

The number of spectators had grown throughout the day.

Several town leaders, as well as the professional militia that used the barracks, joined the crowd. The energetic group had taunted and cheered, giving these mock combats a festive feel.

Lily stood in the middle of the ring. She stroked her chin in thought. She did not answer out loud. *Elisa, this is so cringy!*

Just do it! teased the princess.

Elisa continued her melodramatic address. "Friends! Will you help me encourage her to accept?"

"Yes!" came the crowd's reply.

"Dra-gon! Dra-gon!" chanted Elisa.

"Dra-gon! Dra-gon!" repeated the crowd.

After a few moments, Lily threw her hands in the air. The crowd became quiet.

"Fine, I'll do it. Just quit chanting. I don't want my new nickname!" Lily begged.

The crowd burst into laughter.

"Since you are helping our friends, I get to use any of my magic, correct?" asked Lily.

Elisa agreed and then looked around the area. "Captain Refren, our crowd has grown. Could we move the battle to a more spectator-friendly location? You all would like that, yes?" Elisa asked the crowd.

"Yes!" replied the crowd.

"Yes, Your Highness, let us adjourn to the training field just south of the city," Refren replied.

The assembled crowd and combatants walked out of the city gates to the training field. They were a boisterous lot, and curious onlookers asked what was happening. News of the mock battle spread like wildfire, and the number of spectators grew to almost a thousand.

The training field was an ideal place for the battle. The field was large and level, and the terrain on the city side was sloped, allowing good views for all the spectators. A larger combat ring was set up, which would make it harder for Lily to knock her opponents out of the ring, but it also allowed her more room to maneuver.

The soldiers placed racks of replacement weapons, both spears and swords, at the edge of the circle. They were clearly expecting a protracted battle.

Sergeant Carter resumed his emcee duties. His powerful voice projected well through the crowd.

"Ladies, gentlemen, and children of all ages, welcome to the final mock battle of the day. For those who are just joining us, the soldiers of Vorland have been facing selected warriors from Llanos in tests of strength and skill. Contestants may fight until they are incapacitated, choose to surrender, or otherwise leave the ring. This is a friendly contest, so no long-term injuries, maiming, or killing. But what are a few bruised bodies and egos among friends? The contest will end when one side can no longer fight or ten minutes have elapsed.

"This is a group combat. Representing the home team, I present the dozen lovely warrior maidens of—"

"I'm married!" yelled one of the female soldiers.

"Maidens and matrons of the First Mounted Infantry Company of Vorland, the Valkyries!" announced Sergeant Carter.

The crowd cheered loudly as the Valkyries saluted.

"The home team will be aided and supported by the powerful magics of our honored guest, the guardian angel of Viverna, Princess Elisa of Llanos!"

Princess Elisa saluted and bowed to the crowd. The townspeople were confused—"She is a Llanos princess?" "What about Viverna?" "Why is she helping Vorland?"—so their response was modest, but Captain Refren and his soldiers, including the contestants, gave a hearty "Hoorah! Hoorah! Hoorah!"

Sergeant Carter continued, "They will be facing a single opponent. She is a knight of Llanos and priestess of the Earth Goddess. She held the church in Viverna against a horde of monsters, including a giant, less than a fortnight ago. She is not only undefeated, but also untouched in her battles today. I present to you the Hero of Viverna, the Dragon Lily!"

A chant of "Dra-gon! Dra-gon!" followed Lily to the center of the ring.

An exasperated Lily pleaded with the crowd, "Please don't call me that!"

Gales of laughter answered her pleas.

"Combatants! Prepare yourselves!" announced the sergeant.

The twelve female Vorlandish soldiers gathered around Princess Elisa. Several of them had minor magical abilities, and all of them had been healed by priests before, but none had worked with a priestess of Elisa's caliber. She cast a group enhancement spell on them that would boost their strength, endurance, and toughness. Elisa poured a tremendous amount of mana into the spell. The air around them crackled with power. The excitement in the crowd grew. The women declared themselves ready and moved to their positions along the edge of the circle. Princess Elisa stood outside the ring, facing the crowd on the slope. A couple of her guards stood nearby, and a young man in green, perhaps her page, waited by her side.

All eyes now on her, Lily cast aside her battered shield. She formed another stone sword from the ground. This was the first time most of the crowd had seen this magic. The children particularly liked it. It was a scene from a heroic tale.

Lily then crossed her swords in front of her, and she cast her enhancement magic. Her voice was low, deep, and powerful, and the ground all around her began to vibrate. Nervous anticipation filled the crowd. Lily finished her spell and took her ready position.

Sergeant Carter shouted, "Go!" and the battle commenced.

The Valkyrie women attacked in squads of four, two from the front and two from the back. As they grew weary or were forced to retreat, the next set of four would attack. Their goal was to use their strength of numbers to never allow Lily to rest. Their coordination was precise and focused. When Lily moved to attack the pair in front, the pair behind her lunged at her back.

The first minute was filled with attacks, feints, dodges, and parries. The women refined their coordination and took the measure of their opponent. Lily moved gracefully and purposely around the circle, commanding the area within reach of her blades. To the less-knowledgeable spectators, the blades' movements were part of a free-flow dance. To the veterans, these movements were just teasers for the action to come.

At the one-minute mark, a glow pulsed through Elisa and spread to the Valkyries. Their movements became quicker and their bodies stronger. The Valkyries began to attack in earnest, four wooden swords and four steel shields at a time against the two stone blades. The sounds were wood against stone and stone against steel. The crowd was quiet, and the only voices were the squad leaders calling instructions. Lily had to increase her tempo, but her defenses remained strong, and no attack reached her.

Every minute after the first, Elisa further strengthened her magic, and the Valkyries increased their assault. Four minutes in, wooden swords shattered and were replaced. Shields were dented but held firm.

At five minutes, the Valkyries' movements were so quick they were blurry. A deflected sword hit the ground and left a small crater.

At six minutes, the women changed their attack pattern without warning. They reformed into two groups of six. Six women attacked Lily's left sword at the same time. Amplified by Elisa's magic, the Valkyries' tremendous blows shattered Lily's sword at the cost of all six of their swords. The second group of six immediately lunged forward to capitalize on their advantage. Their blades sliced through the air. With superhuman effort, Lily leaped clear of the entrapment and charged the second group from behind to scatter them.

Lily continued her run around the inside edge of the circle. Still holding the broken stone sword, she leaned down and dragged the edge along the surface of the ground. A deep furrow began to form, and the sound of stone grinding on stone filled the air. Within a few strides, her sword was reformed, and Lily returned to the fray. The Valkyries switched to defense to keep Lily busy, and half their members switched from swords to spears.

At seven minutes, the Valkyries received another surge, and they went on the attack again. Lily stayed defensive while the Valkyries regrouped. This was surprising to the veteran fighters, as it was the first time in the battle that Lily was not being constantly attacked.

Sir Aden was the first to realize how Lily had spent her time. He laughed and said, "It is about to get really interesting." The spectators around him were puzzled until they saw the ground within the combat ring ripple and shatter, uneven and treacherous under the Valkyries' feet.

Three Valkyries near Lily lost their footing and fell to the ground. In an instant, she closed in on them and slammed the flat of her blade against them in quick succession. Each took the brunt of the blow on their shield, but the impact sent them flying. Only quick reactions by their comrades kept them inside the ring. They were shaken, but their magically enhanced bodies kept them in the fight.

Controlling the surface of the field required concentration from Lily, so most of her movement was defensive. However, the Valkyries could not take advantage of Lily's distraction due to the lack of solid ground.

Just before the eighth minute, Lily passed near Elisa's position and delivered a loud, evil-sounding laugh. The ground surged and rolled like the ocean. Half of the Valkyries were entombed in earth up to their chests, and the rest were thrown off balance in their efforts to avoid the same fate. The surge of power amplifying the Valkyries' strength did not occur. Instead, Princess Elisa burned a massive amount of mana in an instant. She sent her own wave of power through the earth to shatter the prisons of the Valkyries.

In the meanwhile, Lily inflicted punishing blows on her untrapped opponents. Only heroic efforts by the now-released Valkyries kept Lily from incapacitating half of the contestants in a moment.

The surface of the field swelled wildly in some locations, only to be calmed moments later when the swells moved to a new part of the field. Lily and Elisa were locked in a magical contest for control of the earth within the combat ring.

The Valkyries regrouped as Lily calmly returned to the middle of the ring. After replacing their broken weapons, the soldiers arrayed themselves near their starting positions. Tension filled the air during this uneasy pause in the fighting. The Valkyries were tired but resolute. Princess Elisa was pale and breathing hard. Dame Lily was covered in a light perspiration, as if she were enjoying a simple morning workout.

Lily broke her silence. "Sisters, our time draws to a close. We are all tired, hungry, and need a strong drink. Well, several strong drinks." Her happy, enthusiastic expression was at odds with her words, but the crowd saw a glimpse of Lily's true personality. She was a big-hearted warrior who was having the time of her life. "We could end this battle in a draw, but that would feel unsatisfying. Princess Elisa has been my arch-rival since I was six years old. When we fight, we always fight for total victory. One of us wins, and one loses. Then we dust each other off and return to being best friends. We have time for one final attack to see who wins today!"

The Valkyries responded with a hearty, "Hoorah!"

Elisa shouted, "You are going down, Lily!"

Thirty seconds remained in the battle. Princess Elisa unleashed a mighty yell—"Now!"—and the Valkyries charged Lily from all directions. Six swords aimed to entrap Lily, and six spears were held high to prevent her escape. A massive surge of magical energy enveloped the soldiers, enhancing them to their limits. The ground was suddenly still as Elisa's magic destroyed Lily's control of the earth. The Valkyries were moments away from their win.

An eyeblink before the soldiers made contact, the Dragon Lily roared. An unearthly sound split both sky and ground. A massive explosion catapulted the Valkyries into the air. They flew high above the battlefield like their famous namesakes. Alas, their direction was away from the enemy rather than toward it. While each of the dozen displayed great skill in their landing, they fell from a great height. Fortunately, the ground beneath their feet softened for their impacts. A quick glance showed a relieved princess; she had used her earth magic to cushion the Valkyries' landings.

Each Valkyrie was immediately ready to charge again. However, they were well outside the ring. The battle was over.

The spectators took a few moments to register what had happened. The shock wave from the explosion had been firm but surprisingly gentle when it had reached the crowd. The spectators had been blown back, but no injuries had occurred.

While the crowd was recovering from the shock, Lily called out to Princess Elisa and to the Valkyries, asking them to join her in the center of the ring.

Sergeant Carter resumed his emcee duties. "Ladies and gentlemen, in all my years as a soldier, I've never experienced such an awe-inspiring sight. You know that I tend to hype contests with a bit of enthusiasm." The crowd laughed in agreement. "However, this time, I undersold the contest.

"Princess Elisa and the Valkyries, please step forward." They did so. "While they did not win today, they gave us a great show. Folsom! Please cheer your home team!"

The crowd cheered loudly, but no one cheered louder than Lily.

After the crowd quieted, Sergeant Carter continued, "Dame Lily, please step forward. Folsom! Here is the undefeated champion of today—the Dragon Lily!"

The chant of "Dra-gon! Dra-gon!" again filled the air. Lily's cheeks were red, but she wore a genuine smile. The embarrassment of such a powerful warrior made her human and approachable.

The combat now complete, the crowd began to disperse. Several children approached Lily, and they asked to see her swords. She placed them on the ground. One of the older boys ran forward and tried to casually pick up one of her stone swords off the ground. It was so heavy he pitched forward. Lily caught him before he did a header into the dirt.

"Are you okay?" Lily asked with concern.

The boy's eyes were large as he looked up at her. "How heavy are the swords?" he asked in awe. Everyone had seen her move them as if they were weightless.

Lily was being swarmed by the children. They thought she was very cool.

Sergeant Carter came to Lily's rescue. He picked up the sword with both hands, one each on the hilt and the blade. The sword was massive—more of a sword-shaped club than an actual sword. "Feels like twenty-five kilos. A normal sword is about one-and-a-half kilos."

The boy's eyes lit up. "Wow, that's amazing! How did you get so strong? Can I get strong like you? Why not use a normal sword? Why are you called a dragon if you don't have scales?" The boy rapidly fired questions at Lily without giving her time to respond.

"Off with the lot of you! Dame Lily said she was hungry. And do you know what dragons eat? Naughty children!" Sergeant Carter growled and taunted the children. This led to squeals of delight as the children ran off to join their parents.

The soldiers and the princess's party returned to the mess hall for dinner. Captain Refren thought Elisa would want fine dining now that she was back in a city. However, she asked to dine with the soldiers. Today had been great for the morales of both her group and Refren's unit. A small party would be a fine way to end the day. The Folsom city mayor and other town leaders were invited to join, and they were happy to accept.

On the way to dinner, the leader of the Valkyries boldly asked if Princess Elisa or Dame Lily would sit with them. The Valkyrie leader never would have had the courage to ask a normal noble, much less a princess, but Elisa and Lily were very approachable. Elisa politely declined, as she wanted to talk with the town leaders. Lily was about to decline as well out of deference to Elisa's choice, but her body language clearly said she wanted to eat with her former opponents.

"William, attend me at dinner this evening. Lily, go debrief with the Valkyries as soon as you get your food," Elisa commanded.

"Yes, Your Highness!" Lily answered with a smile. The warrior women were excited as well.

Sir Aden stopped in the doorway as he entered the mess hall ahead of the group. The princess's escort switched into high alert in case there was danger. Aden motioned to Dame Lily to join him. She froze in her tracks at the entrance, too.

"Sir Aden, is everything okay?" Princess Elisa asked.

Sir Aden turned to face Elisa. His expression was hard to read. "My apologies, Princess. This mess hall breaks a principal tenet of military life: the food is nutritious and plentiful, but it's always bland and cheerless. This smells…delicious."

Elisa started to giggle until she saw the shocked look on Lily's face.

Shock turning into anticipation, Aden led the party to the cafeteria-style serving line. The princess's party piled their plates high with tantalizing food, then joined Captain Refren at a group of empty tables. Captain Refren wore a large smile. He was enjoying the surprise of his guests. The group began to eat, and the surprise turned to joy. The food was amazing.

"This is your standard fare?" Aden asked between bites.

"Today the chef is treating us to the holiday menu, so it is better than normal. Still, the everyday fare is quite tasty. Now you know our secret to soldier retention rate. If you leave the army, you leave the food behind."

"Brilliant. I wonder if I can get Llanos to make this change?" asked Sir Aden.

"Good luck. Food quality is something Prince Ryne was championing a decade ago. Our lord, Prince Nevan, made the switch last year for his troops. Lucky for us, Prince Nevan now sees the value."

"Still, worth a try," said Aden, savoring the soup.

The soldiers finished dinner and switched to drinking. Because the company was scheduled to escort Princess Elisa again tomorrow, the alcohol was limited to one mug each, but Captain Refren had tapped a keg of good dwarven ale, so everyone was happy. They were even happier when Princess Elisa had her maids open several bottles of a fine Llanos wine. There was enough to give everyone a small measure. This wine was seldom exported, so the tasty treat was appreciated by all.

The Valkyries' table was quite lively as the women discussed their battle.

"How did you handle your sword breaking so calmly? I was sure it would have at least caused you to falter," asked the leader.

"Wait, you think I was calm? Really?" Lily asked with a wide-eyed expression.

"Yes, you were in front of us, and then you were gone! The next thing we knew, you were reforming your sword and then charging into the middle of us. It was terrifying!" said one of the squad leaders with a laugh.

"Oh, you have it all wrong. I wasn't expecting you to all attack my sword, and I was totally caught off guard by its shattering. My brain was screaming, 'Oh no, escape!' I guess I reactively leapt. Good thing I did because you all were so close to me. I started running, trying to figure out how to recover. Dragging the sword was a happy accident. Normally it takes time to cast the spell. This time, I guess my desire to replace the blade turned into an instinctive casting. Before I realized it, the sword was good to go. I knew I had to throw you all off guard, so I did what I always do when I'm running on instinct. Charge towards the biggest foe and hope I can survive." Lily shrugged and grinned.

The chief priest of the Folsom's War God temple was sitting nearby at Princess Elisa's table and overheard Lily's description. He interrupted to ask, "Pardon me, Dame Lily, do I have this correct? You cast a ritual formation spell while running, and you performed it instinctively. It just...spontaneously happened?"

"Yes, sir. The mana cost is terrible, but when I panic, most of my magic becomes instinctive."

"Wow. That is just...wow," stated the flabbergasted priest.

"That's not normal?" asked the mayor.

"Instinctive casting is exceptionally rare in humans. Such casting foregoes the control mechanisms that mages have created, such as chants, gestures, and magic inscriptions. Without these controls, mana is consumed too quickly, which can cause the caster to faint. Being unconscious is not a good thing in combat." The listeners laughed in agreement. "But you know who does cast instinctively? A dragon. It's well documented by those who survived a dragon encounter." The priest turned back to Lily. "My Lady, your new nickname fits you well."

A small chant of "Dra-gon! Dra-gon!" spontaneously started. An embarrassed Lily hid her face in her hands.

The party was starting to wind down when the chief priest finally had a chance to talk shop with Princess Elisa. Deep magic discussions were usually beyond the interest of the other town leaders, but the chief priest's astonishment at Elisa's magical skills and power kept them listening.

The priest explained to the others, "Enhancement magic tends to be personal because the spellcaster needs to carefully gauge the effect. Too strong of an enhancement can damage the person you are trying to aid. Their muscles become stronger than their bones can handle. Their body feels numb because of too much magic power coursing inside of them. Using a more modest enhancement prevents those issues, but any enhancement is magically taxing on the caster and physically taxing on the enhanced person. Pushing and bypassing human limits quickly leads to exhaustion. If the caster and the enhanced are the same person, then balancing these effects is much easier. Hence, enhancement magic tends to be personal. If not personal, then the caster and the enhanced are often a team who have worked with each other extensively.

"Now let's talk about Princess Elisa. I'll compare her to what I was capable of during my prime. At best, I could handle three people at once: myself and my two brothers. I was very familiar with the fighters I was enhancing. In comparison, the princess was buffing twelve near-total strangers at the same time. They had never trained together.

"Strength of the enhancement is next on the list of considerations. I could make myself four times stronger than normal while doubling my brothers' strength. That much of a boost made us virtually unstoppable against human opponents and allowed us to take a pair of ogres as a team.

"I estimate that the princess started at a two-times enhancement at the beginning of the battle on the twelve Valkyries. By the end of the battle, five-times, maybe more? And she was not just enhancing strength. The women were faster and more agile. That is not the domain of the Earth Goddess." The priest looked toward Elisa. She wore a mysterious smile and did not reply.

"Now to the magic pulses that happened every minute.

That was the princess recasting the spell to both strengthen the enhancement and remove the Valkyries' fatigue. With those kinds of multipliers, the women should have been exhausted within two minutes, tops. In my prime, I could pulse my team of three twice, so we had about four minutes of full-strength attacks. The princess kept her group of twelve running for a full ten minutes.

"I know that Dame Lily's fighting was amazing, but Princess Elisa's magical strength and control were no less impressive. Oh, and don't forget, they engaged each other for control of the earth within the combat ring. A beyond-amazing performance by both, if you ask me." The priest paused to take a sip of his drink. He turned to face Princess Elisa.

"Your Highness, I've only met one other spellcaster who could approach your abilities. She was also from Llanos, and I fought by her side in the southern wars decades ago. She was also petite and blonde. Might you be related?"

"Are you referring to the infamous Witch of Taronto, Sarai, the Scourge of Llanos, and several more unflattering titles?" teased Lily.

"I do not wish to offend, but yes. The leadership of many nations feared her, but the soldiers who served with her loved her. She was the greatest spellcaster I've ever met. Until now, at least."

Elisa responded, "You flatter me, sir, and I thank you. She was my aunt, Goddess rest her soul. Most who compare me to her do it as an insult. Your kind words are most appreciated."

Elisa excused herself and sought her bed a few minutes later. She was exhausted, but her goal for the day was reached. The legend of the Dragon Lily, Hero of Viverna, continued to grow within Vorland. Her own reputation was not doing badly, either.

Lily and William, good work today. We put on a show that no one here will soon forget.

Elisa, you are a natural showman if you ever tire of being a princess, teased William.

I just want to be Lily. Not Dragon Lily. Just plain Lily, complained the female knight.

Chapter 8

The third and final development before the combined group reached Ryne's territory involved the dissolution and renewal of the mental bonds.

The morning after the mock battle at Folsom, Lily slept later than normal. The room was silent when she woke. A moment later, she realized her mind was quiet as well. She thought at Elisa and William, but no one answered. On the eighth day of the resumed trip, the mental link binding Lily to the others was gone. Lily was elated. Her thoughts were hers and hers alone.

The previous two weeks had been mentally draining. Lily had tried to shield her thoughts from first William and then Elisa, but that was not her strength. Lily had been honest when explaining her fear of sharing thoughts, but she had left something untold.

Her daydreams about hot guys like Sir Aden were enjoyable in private, but completely humiliating to share with others. More importantly, Goddess forbid that Elisa ever learn about Lily's recurring dream of "Save the Princess." The locations and villains changed, but there was a common theme. Lily saved the beautiful Princess Elisa. The grateful princess then awarded her savior a kiss. The dream kiss usually woke Lily, but when it did not, her memory was hazy after waking. Lily felt like she had done something naughty, which was both thrilling and mortifying. Lily was afraid of Elisa's reaction if Elisa ever found out.

Elisa, Lily, and William had discussed renewing the linking magic. As they had discovered, the shared mental space was tied to the massive increase in magic power that the trio shared. After much discussion, Lily agreed to renew the magic if there was a catastrophic event or if Elisa's life was in serious danger. However, using the power to entertain the citizens, soldiers, and leaders of every village and town they passed through was not Lily's idea of fun.

Lily had been a dutiful servant of the princess the previous day. Lily had done as the princess had instructed. Lily even enjoyed the battle, but she had not faked her embarrassment at her new nickname. The cringing she felt when playing the invincible hero was also real. Lily trusted that Elisa had a long-term plan, but the short-term mental trauma was almost more than Lily could handle.

Lily dressed and headed downstairs to check in with the princess's group. Preparations were well underway to leave the city and travel northwest. Perhaps it was her imagination, but the soldiers were even friendlier than they had been before. Everyone greeted her and wished her a good morning.

Today is turning out to be a nice day. Lily hoped she did not just jinx the group with that thought.

Princess Elisa was eating breakfast when Lily walked into the mess hall. Elisa waved to her friend, then continued to study the way the soldiers treated Lily. Before the mock battle, the commoners had treated her politely and with the respect due to a senior officer and knight. Today, the respect was still there, but now the soldiers were more friendly and open with Lily. The battle had demonstrated Lily's amazing fighting skills and magic. The party afterward had shown Lily's open and happy attitude and her kind and caring heart. The soldiers' respect had blossomed into admiration, just as Elisa expected. Elisa was satisfied with the way Lily's reputation was developing.

For Elisa, the war priest's words had been a fortunate happenstance. The discussion could not have gone better last night if she had planned it. Vorland was a much more welcoming country than Llanos, and Elisa planned to use that openness to cement their reputations in their new country before Elisa's enemies could undermine her.

Unlike Lily, Elisa was annoyed by the loss of the mental link. Long years spent fighting in Llanos politics had trained Elisa to hide her thoughts and intentions. Elisa had not felt as mentally exposed as Lily in the shared mental space. Combined with the convenience of immediate and secure communication, as well as the vast magical power boost, the advantages outweighed the disadvantages for the princess.

Princess Elisa literally knew how Lily had felt during the mental linkage. Elisa had suspected the doubts that troubled Lily, but now she knew them in detail. Despite Lily's warrior exterior and attitude, she had many of the same doubts and fears as other young women her age. Lily did not fear walking unescorted around town, but she did worry about whether people liked her and if she would ever find a husband. Lily did not understand these were common fears and concerns. She had many male friends among the Varangian Guard with whom she had trained, but female fighters were rare in Llanos. The few women there considered Lily to be a rival and nothing more, even when Lily had reached out to try to help them. Lily had been popular among Elisa's household staff, but these women were in awe of her amazing stature, never seeing the timid and sweet girl inside.

Now that Elisa was aware of the problems that Lily faced, the princess knew what she needed to do. She would continue to make plans and seek opportunities to demonstrate how Lily was both a legendary combatant and an approachable friend. Elisa saw this as a chance to share her awesome best friend with this new country. Elisa hoped both her friend and her new country would see the benefits in the future.

Whereas Lily was an open book, William was a closed fortress. Elisa trusted her instincts and magical eyes—William was an ally, not a threat. However, William was a most inscrutable person. Despite her best efforts, Elisa had made little progress in understanding William's motivations and abilities.

William proclaimed himself a servant of Prince Ryne, and he had gone to great lengths to secure Elisa's safety as well as satisfy her whims. Building the wall around Viverna was one of Elisa's crazy ideas that had come to completion. Lily had complained when Elisa explained her idea. William had asked questions in order to refine it. Lily could understand the impact it made on the villagers' lives, but she did not see how it fit into Elisa's greater plan to spread their fame and gather fans and allies during the trip through Vorland. William acknowledged the value of such a plan with a smirk, sensing the game that Elisa was playing. He had worked tirelessly to help her accomplish it.

The previous day's training battles had been a spontaneous opportunity for Elisa. The shared mental space had still been active, so Elisa had been able to orchestrate an amazing mock battle between the Valkyries and Lily. Lily had been reluctant at first but quickly warmed to the idea when she realized the fun of such a battle. Elisa had been worried about the final attack, but Lily's power, guided by Elisa's control, had generated an earth-shattering explosion that did no real damage to either participants or spectators.

William's part in the battle had been invisible to all but Lily and Elisa. He had coordinated the magic on the Valkyries and monitored their conditions for the best effect. This had allowed Elisa to concentrate on just supplying the next pulse of magic while she directed Lily around the ring. William also had monitored and ensured that the magical earth-control contest between Lily and Elisa had not gotten out of control, potentially harming the Valkyries or the spectators. Finally, William had supplied the agility-enhancing magic used by all the contestants. While the fight would have been impressive with just strength enhancement, the increased mobility and agility of the contestants had made it truly spectacular. Again, William had supported Elisa without complaint.

Elisa had woken early this morning. The now-familiar buzz of dreams meshing was gone. Her mind was too quiet, and she sensed something had changed. The mental link was gone.

Elisa was able to intercept William before he left for scouting. Without the bond, their conversation could now be overheard, so they took care to be quick and quiet. Elisa wanted to renew the mental link with just the two of them this time. She saw it as an opportunity to continue their spell discussion and perhaps improve her knowledge of the Elvish language. William was reluctant and said he needed to seek permission. Elisa asked if Prince Ryne was the one he would ask. William said yes. He was uncomfortable continuing to form such an intimate relationship with the prince's future wife, particularly without a chaperone. They agreed to talk more that evening.

The day passed quickly. The combined company was in good spirits after yesterday's entertainment, and they arrived at their next stop on time.

After dinner, Princess Elisa summoned William. She intended to speak to him alone, but he politely refused. One of the conditions he had received from Ryne was that Dame Lily had to be aware of the mental link even if she was not part of it. Elisa relented and brought Lily into the conversation.

Lily was concerned about Elisa but not surprised. "Why do you need to renew the link? Didn't we already have this discussion?" she asked.

"We did talk, and you expressed your unwillingness to

continue it. I do not have such qualms," replied the princess.

"Have you asked William his opinion?"

"He sought permission from Prince Ryne as a condition for renewing the link. We are having that discussion now," answered Elisa. She turned to William. "What did Prince Ryne say?"

"He is willing to let it happen, provided we meet several conditions. Lily is to monitor and limit all physical interactions that you and I have. He does not want to risk your reputation with the appearance of inappropriate behavior."

"Done. Lily is already performing that role. Next?"

"When the link first occurred, I suspended myself from Auraria's communication network because of the security risk. Now that we know the link is limited to only its participants, I will be readmitted. While the network is not telepathic, it requires my conscious thought to participate, so you will be aware of all communications. Since you are to be wed, the prince is willing to take the risk."

"Was he worried I would spill state secrets?" taunted Elisa.

William smirked and said, "No, he is worried that the humor and informal speech that we use may be offensive."

Elisa snorted in a very unladylike way. "He must be unfamiliar with Aunt Sarai's humor."

"He is quite familiar with it. He is just unsure if you appreciate it or not."

"I'll be fine. Wait, what? Just how well did he know Sarai?" Elisa asked.

"That is his tale, not mine."

"Then I will follow up with him. Next?"

William continued. "Finally, he figures you wish to interrogate me for the next several days. He is fine with that, but I'm given discretion on how much I answer. For example, elven secrets are out-of-bounds. Learning Elvish is fine."

"I can live with those terms."

William cast the spell, and then he and Elisa performed

their prayers. The link reestablished itself immediately. Perhaps the repeated casting each day when they had been rebuilding the village made the link easier to form. They informed Lily they had been successful, and then William left since they did not need to be next to each other for the link to work.

All right, what are the requirements that you did not want to mention in front of Lily? asked Elisa.

Thank you for waiting to ask. The prince will appreciate your cleverness and intuition.

Elisa's mental smugness was clear through the link. *Why, thank you, William.*

The last item is for my personal comfort. I spent a great deal of effort during the previous link on keeping my thoughts as pure as possible so as to not upset Lily. The emotional calming spells I used felt like leaping in ice water—effective but unpleasant. I don't resent Lily for her easily embarrassed nature, but I don't want to spend another week walking on eggshells for fear of making a mistake.

Elisa laughed. *We both spent the last two weeks controlling our thoughts and emotions, but Lily could not control hers. Bless her, she tried, but the girl simply has no mental filter.*

William asked, *How many times did Lily admire your posterior? Then feel jealous that your rear was more desirable than hers? Then feel bad for being jealous? Then feel mortified for objectifying the royal rear? Then feel horrified for betraying her best friend? Did I forget anything in that circle of thoughts?*

Just one—where she felt she betrayed the Earth Goddess by "lusting" after a woman rather than a man. Oh, by the way, "the royal rear"? What an interesting turn of phrase.

Well, it is a national ass-set, replied William matter-of-factly.

Elisa paused for a moment. Then she got the giggles. This led to her laughing in front of Lily, who gave her a stern look in rebuke. Elisa apologized and got control of herself.

William, are you teasing me? Maybe you are flirting with me. Elisa discovered that the expression of a raised eyebrow transmitted surprisingly well through the link.

Just testing the limits, Your Highness. If you don't appreciate my dumb jokes and irreverent humor, the next week won't be much fun. Just to be clear, while my age says I am an adult, you are subjecting yourself to the idle thoughts and urges of a teenage boy.

Any worse than being the subject of a "Save the Princess" dream on a nightly basis? I think you were the "damsel in distress" at least once or twice, teased Elisa.

Elisa could feel William's involuntary shudder. *No, Princess, nothing that emotionally draining.*

Then I think I will be fine.

The next morning, William introduced Elisa to the Aurarian communication network. William left the combined company to gain privacy, then produced an odd magical device from his pocket. William was deliberately thinking through each action so that Elisa could "see" it as well. The device looked a bit like a seashell. William poured mana into it, and the device disappeared from view, but the weight of it was still in his hand. He placed it on the right side of his head. Elisa could feel it fitting snugly against his ear.

‹Morning, everyone; this is William.› Elisa heard him add a different emphasis to his name through the comms link.

Several voices immediately replied in a combination of well-wishes and good-natured taunts: ‹Good morning!› ‹Welcome back, chief!› ‹Did you enjoy your vacation, Will-i-am?› ‹Boss-man let you out of jail, huh?›

William proceeded to fill them in. ‹Ryne should have explained the details last night, but here is the quick summary. The princess is on comms with us through me as the intermediary. She can hear everything you send to me, but she won't be able to reply directly until we get her a device. No security limits, but please at least think before you speak. Conrad, this means you—don't scare her away before she has a chance to meet the prince. Everyone, please say hello to Princess Elisa of Llanos and introduce yourselves,› said William. Elisa had noticed the lack of an honorific when William had first said the prince's name.

William barely finished speaking before a woman's voice blasted through the earpiece. ‹WILLIAM, ARE YOU AND THE PRINCESS USING TELEPATHY? DID YOU SOLVE THE PROBLEMS? CAN WE IMPLEMENT IT FOR THE NEXT-GEN COMMS? OH MY GODDESS, THIS IS EXCITING!›

The comms link was silent for a few moments. The same woman spoke again, but her voice was now quiet and timid. ‹William, are you still there? I got carried away again, didn't I?›

‹I'm here, Runera. Just repairing my eardrum. I share your excitement even if I lack your enthusiasm. So why don't you introduce yourself first?›

‹Hello, Your Highness. I am Runera. I am a magician in the service of Prince Ryne. I focus on magical items and new spell development. This is my first time performing fieldwork, and it is exciting. I'm very pleased to meet you!›

A deep voice talked next. ‹Hey, half-pint, remember that the princess cannot see you. You must describe yourself too. Don't worry; I've got you covered. Runera is a female halfling. She is nineteen years old and the size of most five-year-old humans. But don't let her size fool you. She is wicked smart and can drink most dwarves under the table.›

Runera was annoyed. ‹Everything you said is true, but you could have spoken more eloquently, YOU HORSE'S ASS!›

The deep voice replied, ‹Runera, that is unfair. I have a horse's ass, but I'm the very definition of male sophistication.› Comms erupted in laughter at this last statement.

The deep voice continued speaking. ‹Princess Elisa, my name is Conrad. As you may have guessed, I'm a male centaur in the service of Prince Ryne. I handle fieldwork and command the other scouts. I'm twenty-five years old, and I'm very pleased to meet you! Oh, William, guess what? Guess what?›

William replied in the voice of the long-suffering, ‹What, Conrad?› although he clearly knew the answer.

‹New people are joining us! I get to trot out all my centaur jokes again! Here's one—hey, Princess, how am I like a holiday stocking? We are both *well hu—*›

‹Conrad! Bad horsey!› interrupted Runera before Conrad could finish.

Princess Elisa was preparing to board her carriage while this conversation was occurring. Because she was hearing it through telepathy, no one else around her could hear it. Up until Conrad's joke, she had kept her mirth inside the shared mental space. She might have been able to handle the joke, but Runera's response caused Elisa to lose it. A full spit-take was followed by gales of laughter. The soldiers nearby paused in an awkward silence, and Lily was horrified.

Elisa, Princess of Llanos, sheepishly looked up at everyone. "Sorry, I just remembered the punchline to an old joke. Please carry on." Elisa quickly ducked into the carriage to hide her embarrassment. Although she did not realize it, this event endeared her to the First Mounted Infantry Company even more. She was a royal who cared about her people and did not take herself too seriously. Several of the soldiers wished she was destined to be the princess of their duchy.

While Elisa was regaining her composure, William told the others what he felt through the link. Sensing that she could focus again, William said, ‹Perhaps we should move to the next introduction.›

‹Hello, Princess Elisa, my name is Petras. I am a male dwarven engineer in Prince Ryne's service. I'm just shy of a hundred years, so I'm relatively young for my people. I'm currently in Auraria to handle the rebuilding efforts. Your fame precedes you. I look forward to discussing your recent building project in Viverna.› Petras's accent was strong, but his tone was open and friendly.

‹Beware, Princess! Once Petras has had a drink or three,

he will drone on and on about all kinds of boring things. Blah blah blah, ancient architecture,› injected Conrad.

Petras huffed. ‹You sleep under trees, you heathen! I try to introduce you to culture, and my words pass from ear to ear in your empty skull!›

‹Conrad, are you going to provide commentary on everyone?› asked William.

‹Of course! The princess needs to know what her new vassals are like.›

William let out a long sigh. He knew a losing battle when he heard one.

‹Princess Elisa, my name is Owen. I command the duchy's troops for Prince Ryne. I'm a male human, age twenty-four. I had the honor of serving His Highness in the last three military campaigns, as well as the battle to retake Auraria from the invaders. I look forward to meeting you and your knight, Dame Lily. My group will be providing escort after Captain Refren withdraws at the duchy's border.›

Conrad asked, ‹Hey, Owen, guess what? My idea for magician-equipped light cavalry centaurs is working great!›

‹Good lord, poor Runera! How are you holding up?› asked Owen.

Runera replied, ‹Better now with the anti-nausea medicine, but I don't think halflings are meant to ride horses. I've already fallen off twice.›

‹Conrad, you better not let Runera be injured,› Owen growled.

‹It's fine. Everything's fine. You worry too much,› replied Conrad. Owen did not seem convinced.

A new voice popped up. ‹This seems like a good time to introduce myself. Hello, Your Highness, I am Edmund, the majordomo for Prince Ryne. If you have questions or need anything, please contact me. I am a human male, age forty. His Highness wanted to join us today, but he is currently occupied with other matters. He looks forward to seeing you soon.

William, I will send you comms devices for both Princess Elisa and Dame Lily.› Edmund's voice was calm and soothing.

Comms were quiet for a few moments.

‹Conrad, no snide comments?› asked William.

‹Even I know not to bite the hand that pays me.›

The others laughed.

William continued explaining things to Elisa. ‹These are the main people who use the comms network. Ryne will join us when he can. We also add additional people for special ops. Most of our communications are direct, person-to-person, but we initiate group-wide comms as the need arises. For the next two days, we will mostly be working with Conrad and his team. Runera as well, since she is on the scouting op. If all goes smoothly, we will not see them, as they will be protecting us from afar. Everyone, thanks for your attention. Conrad, deploy the team as a standard screen. I'll run a roving position again. We will start moving in twenty minutes. William out.›

Elisa felt the comms connection break on William's end. While she had sensed William using the communication magic in the past, this was the first time she was physically close enough to William for their bond to let her "listen" in on the comms.

Elisa was impressed with the Aurarian communication network. She was unaware of any similar system in use by Llanos. She was further impressed by the camaraderie the members shared and asked William why they were so close.

William explained, *Retaking Auraria from the monster horde was a monumental task. At all times, we had a severe numerical disadvantage. What we did have was a close group of exceptional individuals who had fought countless battles together. We lost many good friends along the way, but we succeeded in the goal to recapture Ryne's city. We are all driven to make Ryne's vision of the future a reality. Before you ask, he wants to talk about it to you personally. He believes that you, as well as Lily, would be valuable assets to his team.*

Elisa replied, *Then I look forward to meeting him again. Perhaps* he will tell me why you use his name so casually. Oh, Lily is giving me the evil eye, so I better go for now. Can we begin the language lesson after we get on the road?*

Yes, Your Highness.

The next two days passed quickly and without incident. Well, Lily was annoyed with Elisa on the first evening. The Elvish language lesson had been going well, and Elisa asked William to show her his elf-made armor and bow. Lily did not think such contact was necessary, but Elisa was insistent, and in the end, Lily could not deny her princess.

He magically removed his armor and placed it on the table in front of Elisa and Lily. He did the same with his bow. Lily's annoyance was soon forgotten, as she was entranced with the beautifully crafted items.

"May I pick up your bow?" a reverent Lily asked.

William smirked. "You are welcome to try."

Lily was puzzled by the comment, but she gently reached out to grasp the bow. Her fingers passed through it as if it were a mirage. Lily was startled and looked at William.

"Elven goods are crafted so that only an elf, or a person with substantial elvish blood, can use them. They simply don't exist for everyone else."

Lily tried again but to no avail. "Wow, that's impressive."

Elisa watched her friend fail and remembered how Sarai had told her about elvish items not being human-friendly, but she decided to try herself. She grabbed the bow without issue. It felt warm and pleasant in her hand. The grip was a bit too large for her hand to close around, but she felt the wood flowing in response to her touch. Within seconds, it fit her hand perfectly.

Elisa turned to face the others. Lily was staring with her mouth open, while William wore a thoughtful look. Elisa's heritage was well documented for many generations. There was not a drop of elvish blood in her veins. Llanos considered non-humans to be tainted, and their presence was barely tolerated outside of the Taronto Water Gardens.

After a few moments, William nodded. "It's the link," he said with a smile. "Let's try something." He summoned his armor from the table. One moment, it was lying there, and the next moment, it covered his body. Elisa had felt a small bit of mana flowing through William, but he had not cast a spell. She was impressed.

William placed his hands in the air, clearly visible to both women. "Ladies, do I have permission to move my armor to the princess?"

Elisa agreed immediately.

Lily delayed her approval. "Do not touch or remove her clothing."

William agreed. Elisa sensed the mana flow again. A comforting weight covered her body. The armor was too large, but like the bow, it changed to accommodate her smaller, more curvy stature. The armor felt like a comfy robe. She danced about the room, checking if the armor constricted her movements. It did not.

William was happy. Lily was more subdued and perhaps a bit envious.

"Both my bow and my armor recognize you. I think we have found another benefit of the link. This may open...several possibilities," concluded William.

Later that night, Elisa sensed William talking to someone else in Elvish. Her command of the language was not strong yet, but she knew William was excited.

CHAPTER 9

At the end of the second day, the combined group of Captain Refren's company and Princess Elisa's escort unit arrived at a small village on the border of the two duchies. Commander Owen's troops were a couple of hours away but expected to arrive before sundown. Escort duty would officially switch the following morning.

About an hour before Owen's arrival, the Aurarian communication network went active. Conrad's scouts had found a large group of humans crossing the duchy border half a day's march to the west of the village. Their motley and unmatched dress indicated bandits, but their arms, as well as their orderly discipline, belied that appearance. They numbered over a hundred, so they were a clear threat to the princess.

Assuming the enemy had eyes on their movements as well, Owen's group arrived in the village as planned. The leaders met to discuss the threat. By this point, William had joined the other scouts and was actively tracking the enemy's movements. The "bandits" showed no signs of stopping for the night. On their present trajectory, they would arrive at a small thicket of trees near the road to Auraria before morning. The thicket would provide adequate cover for an ambush. The enemy appeared to be using non-magical scouts. Small groups of lightly armored soldiers departed the enemy detachment at regular intervals while other groups returned. William relayed this information back to the Vorlandish leaders.

After considering several options, the princess and her protectors decided on the following plan: In the morning, Owen's group would leave on schedule with the princess's carriage containing a decoy princess. Captain Refren's company would delay their departure from the village. The company would perform training and drills outside the village so that their lack of departure did not seem suspicious. Owen would attempt to trigger the ambush, then retreat toward the village. By this time, Refren's soldiers would have moved into position for a counterattack. The princess's group, including Lily and William, would remain in the village. Owen secured a second, much less elaborate carriage for the princess to flee in if needed.

The next morning, the combined force executed the plan. The Aurarian scouts confirmed the "bandits" were preparing an ambush at the expected location. The invaders appeared tired, having marched through the night, but they were still battle-ready. These were professional soldiers from either an enemy army or a mercenary group. Commander Owen predicted they would soon know which, depending on how the enemy reacted when confronted with Refren's counterattack.

Princess Elisa's group waited in the village, some more patiently than others. Sir Aden and the guards were trained professionals—they were acquainted with long hours of boredom punctuated by occasional moments of deadly excitement. The remaining lady-in-waiting and the two maids were fearful. They had neither the training nor the disposition for such an overhanging threat. Princess Elisa kept them calm with kind words and challenging tasks to keep their minds occupied. They learned to embroider Prince Ryne's coat of arms and were happy for the distraction. The attendants—the group of young men who took care of the horses, carriage, and wagons—found the impending battle exciting. Their victory against the modest force of monsters that had attacked the stable in Viverna emboldened them.

William was silently coordinating with Conrad and his scouts, Commander Owen's bait-decoy group, and Captain Refren's company. Conrad had embedded one of his scouts with Refren to allow for quicker communications. Dame Lily stationed herself near Elisa. Her aura was filled with patient and resolute violence, which further reinforced her new nickname.

At just before eleven o'clock in the morning, William was notified the ambush had been sprung. Owen's group feigned disarray before quickly retreating. The enemy had chosen their hiding spots wisely. Had Owen's group not been forewarned, the ambush would have succeeded.

Owen's group was mounted on horses, while the enemy was on foot. The enemy had two groups that flanked and pinched them from behind, completing the encirclement. Reversing course was still the best option, but Owen was likely to lose several cavalry soldiers during the break through the enemy's ranks. As feared, the attackers were professional soldiers who did not run from a cavalry charge. These soldiers set their spears and waited. They were willing to trade some of their own lives to capture the princess. Owen's group of forty was outmanned by at least three to one. Refren's relief was close, but the battle would be well underway before his soldiers would arrive. The battle was shaping up to be bloody for both sides.

The enemy leaders could feel victory within their grasp. The princess would soon be theirs for the taking. Their hopes were dashed a moment later by a most comical sight. A single lancer came charging around the bend in the road from the south. A small figure was bouncing wildly on the horse's back. A single knight would have little effect on their troops. Several spearmen in the back row had already pivoted to deal with the solitary threat. The single mounted lancer had started hundreds of meters from the troops, but they were closing much more rapidly than should have been possible. As the figure got closer, the threat seemed even less real. The lancer was not a mounted knight but a lightly armored centaur with lance and shield. The child on the centaur's back was screaming at the top of her lungs, "Too fast! Slow down! I'm going to huuurrl!" The centaur was laughing as he thundered toward the enemy troops blocking the road.

Perhaps the spectacle caused the enemy archers to hesitate, but they were clearly not ready for what happened next. Conrad, the centaur lancer, and Runera, the halfling magician, introduced themselves to the enemy troop with lightning and thunder. Runera cast her spell at near point-blank range. Lightning arced through the nearby troops, stunning them. A moment later, the shock wave of thunder bowled the soldiers over. In an instant, a passage for Owen's group opened.

Conrad continued his charge along the now-empty road. Piles of moaning armored opponents lay on either side. Conrad continued his run through Owen's rapidly approaching group. As they passed, Owen's soldiers shouted, "Huzzah!" while Owen taunted, "Showoff!"

"Wave of the future, baby!" was Conrad's reply.

"Too fast," was Runera's heartfelt plea.

Conrad turned around at the end of the group and began providing rear cover. Seconds later, Owen's group cleared the enemy's line and continued toward Refren's prepared soldiers. The enemy recovered quickly and gave pursuit.

Back in the village, William and Elisa were using the communications network to follow the flow of the battle. Owen provided the play-by-play, Conrad the color commentary, and Runera the comic relief. Elisa could sense their emotions through the link with William. Owen had been afraid he was going to lose soldiers to the enemy attack. Conrad had heard that fear in his voice and responded. Runera, who had just been thrust into her first battle in a ridiculous way, overcame her fear to provide the protection that Owen needed. She had cast her spell to maximize impact on the enemy. Perhaps one or two had been killed, but the survivors would not be incapacitated for long, though still long enough for Owen to break through.

Your friends are crazy, Elisa told William.

Yes, they are. At least you are getting a sense of how Prince Ryne's vassals operate. Have we scared you away yet? "Yes" would be the sane answer, William teased.

Real friends facing danger together. I think I could get used to this.

Thirty minutes later, William got the signal to proceed. The enemy had retreated to the west, away from the village. Both Refren and Owen were in pursuit. The enemy was very disciplined and well-led, and they were now performing a tactical retreat. While they did not appear to have magical personnel, they did have magical support. They should have been exhausted from the overnight march and pursuit, but they were still fighting at full strength. Owen suspected they had access to at least recovery magic. In any case, the combined allied forces were sufficient to force the enemy's retreat.

The princess's group decided to leave the village. Their way had been cleared in front of them, and the small village did not have any significant defensive structures. Thus, the best course of action was deemed to be traveling to the next town, which was just over a day and a half away. Owen's forces would follow and meet them. Runera stayed with Owen's group to assist with the enemy soldiers, while Conrad and his scouts joined Elisa. William was again the rover, staying between the outer screen of scouts and the princess. Due to the late start and the distance involved, the princess would have to travel through the night to reach the next town, but this was considered an acceptable risk due to the strength of escorts and scouts. Still, Sir Aden paced the group carefully to ensure the animals were not overtaxed. In an emergency, he needed the horses to be fresh enough to withstand a short run if required.

The princess's group stopped briefly at the ambush site two hours later. Two of Owen's men had lost their horses in the battle. Owen had ordered them to stay and wait for Elisa's group. Sir Aden had spare mounts, and the extra fighters were a welcome addition. The men had wisely used their time while waiting. They had inspected the deceased enemy soldiers. Each of the dead men bore good-quality weapons with no maker's marks. Their armor and clothing similarly lacked insignias, but they were also of good quality. Clearly, not the equipment of bandits. Through the mental link, William speculated the enemy was likely a mercenary company from Polis, which lay to the south of Vorland. The near-constant warring between the Polis city-states generated many such mercenary groups. If Refren and Owen were able to capture a mercenary leader, then they might learn the name of their enemy's sponsor.

Near dusk, Elisa's group stopped to rest and rotate their horses. The group ate a quick, cold meal as they did not want to take the time to cook. As he did each evening, Sir Aden removed a magical device from his saddlebags. As the leader of Princess Elisa's escort, he reported on their status to his Llanos superiors each evening. While Aden possessed only minor magical abilities, the device allowed him to transmit and receive a small number of short messages. Whenever possible, Aden used the device in either Elisa or Lily's presence for the sake of transparency. The device was considered secure, as both ends were controlled by people loyal to Elisa's father, Prince Miller.

Sir Aden activated the device and dictated his report. He waited for confirmation that his message had been received. Normally, any response was rapidly delivered, but tonight was different. After a few minutes, the voice was different than the one that normally replied and said, "Stand by for further instructions."

Sir Aden was puzzled and looked at Princess Elisa. She shrugged in return.

Dame Lily was sitting beside Elisa when this occurred. She took a last bite of food, then put her plate aside. Lily stretched, popped her neck, and casually surveyed the area. While Lily looked calm, Elisa knew her friend well. Lily was preparing for a fight, and everyone was a potential threat to Elisa. Sir Aden recognized Lily's stance as well. He slowly backed away to give Lily more space.

Elisa used the mental link to inform William. He was scouting forward of the escort group by several minutes. William used comms to brief Conrad, and then he ran to join Elisa and Lily.

Aden's communication device activated, and a new voice spoke from it. "This is General Johnson. The king died today, and Prince Logan has now assumed the throne. By King Logan's royal decree, Lady Elisa is hereby ordered to return immediately to Taronto. Sir Aden, confirm receipt and acknowledgment of these new orders."

The atmosphere became tense around the princess. Lily's right hand was on her sword hilt, and a throwing dagger was already in her left hand. "That is not going to happen. We are going to deliver Elisa to Prince Ryne. End of story."

Sir Aden had his hands in the air to show that he was not a threat. "Dame Lily, that was General Johnson's voice. He commands all of the Llanos forces. He has given us a direct order from our new king. We must do as the king commands."

Lily responded, "King Logan wants a hostage to use against his brother, Prince Miller, Elisa's father. Remember Prince

Miller, Aden? He is your liege lord. Be a good soldier and honor the orders of the former king. He commanded us to safely deliver Princess Elisa to Prince Ryne. Besides, General Johnson is the son of Count John, the man who brought false accusations against Princess Elisa. Johnson is not to be trusted."

Elisa was transmitting the conversation through the link. William cast agility magic as he ran, and it affected both Elisa and him. He began racing at breathtaking speed to reach Elisa. Elisa felt a second surge of magic. A comforting weight covered her body. She was wearing her travel cloak, so no one else noticed. She silently cast her own strength-enhancing magic.

The communicator sounded again. "Sir Aden, confirm receipt and acknowledgment of these new orders immediately," the general demanded.

The other escort fighters moved to support Sir Aden. Aden motioned them to hold. "Dame Lily, this is an order from the king. We must obey. I cannot defer to Duke Miller or Princess Elisa. The line of succession has changed. We must obey the king." Aden was distraught. His words did not match his body language. He clearly did not want to follow the new orders, but he was unable to contradict them. "Princess Elisa, please understand…"

Elisa spoke. "Sir Aden, your loyalty is honorable, but your leaders are not. Who do you think paid for the fighter that Lily defeated in the trial by combat? The fighter was one of Johnson's subordinates. Both are followers of Logan. My enemies are moving against me. I will not submit to a death sentence."

Sir Aden shakily drew his sword. He stared at Elisa, and then he violently threw his sword to the ground. He fell to his knees. He looked at Elisa with tears in his eyes. "I can't take arms against you, Princess."

The tension started to dissolve. The general's voice issued from the device a final time. "Feed your hunger for revenge," he commanded. The world exploded in bright light.

Elisa saw only white. The brilliant flash blinded her. A second later, something slammed into her back. The sound of metal on metal rang in her ears. Both her agility and strength were massively increased, and she jumped more than twenty meters to the side out of instinct. Her eyes were useless, but she had other senses. As an earth priestess, she could cast vibration-sensing magic. It made her overly sensitive to loud sounds, but it allowed her ears to "see" movements on the ground and in the air. She was out of immediate danger.

Lily had not moved. The brilliant flash had caught her by surprise, but years of careful training made blind fighting second nature to her. Two figures charged her from the front and one from the back. Two of the fighters and one of the maids were attacking her. She used the flat of her blade to keep from severing them in half, but Lily did not pull her blows. All three were soon lying on the ground, incapacitated and dying. Lily oriented herself and felt Elisa a few meters away from her. Another slight figure, perhaps one of the attendants, was closing on Elisa. Lily charged forward and backhanded the person. Lily's magically enhanced fist sent the figure crashing into a tree several meters away.

The cries of the wounded filled the air. As Lily guarded her, Elisa cast healing magic to remove their blindness. The magic helped, but it was not strong enough to fully clear their vision.

The pair of women heard someone in extreme distress. The sound was of someone choking. It was coming from Aden's last known position. Elisa wanted to give him aid, but Lily refused to let her leave their relatively secure area.

Elisa felt another surge of magic from William and then heard him curse.

Elisa, I'm still a minute away. Let's try something. Remember this feeling. William withdrew a potion from his extra-dimensional space. His hand felt a slight resistance as magical energy swirled around his fingers. It felt like plunging a hand into a refreshing waterfall. The potion vial was waiting just inside the space. Elisa could see the shape and color of the vial, as well as the glowing blue liquid inside. William pulled the vial out, looked at it, then returned it. The entire action had taken a couple of seconds. *Now you do it!* commanded William.

Elisa reenacted the motions, energies, and feelings. The space became visible to her, but the waterfall kept her from reaching in. William injected his own mana, and the waterfall parted. Elisa grabbed the vial and pulled it to her. *I've got it!* she acknowledged.

Drink a sip, then give Lily a sip. Your vision should clear immediately. If you want to save Aden, give him the rest.

Elisa followed the instructions. Within seconds, her vision was restored. Lily followed quickly after. The pair surveyed the scene. The rest of the escort party was disabled, either from an attack or the flash of light. Aden was writhing on the ground, his mouth covered with foam. His movements were rapidly getting weaker.

Poison! Elisa told William. Aloud, she said, "Lily, I'm going to try to save Aden. I do not sense any ill will from him."

"Understood, Your Highness."

Elisa ran to Aden while Lily guarded her. She poured a bit of the glowing blue liquid on the small wound at his side, then rolled him over and poured the rest into his mouth. Unlike the flash blindness they had suffered, the poison was taking longer to fix. Elisa cast her own healing magic to assist. After thirty seconds, the healing began to take effect. Aden's distress lessened.

Elisa felt William approaching, and she warned Lily in order to prevent a friendly fire accident.

Upon arrival, William moved immediately to the Llanos communication device and smashed it. "Runera will just have to study the pieces. We can't afford any more mischief from our Llanos 'friends,'" he said.

Aden was now in a deep but peaceful sleep. They moved him into the carriage. The trio had to decide what to do with the other escort members. Four were clearly assailants—the two fighters and the maid who had attacked Lily, as well as the attendant who had assaulted Elisa. All four were unconscious and heavily wounded. The remainder of the party—the other maid, attendants, and the rest of the guards—were unconscious and appeared unwounded.

Lily concluded from the size of Aden's wound that one of the fighters had stabbed Aden before moving to her. All the hostiles appeared to be determined.

Lily took charge of the scene. "Princess, use your special sight to look for magic and hostile intent. You will stay away from everyone. I will guard you. William, you will approach and check each person. I'm going to restrain the hostiles for now. Let's start with others. We are in open and potentially dangerous terrain. We need to move quickly. Agreed?"

Both William and Elisa agreed.

Lily used earth magic to encapsulate each of the four hostile party members. William then began to check the others, starting with the fighters. He first searched and removed weapons, then checked each person's health. Moving swiftly, William finished in a few minutes. Each was physically okay but bewitched with strong sleep magic.

"This is very powerful magic. Had you both not been very strong-willed, you would have succumbed as well. The healing potion that you used earlier will help them recover. A couple of vials will be sufficient. Lily, do you want to wake them now?"

"Let's hold off until we handle the four hostiles. Fewer moving people, less chance for surprise. However, let's move them away from the hostiles."

"Will do." William moved the sleeping people behind the carriage. "Princess Elisa, our next action is your call. The best way to handle the hostiles is to dispose of them. I prefer this method. The downside is we lose information on how your enemies caught us off guard. That information is valuable enough to consider examining and interrogating a hostile while they are still alive."

"The knowledge is worth the risk. Procee— Wait, hold a moment. William, take back your armor," Elisa commanded.

William hesitated.

"Do it. I have Lily to shield me. We cannot risk you getting hurt."

"Yes, Your Highness." William moved to examine the first of the fighters. "Princess, your passive magical skill allows you to detect hostile intent and magical influence, correct?"

"Yes, although not as well as if I actively use my eyes. Focused use of that passive skill consumes significant mana, so I only use it when I need to. Like when we first met. However, I've periodically scanned everyone in the party, and no one has ever shown issues. Well, Lady Philippa did, but she never really concealed her hatred of me. She was sent to be an active thorn in my side."

William said, "Your enemies likely understand your abilities and took steps to shield their agents against you. If concealing magic was being used, we may find traces of it. The next question is whether these hostiles were even aware of their conditioning. Lily, when we are ready, please remove the stone cocoon on this fighter. Please keep his hands and feet bound, but we need to check his body for magic. Princess, stay behind Lily and position yourself where you have a clear view. Your detection magic is much stronger than mine, and I don't want to miss anything."

William drew a dagger. If the person moved, William would end his life immediately. Lily removed the stone cocoon, and William used his knife to slice through armor straps and clothing to expose the man's bare skin. The man was lying on his stomach, so his back was now visible.

"Whoa, are you seeing this?" asked William.

A series of intricate tattoos covered the man's back. There were two distinct sets—an outer ring that was beginning to fade and an inner circle that remained intact. Crude but effective magical inscriptions composed both markings.

William smelled an odd metallic odor. "The outer ring is likely the concealment magic. The inner circle is a geas—a magical compulsion. The enchantments are very powerful but sloppily done. The caster was either in a hurry or did not care what happened to the recipient. I bet the latter. This man is a disposable pawn."

"William, the inner circle inscriptions are hard for me to examine. The writing is...foul," Elisa explained.

"The enchantment looks like a servant binding that I've seen before. Humm..." The metallic odor suddenly grew strong. "Drop!" yelled William.

Lily grabbed Elisa and hugged the princess to her chest, then dropped to the ground while facing away from the man whom William had been inspecting. Lily felt something bump her neck and head, and then the sky burned above them with fire. Only a thin, multicolored bubble kept the heat at bay. A shock wave from the explosion shook the ground. A second and a third explosion followed soon after.

Chapter 10

Lily's awareness returned. Elisa was safely snuggled in her arms. A magical shell of rainbow-colored lights hung in the air a couple of meters above Lily. William was huddled over Lily's body, his face mere centimeters from hers. She saw the concern on his face. The bump she had felt was William using his body to shield her neck and head. Perhaps it was just the adrenaline talking, but right now, William seemed very manly. She calmly stared him in the eyes and mouthed, "Thank you."

His answer was a warm smile as he pulled away and stood up. Lily followed and returned Elisa to a standing position.

"You two need a moment?" teased Elisa. Her eyes were sparkling as she glanced at Lily and William. "Shared danger and mutual admiration are quite the potent aphrodisiacs."

"Elisa!" scolded Lily. "We are still in danger!"

"Okay, later then," the princess quipped.

Lily scowled, and William carefully studied the ground, but the tension from the near-death experience had been broken.

The rainbow shell continued to protect the trio.

"William, you never cease to amaze me. What a gorgeous shield."

"Thank you. It is burning a lot of mana, so I need to drop it. Everyone ready? Dropping in three...two...one...now," William said.

The sky surrounding them returned to a late evening hue.

The area around them had been destroyed by a series of small but powerful explosions. All evidence of three bodies—the two fighters and the maid—were gone. A pile of debris had gathered around the edge of the shield. Lily recognized it as the rock she had used to encase the other two bodies. Had the magical shield not intervened, deadly shrapnel would have punctured the trio. The former locations of the bodies were obvious from the depressions that the explosions had formed in the earth.

"What set off the explosions? Was it because we examined a body? Was it time? Or did someone do it remotely?" asked Lily.

"I don't think it was strictly time; otherwise the attendant would have exploded as well. Remote detonation is possible, but I would expect the bomber to have chosen a time when the princess was more vulnerable. I'm guessing it was the examination for the first, and then the other two were detonated by the shock wave of the first. The attendant was outside the blast and thus unaffected."

"That makes sense. We need to dispose of the attendant. Too dangerous for another detailed inspection," Lily concluded.

Unlike the fighter, the attendant had not worn armor. William shot an arrow into the man to confirm he had expired. Lily used earth magic to dig a deep hole, and William used wind magic to shove the body into the hole. A few minutes later, flames shot skyward out of the hole, and the ground shook. The trio stood a safe distance away. The immediate issues had been addressed.

William said in the shared mental space, *Princess, if you don't mind, I'm going to ask Lily to rejoin our mental link. The unknown dangers we face are more important than our individual comforts.*

Elisa answered, *Please do. If I ask, she will consider it a command. I don't want to force her, but I suspect she will agree with your assessment.*

"Lily—" said William.

"William—" said Lily.

The two had spoken at the same time.

William offered, "My apologies; please go ahead, Lily."

"Thank you. I know I made a big deal about it before, but may I be added back to the mind link? I need it for the princess's security. I'll try not to be such a burden this time."

Elisa walked up to Lily and hugged her. "William and I both want you to join."

Lily looked at William. He nodded and smiled.

The trio renewed their ritual of spell and prayer.

Can you hear me? asked Lily.

Loud and clear, replied Elisa.

Elisa and William felt Lily's sigh of relief. *If I'm honest, I was getting envious of you two, not knowing what made the princess laugh so much. I felt a bit lonely,* admitted Lily.

Elisa laughed. *The banter among Prince Ryne's crew is...interesting. Loneliness will not be an issue.*

William used his comms device to reach Conrad. The centaur and his team were still providing a defensive screen around the princess. William asked Conrad to come to them to provide more immediate support.

The party now had three nearby and conscious people they knew they could trust for escort duty: Lily, William, and Conrad. The rest of the scouts needed to stay in position to check for approaching threats. Sir Aden was likely an ally, but he was unconscious and still recovering from the poison. The rest of the escort party was still in a deep sleep from the stunning device.

Lily was the acting leader of the party. She was unwilling to risk the princess's safety until they had time to adequately screen each of the sleeping party members. The group was still hours from the town, and there were no defensive structures to aid them out there in the open. Lily did not want to leave party members behind, but she also did not have a good way to transport them.

Elisa provided the answer. "Let's load them into a wagon, and I'll drive while you all provide security. William, why don't you ride with me and provide cover from the wagon?"

"You can handle a team of horses, Your Highness?" asked Conrad.

"I can. Lily will vouch for me."

"Princess, your carriage has all the magical protections. I'm not comfortable having you in the open," stated Lily.

"Will this be acceptable?" William said, transferring his armor back to Elisa.

"That will work," replied Lily.

Conrad's eyes grew really large when he saw William's armor on the princess.

Elisa got to work calming the horses and attaching the freshest ones to the wagon. She secured the spare horses to the back of the wagon. Seeing the tiny woman work so comfortably around the huge beasts surprised both Conrad and William. "I had a great mentor," was Elisa's only explanation.

The group had to leave the other wagon and the princess's backup carriage behind. Those would have to be retrieved later.

A few minutes later, the party was underway. Elisa's skill with the horses prompted several outrageous jokes from Conrad. Lily was unfamiliar with the centaur's normal chatter, so she was taken aback that he would tease the princess. It did not help that Elisa quickly made things worse by adding her own tawdry puns. Lily looked at William for help, but he just shrugged his shoulders.

William initiated a group-wide comms channel within the network. After briefly mentioning that Lily was now listening, followed by a quick round of welcomes, William gave his report. A Llanos general had just initiated a direct attack on the future bride of a prince of Vorland. Such a bold move could easily create a war between the two countries, so it was unlikely that this was an isolated incident. William wanted to alert the network to look for additional threats.

Edmund, Prince Ryne's majordomo, was very concerned about the surprise attack. ‹General Johnson tried to kill Princess Elisa, not capture her. He must feel that her value as a hostage is no longer needed. That seems like trouble for Prince Miller and his duchy. I will contact one of our agents to warn the prince.› Edmund dropped off the comms channel.

Commander Owen reported that he and Captain Refren were still dealing with the suspected foreign mercenaries. The enemies had retreated into Nevan's duchy, so Refren was able to request local support from Folsom. Owen hoped to have the issue resolved within the next day, but for now, at least, he was unable to support Princess Elisa.

Runera, who was currently riding with Owen, had been a huge help. However, she was getting tired of fieldwork and wanted to return to the safety and sanity of her laboratory.

While they waited for Edmund to return, William and the rest of the group discussed the next steps for Princess Elisa's escort. The escort was currently headed for the nearest town, Golden. At their current speed, they would arrive about an hour before dawn. The gates of the town would be closed at that time, and while a royal entourage would not be denied entrance, it would bring significant attention to the group. Lily wanted to avoid such attention, at least until the party had fully recovered.

Fortunately, this was Prince Ryne's duchy, so they had allies both inside and outside the town. A retired army captain who was a former subordinate of Ryne's had a small manor a few miles outside of Golden. At William's suggestion, Lily ordered that the group would approach the man for help.

Those on the group-wide comms channel remained on standby. An hour passed, then two, and Edmund had still not returned. Finally, just before midnight, Edmund rejoined the comms group. He was not alone. Prince Ryne himself joined the discussion. After a quick welcome, Edmund began his report. The news was dire.

Prince Logan had killed his father, King Friedrich, in a fit of rage earlier in the day. While Logan was the crown prince, he needed approval from the Llanos Senate of Lords to ascend to the throne. Many of the current lords viewed his regicide with horror, so Logan decided to reform the Senate by pruning it of those who did not support him. The streets of the capital city, Taronto, ran red that night.

William asked about the status of Prince Miller, Elisa's father. As second in line to the throne, Miller was a direct threat to Logan's ascension. The crown prince and his supporters would have moved quickly to end the lives of Miller and his descendants. This likely explained why General Johnson had executed the kill command against Princess Elisa.

‹William, Princess Elisa can hear me through you, correct?› asked Prince Ryne. His voice was deep and resonant.

‹Yes, Ryne,› William replied.

‹Princess, your family is now safe, but many of your family's retainers lost their lives to provide your family safe passage. Your father, mother, and brothers are en route to your family estate and are planning their next steps.

‹Your father has survived a grave attempt on his life. Assassins struck him unaware, but he endured the attack. Your older brother was nearby and aided your father. During the fight, your brother was struck with the same poison that was used against you and your party. Because you, through William, were able to warn us after your attack, we had sent one of our best agents to aid your father. She arrived after the attack began but swiftly came to your family's aid. She gave your brother the antidote that saved his life. She is now traveling with your family and will relay more information when possible.›

William sensed Elisa letting go of her breath. The prince's

words had calmed her. She relayed her thanks to the prince through William.

Prince Ryne continued, ‹William, the next instructions are for you. Galene, the keeper of the Taronto Water Gardens, is missing, and the property has been sacked and looted. We believe that someone used the confusion in the city to kidnap her. I've been in touch with Willow. She has ordered you to proceed to Taronto, find and secure Galene, and escort her safely out of Llanos.›

Elisa and Lily were shocked by the news. Galene was the kind half-elf who had sheltered them in Taronto after Sarai died. The two women felt the mental link go ice-cold. The friendly and kind William they knew disappeared, replaced by a calm and calculating persona.

‹Is this just a rescue?› William asked.

‹No. Rescue of elven personnel is the primary mission. Once Galene is safe, Willow and I have agreed to send a message to the new king of Llanos. You will punish all parties responsible for interfering with Elven sovereignty. Currently, we have no evidence to indicate that the new king or his direct supporters are responsible for the attack. If they do not interfere with your operations, you will ignore them. If they do interfere, you are authorized to take any actions you deem necessary.›

‹What are my resources?›

‹Willow petitioned Dreki-hratt for transportation and support. He has agreed. Willow is sending Lahat Chereb and Orvar-Oddr for your use,› Ryne explained.

William whistled. ‹Sweet Goddess, just how big a message do you want to send?›

Ryne's voice was filled with passion. ‹Logan and his flunkies just tried to kill my future wife. They may have been behind the attack on Viverna, and they were certainly the ones who hired the mercenaries that Owen is currently chasing. Logan is attacking through intermediaries and will deny knowledge of these attacks.

‹We need to slap Llanos hard enough that they think twice about taking such rash actions again. If we move directly against Logan, both countries will go to war. However, our allies, the elves, are going to punish the culprits responsible for attacking Elven sovereign holdings in Taronto. Even Logan should understand that message—he can be destroyed with no advanced notice. Hopefully that will keep his politics confined to his own borders.

‹Our support of Prince Miller will be more subtle, as we don't want to undermine Miller's position within Llanos. Mizu, our agent who coordinated Princess Elisa's joining us, is currently with the prince. She will continue to act as a liaison between Vorland and Prince Miller.›

William replied, ‹Ryne, you mentioned that the elves are punishing the guilty. You and Willow are sending me. How should I interpret that?›

Prince Ryne snorted. ‹Sending Shadow Prince William would not be much of a message. Your magic would make them forget you before you ever left the city. For this mission, Witch Queen Albrun is a far more appropriate choice.›

William sighed. Even through the verbal link, everyone could feel William's facepalm. After a moment, William asked, ‹Why…why do you do this to me?› The disgust was plain in his voice.

‹What ever could you mean?› asked Ryne. The innocence of his question was undermined by the humor in his tone.

‹You darn well know what I mean! Not one, but two new nicknames. What is wrong with you?›

Elisa and Lily could feel William's annoyance through the mental bond.

The comms link erupted in laughter. William growled in response.

‹William, your titles aren't exactly new. Remember that meeting you missed at the end of last spring?› asked Ryne.

‹Yes, I remember,› William said with a sinking feeling in his stomach.

‹The team decided you needed new, more fearsome titles. Conrad suggested "Shadow Prince" for William. Your mother, Elven Queen Willow, granted you her old title of "Witch Queen." The rest is history. The bards have been spreading rumors of your exploits for the last season. I hear the songs are very popular.›

More laughter filled comms.

‹I hate you all, but I hate Ryne most of all!› William screamed.

The laughter just got louder.

After a few minutes, order was restored. ‹Any other questions?› asked Prince Ryne.

‹What about the mission to protect the princess?› asked a mildly grumpy William.

‹I'm taking over escort duty from you. Princess Elisa and I have many things to discuss, and I'm looking forward to meeting her again. I will be there before morning; Dreki-hratt is giving me a ride. You will depart for Llanos after that.›

I have so many questions, I'm not sure where to start, Elisa told Lily and William.

Sorry about all of this. We were hoping your trip to Auraria would be less...eventful, said William.

Elisa replied, *Please don't apologize. I might have died several times on this trip without you and Lily. Thank you.*

You are welcome, Your Highness, said William.

You keep using my titles, but you seem to forget your own. Prince Ryne said Willow, your mother, is the Elven Queen. Does that make you Elven royalty?

Elves are much less formal than humans when it comes to leaders. Mother is the current queen, but she will pass it to another elder at some point in the future. Just being her child does not give me a path to the Elven throne. Elves also lack the noble titles that humans hold so dear.

I have been told that only exceptional humans are accepted among the elves. Given his age and closeness to the elves, Prince Ryne is your father, isn't he? asked Elisa.

What makes you so sure? asked William.

Only a father could make his child as frustrated as Ryne made you.

That is a good guess, but Ryne is not my father.

But given how close you are—did he adopt you? Are you his heir? Elisa questioned.

William replied, We are close, but I will defer to Ryne to explain our relationship. No, I am not and cannot be his heir. Vorland is more tolerant of non-humans than Llanos, but this country would never acknowledge a non-human leader. Ryne needs an heir that this country will accept. He needs someone like you to produce such a child.

You heard General Johnson. My value to Prince Ryne is gone.

William stated, The question of your status has yet to be resolved. Moreover, if Ryne just wanted a pretty, young wife, he had many choices available. He sought you for a reason. He wants an equal to share his life with him, not just a lovely face who gives him children. Talk to him as you travel. He will share his vision of the future with you. Hopefully it is something you will value as well.

Thank you, William. You are very kind, replied Elisa.

The mental link was quiet for several minutes.

William finally broke the silence. I'm sure you both have many more questions. Some of them I'm going to leave for Ryne to answer. Other answers will become obvious in the morning. I hope you will forgive me when you learn the truth about me.

Elisa and Lily could feel a wave of sadness pass through William.

Princess Elisa's group reached the manor outside Golden an hour and a half before dawn. The retired captain was surprised to see the group but quickly adapted and welcomed them into his home. Now would have been a good time to awaken the sleeping escort members, but William asked to refrain from doing so. Ryne was arriving shortly, and William did not want the Llanos retainers to see what was soon to transpire. William, Lily, and the captain moved the sleepers into the front hall and made them comfortable on the floor. They placed Sir Aden on a spare bed. Conrad stayed outside to redeploy his scouts around the manor.

A few minutes later, Ryne called to William and Conrad through the communicator. He said he would be arriving shortly. The captain requested that the prince land in the western field. The crops had already been harvested, and the area was screened by a thick hedgerow. The field would provide good cover from curious eyes.

The captain led Elisa, Lily, William, and Conrad to the field. The moon had already set, but the stars were bright, so the group was able to walk without additional light.

Lily could feel rather than see the grin that was forming on William's face. "What's so funny?" she asked with suspicion.

"How much have you told them?" asked Conrad.

"Nothing. I'm not going to undermine the old man's grand entrance."

Conrad and the captain laughed in appreciation. Lily was annoyed they were hiding a secret. Elisa was intrigued.

The group stood patiently at the edge of the field, some more patient than others.

One moment, the sky was empty, and the next, it was filled with a shadow that blocked all the stars in the sky. The shadow descended onto the field with barely a whisper. Both women were shocked by the sudden appearance, but each was immediately prepared to fight despite the intense magical aura of intimidation emitted by the massive shadow dragon that lay before them.

A voice called out from atop the shadow dragon. "Well met, friends. Please forgive my little rite of passage. You truly are as exceptional as William has told me." A massive human figure detached itself from the shadow and walked toward the group. A warm, soft light began to glow around him. First, he approached and greeted Elisa. He took her hand in his large fingers, then bowed before her as he kissed the top of her hand. "Princess Elisa, I am Ryne. Welcome to the Duchy of Auraria. You are even lovelier than when we last met." Ryne was a very large man, but his movements were as polished as a dancer's. His features were rugged and very handsome. His eyes were a startling ice-blue.

Elisa felt herself drowning in his eyes. With great effort, she recovered enough to return his greeting. "Prince Ryne, I am Elisa. Thank you for granting us refuge. I hope we will prove worthy of your trust." Elisa's words were even and polished, but her heart was beating fast.

"I look forward to our time together, Princess." Ryne then turned his attention to Lily, who was kneeling on the ground before the prince with her eyes cast upon the ground. "You must be Dame Lily. Please stand and raise your head so I may have a better look at you."

Lily did as the prince instructed. For the first time since she had become an adult, Lily had to tilt her head up to meet someone's eyes, those of the prince.

Ryne offered his forearm in a warrior's embrace, and Lily gladly returned the gesture. "Your Highness, I am Lily, servant of Princess Elisa. Thank you for your kindness." Lily lacked Elisa's emotional control. Her voice cracked as she offered her greeting. A look of awe spread across her face as she gazed into the prince's eyes. With a sudden gulp, Lily realized what she was doing. Her face grew red with embarrassment, but she could not break eye contact with Prince Ryne.

Ryne released Lily's forearm, then grabbed her hand in his fingers. He brought the back of her hand to his lips without breaking eye contact. "The rumors of the Dragon Lily are true. You are as beautiful as you are strong. I am Ryne, and I welcome you."

Lily's knees buckled, but Ryne caught her before she fell. She found herself cradled in the prince's arms. Fearless against the intimidation mere moments ago, Lily now found herself powerless in Ryne's embrace.

"Ryne, stop it!" ordered William.

"Stop what?" asked Ryne. He seemed genuinely confused. Lily was still limp in his arms.

"You've made your grand entrance. Let the poor girl go!"

Elisa interrupted, "Lily is quite happy where she is. This is the first time a handsome man, literally a prince, has swept her off her feet."

Through the link, William felt Lily's overwhelming emotion. Lily had fallen head over heels in love with Ryne. Love at first sight was a truly spectacular emotion. While Lily was a battle-hardened warrior on the outside, she had the soul of a young maiden wanting to experience her first love.

Elisa said in the shared mental space, *William, it is okay. Let it go. Ryne has done nothing wrong. Lily has been wishing for a moment like this her entire life.*

Yes, Your Highness. Just know that Ryne is clueless about his effect on women.

That is part of his appeal. If he was an intentional flirt, he would be far less charming.

A deep "HRUM" echoed through the field. The noise had come from the shadow.

"Good to see you again, Lord Dreki-hratt. Thank you for helping us in our time of need," William said to the shadow dragon. The light around Ryne did little to distinguish the form of the creature.

The dragon's voice was deep and powerful. "You too, my young friend. I'm going to feed. I'll be ready to depart in thirty minutes."

"I'll be ready, too."

The shadow departed in silence. The creature's exit was enough to break Lily's trance.

"Thank you, Prince Ryne," Lily said as she extracted herself from Ryne's arms.

Chapter 11

Prince Ryne, Princess Elisa, Lily, and William took shelter in the retired captain's barn. They did not want to risk unfriendly eyes or ears spying on their discussions.

"First, let's add Elisa and Lily to the Aurarian communication network. Here you are, ladies," Ryne said as he handed them communication devices. "These will allow you to communicate within our team. We have several eclectic individuals; you should get to know them as you consider your own roles within the group."

Elisa and Lily poured mana into the seashell-like devices, which then turned invisible. They each attached one of the devices to an ear, as instructed by the prince.

Ryne continued, "Second, I need to apologize to you. William told me you ladies were fearless, so I thought I would test you. Perhaps I went a little overboard—"

"Way overboard!" injected William.

"Okay, way overboard by exposing you to a true dragon's fear. Still, your responses exceeded my expectations. Princess Elisa, you remind me of your aunt. Sarai must have trained both you and Lily well. I look forward to discussing Sarai during our trip to Auraria.

"Third, William needs to get ready for his new assignment. Where would you like to prepare? Do you wish us to leave?" he asked William.

"The barn will do fine. Twenty minutes should be sufficient.

I do need peace and quiet, so please go outside if you wish to converse. The mental link makes it impossible for me to hide this ritual from Elisa and Lily. In any case, they will see the result. Stay or go as your mood dictates."

While talking to the others, William had been steadily removing his clothing. As he removed each layer, he carefully cleaned and folded the items and then placed them into his extra-dimensional space. One of the final items he had to address was the elvish armor. Instead of asking for it back and storing it, he asked Elisa if she would be willing to continue wearing it until he returned. She replied yes, then removed her cloak so that the armor was visible. Seeing the armor on Elisa made Ryne very excited. William just chuckled.

"Now do you believe me?" William asked.

"I never doubted you. But this...this is quite exciting. So many possibilities," replied Ryne.

"Now that the link is active, Lily should try again. Princess, pull my bow from storage. If she can handle it, then have her try the armor as well. For now, I must focus on the ritual."

William placed a linen sheet on the floor of the barn. He energized it with mana, and the sheet flattened into a smooth, level surface. A highly complex magic circle was inscribed on the sheet. William removed the rest of his clothing and donned a robe to ward off the late autumn predawn chill. He stepped inside the magic circle, sat down, and poured more mana into the circle.

The sight of a naked William did not faze Lily. She had trained with the Varangian Guard for the last decade. Constant drills, extended marches, and cramped quarters had exposed Lily to far too many bare bottoms and male body parts than she cared to count.

However, Lily had to revise her assessment of William. While his build was slight, the muscles in his front and back looked like they had been sculpted from fine marble. There was no excess fat on him. His "manly parts" were surprisingly well-endowed. Lily moved him from the "looks like a little brother" category to the "oh wow, he is actually kind of handsome" category.

Elisa said through the link, *Lily, while I'm sure William is flattered by your new appreciation, you are not helping him focus right now.*

Lily panicked. She had forgotten the link. She grew bright red and exited the barn. Ryne and Elisa followed.

Outside, the three talked quietly. Elisa helped Lily calm her nerves and thoughts so she would not disturb William. Through the link, Elisa could feel William's focus. He was using his mana to slowly change the odd magic that made him so forgettable. Strand by strand, he untangled the impossibly complex web.

Elisa decided to follow William's advice. She reached into his extra-dimensional storage and withdrew the elvish bow. William must have already unlocked the space, as Elisa retrieved the item much more easily than before. Elisa presented the bow to Lily, and Lily gingerly reached out to touch it. Unlike before, the bow now had substance beneath her touch, and Lily took it from Elisa. The grip was too small for her hand, but it quickly began to flow and adapt. Within moments, the bow felt like it belonged to Lily.

Lily was exhilarated, and both Ryne and Elisa found it difficult to contain their excitement. With a bit of regret, Lily handed the bow back to Elisa. She would have liked to try it, but shooting a bow in the darkness would have been reckless. *Perhaps I can try it later,* she thought.

Definitely, was Elisa's mental reply. "Now it is time to try the armor."

Lily was reluctant at first, as she was unsure if it would fit under her normal armor.

Ryne provided the solution. "Remove your armor and don the elvish set as you would a set of leather. Give it a chance to adapt to your body. If it fits, it will remember you. Then you will be able to do the same instant-on, instant-off trick that

William and Elisa do. I will protect the princess while you change."

Even with experience and help, the removal of Lily's normal armor was an ordeal lasting several minutes. The process would have been faster had she accepted Ryne's offer of assistance. She would have liked to do so, but she was afraid his attention would have been too exciting for her. *Dear Goddess, the man is handsome*, she thought before she could stop herself.

Elisa giggled and nodded in agreement.

"Humm?" asked Ryne.

"Nothing. Nothing at all, Your Highness," replied Elisa.

Finally, it was time for Lily to try the elvish armor. Elisa removed it in an instant, leaving the finely crafted metal in her hands. The set's top was like a long tunic. Lily took the set into her own hands, which were trembling with excitement. She then lifted the armor over her head and let it slide onto her body. The initial fitting took a few minutes. Lily was much larger than either Elisa or William. The magic worked, and Lily marveled at the warm, comforting feeling that the armor provided. She then donned the leggings that completed the set.

Ryne suggested that the women try the quick exchange with each other. This proved a good distraction, as William had begun using a new type of magic, deploying a deep and powerful transformation magic. The process was slow, so it was not uncomfortable. However, the procedure did create many odd sensations in both Elisa and Lily. Weirdest of all was the change in their shared mental space. William was slowly disappearing, being replaced by someone else.

After a few more minutes, Elisa felt not-William cast cleansing and purifying magics. Not-William then announced they were done. Their voice through the link had changed. The pitch was higher, and the tone more melodic.

Ryne, Elisa, and Lily reentered the barn. The androgynous figure contained within the magic circle was not William.

Their hair was shoulder length and the color of silver. Their shoulders were narrower, limbs longer, and gentle curves appeared where none had been before. Their skin was dark and flawless, and their face was gorgeous. The figure gracefully stood and exited the circle.

As the figure donned their new undergarments and clothing, Lily's curiosity got the best of her. Not-William noticed her glance and paused, allowing enough time for Lily to see female features.

I'm sorry! was the knight's quick apology.

The wonderful feeling of elvish laughter filled the shared mental space. *No worries. Not much to see.*

Ryne stepped beside them and performed introductions. "Princess Elisa, Dame Lily, this is Albrun Willowdóttir." Prince Ryne had a fierce pride in his voice.

Elisa had a sharp look on her face. She had been expecting a surprise, but not this one. She understood the special shielding magic allowed "William" to avoid recognition as he moved through the world.

Ah, realized Elisa; an elf, particularly one as stunningly beautiful as Albrun, would cause a stir wherever she went. Being Ryne's agent in the human world required Albrun to forego any recognition for her accomplishments, as well as her sense of self. Such a price seemed tragic and made Elisa feel sympathy for Albrun.

Albrun heard Elisa's thoughts. She replied with a small nod of acknowledgment.

Lily stood still in shock next to Elisa, her brain struggling to process what she was seeing. Eventually, she startled herself into motion. "Your eyes…" Lily said in amazement.

Ryne and Albrun were now standing next to each other, facing Elisa and Lily. The human and the elf were a study in contrasts. Their sizes, builds, hair colors—almost all their features were at opposite ends of the spectrum. But their eyes were the same. Albrun had Ryne's gorgeous ice-blue eyes, but her dark skin and fine facial features made her eyes even more striking.

"With those matching eyes, you still say you two are not related?" asked Elisa.

Albrun raised an eyebrow at Ryne.

"I'll explain later," Ryne said.

Albrun began to speak. Her voice was even more enchanting when speaking aloud. "I apologize for surprising you, but circumstances did not allow me to present myself more appropriately. I hope you will forgive me," she said as she bowed first to Elisa and then to Lily. When she saw Lily still wearing the elven armor, Albrun smiled. "The armor looks good on you, Dame Lily. Please take care of it while I am gone."

"Really?" blurted Lily. She became very self-conscious. Elisa had complimented her earlier, and Ryne's acknowledgment felt overwhelming. "Thank you, Willia—I mean Albrun; oh, I'm sorry." Lily became flustered and hung her head to hide her embarrassment.

Lily sensed Albrun calmly walking toward her, then felt small hands grasp her large ones. Their grip was soft and warm.

"Lily, look at me," Albrun commanded. Lily raised her head, but only a little. The elf was more than a full head shorter than the tall warrior. "While I am gone for the next few days, please take care of both the princess and the prince. Ryne is a visionary—he has amazing dreams for the future. Elisa is smart and shrewd. She can refine his dreams into executable plans. They will need to be managed so they don't start anything crazy. The rest of the team will just encourage them. Will you be the adult supervision while I'm gone?" Albrun's expression was earnest.

The elf's words lifted Lily's mood. "Yes, Albrun," she replied. She still felt a bit odd calling not-William by this name.

Albrun sensed the hesitance. "Lily, I'm still me, just a slightly different version," the elf said with a laugh. She released Lily and turned to Princess Elisa.

The two women made eye contact. Elisa's gaze was steady and intense. "You continue to surprise me, Albrun. Have I found the real you? Do your secrets run deeper?" asked Elisa.

"You give me too much credit, Your Highness. I am a simple person. I merely become what my people need me to be."

Elisa laughed. "That's not simple at all. You are intriguing, and I love a good mystery. We will talk more when you return."

Albrun bowed to Elisa, then turned to Ryne. "May I have Mother's package?"

Ryne handed a small magical satchel to Albrun. She opened it and retrieved a one-and-a-half-meter-long sword in a scabbard and a full set of armor. Albrun donned the armor. Whereas the elven mail was composed of fine interlinking chains, this armor looked like metallic silk. Ornate runes and inscriptions covered its surface.

"This is the legendary armor Orvar-Oddr. It is Queen Willow's personal armor. She wore it while dealing with the Catastrophe three hundred years ago," explained Ryne.

Next, Albrun buckled the sword's scabbard across her back. Including the hilt, the sword was taller than Albrun. Such a large weapon on so slight a body should have been awkward, but Albrun bore it well. Her movements were natural and not hindered. "This is the sword Lahat Chereb. Queen Willow used it to end the threat of the Catastrophe."

Elisa and Lily beheld the armed and armored Albrun. Before, she had been a beautiful maiden. Now, she was a warrior angel, a messenger of retribution from the gods.

"Prince Ryne, your message to the new King Logan and the citizens of Taronto lacks...subtlety," Elisa commented.

Ryne said, "Logan was boorish and ill-mannered as a prince, and being king will only make him worse. We hope this show of force will be sufficient for him to turn his warlike tendencies elsewhere."

Albrun tilted her head. "Dreki-hratt is back. Please excuse me. I must go."

Ryne, Elisa, and Lily followed Albrun out of the barn and back to the field. Inky blackness lay in front of them. Albrun bowed to her three companions, then walked forward into the darkness. The shadows swirled around her until she disappeared.

"Dreki-hratt, please take care of her. I can't afford to lose her," Ryne pleaded with the darkness. His voice was strong with emotion.

The shadow dragon shook with laughter. "You worry too much, Ryne. Take pride in Albrun; she is every bit the warrior her mother is." The shadow silently and swiftly departed, leaving Ryne, Elisa, and Lily alone.

Elisa was standing next to Ryne and heard him sigh deeply. His expression was conflicted. Elisa was a very good judge of character. He clearly was proud of Albrun but was equally worried about her safety. Elisa reached out and rubbed his back, comforting him.

Ryne was startled out of his silence. "My apologies, Princess. I would rather you not see my weakness." The huge man wore a self-effacing grin.

Elisa's reply was warm and soothing. "I have been surrounded by physically strong but emotionally brittle men my entire life. They shatter under pressure—lashing out with anger and violence against loved ones. Finding a man who can deal with tough emotions in a caring way—that is a man worth receiving one's heart."

Ryne stood in silence for a few more moments. "Your kindness and perception are equaled only by your beauty, Your Highness."

Ryne escorted Elisa and Lily back to the manor house. The night had been long, and they needed sleep before facing the new day.

Aden, knight of Llanos, woke in a comfortable bed. The room was small but well-appointed. The window was open, and fresh air and light bathed the room. Aden had no idea how he had arrived here. His last memories were of the conflict over the princess, followed by a bright flash, then nothing. Much must have transpired since then.

Aden rolled out of the bed. He was bare to the waist, with only his underclothing on below. His side was a bit stiff from a recently healed wound. His armor and other gear were arrayed next to the bed. He began to dress, then made his way to the window. A pleasant countryside view greeted him. The time appeared to be noon, as the sun was high in the sky. He must have been recovering from the injury, as he never slept this late.

Aden left the room and followed the sound of conversation. He arrived in a large hall filled with people eating lunch. Lily saw him in the doorway, and she motioned for him to join her.

"How are you feeling, Sir Aden?" asked Lily.

"Well rested, but very confused. Is the princess okay?" was his reply.

"She is," assured Lily. Lily spent the next several minutes explaining the situation to Aden, omitting only sensitive details like William's change and new mission. William's absence was not a surprise since Prince Ryne had now joined the group.

Aden was very worried about his father and fiancée. Both were loyal followers of Prince Miller, Elisa's father.

Prince Ryne and Princess Elisa joined Lily and Aden a few minutes later. After introductions, Ryne had good news for Aden. Both his father and fiancée were safe. Neither was in the capital, and neither was high-profile enough to warrant assassins.

"I have more news to share," began Ryne. "Taronto has entered a stalemate. Forces loyal to the old king now support

Prince Miller. They control about half the city—the Merchants and Commoners Districts. Prince Logan controls the other half, including the Nobles and Government Districts. Logan convened the Senate of Lords last night during the chaos. His hand-picked nobles affirmed him to be the next king, but the voting was a sham. The Senate did not have a quorum. Nevertheless, Logan has declared himself the new king."

"Thank you, Prince Ryne. My update is about last night's magical ambush. Aden, Lily has apprised you?" asked Elisa.

"Yes, Your Highness," replied Aden.

"We believe the issue was two-fold. First, the sleeper agents were designed to foil detection, particularly by me. Now that I know what the signatures look like, we should be able to prevent future infiltration. Second, the communication device between my father's retainers and you, Sir Aden, was secure until last night. We believe it was hacked by wizards loyal to Logan, potentially the same ones that generated the monster horde and the attack on Viverna. They are still at large, so we will need to be cautious.

"With help from the prince's retainers, I have finished examining the rest of my escort group for the magical runes that triggered the sleeper agents last night. None of the survivors, including yourself, Aden, are affected. We have also gone through all our goods and belongings, checking for communication devices and unusual magical instruments. Everything appears clean. Now we need to decide how to move forward."

"The first question is for Aden," began Ryne. "You have successfully accomplished your mission—Princess Elisa has safely been delivered to me. Your original plan was to return to Llanos, but the situation has changed. Princess Elisa trusts you, and I believe she is an excellent judge of character. I am prepared to offer you sanctuary here in Vorland if you wish to stay."

"Your offer is very kind, Your Highness, but my family needs me. I will return to Llanos."

Elisa said, "You are a good man, Sir Aden. Llanos does need you. I asked the other survivors of the escort group, and they each expressed their desire to return as well."

Ryne added, "I will provide troops to see you safely to the Llanos border. I understand that Lady Philippa is waiting in Viverna. Will you take her to Llanos as well?"

"I will, Your Highness. She and her family are supporters of King Logan, but I will see that she faces no harm. She has great value in a hostage exchange between the two Llanos factions."

"Thank you, Sir Aden. I wish you the best of luck," stated Ryne.

Aden turned to face Lily. "Will you be accompanying me, Dame Lily?"

"No, my place will always be at my princess's side." Lily's earnest response made Elisa smile.

Aden looked a bit wistful about what might have been had he met Lily earlier. He turned back to the prince and princess. "By your leave, I will prepare the group to leave in the morning. It has been my great pleasure to serve you, Your Highnesses." He bowed, then left.

After lunch, Ryne, Elisa, and Lily withdrew to a private office in the manor. Elisa cast defensive magic on the room to ensure their privacy. They had only gotten a couple of hours of sleep last night, so all three were tired, but several matters required their attention.

Elisa and Lily used their mental link with Albrun to check her location. The link still worked, but it now required mana to function. The upside was that Albrun no longer overheard casual conversations between Elisa and Lily.

Albrun was hundreds of kilometers away and would reach Taronto a couple of hours after sunset. The elf had slept for several hours and was now planning for her mission once she reached the city.

Ryne described a new complication within Taronto. The chaos within the city had led to high-value targets being attacked. This included the embassies of several countries. Their buildings often contained valuable works of art, and their personnel could be held for ransom. At this point, only the unofficial Elven embassy, the Water Garden, had fallen. Larger countries, like Vorland and the Osman Empire, had sufficient personnel to ensure their safety. Many of the embassies from smaller countries, including several of the city-states from Polis, were at great risk of being overrun. All these embassies were in the Government District controlled by King Logan.

Whether through apathy, incompetence, or corruption, King Logan's government was unwilling to protect the foreign embassies. Considering Llanos's position as a nation of merchants, with Taronto as the primary trade hub on the continent, Logan's lack of support was unfathomable.

Vorland was asked by several countries to help escort their people safely out of the city. Ryne saw this as an opportunity to make new allies. Vorland could not respond quickly, but Albrun could.

Ryne contacted Queen Willow to get permission from the Elven nation. She fully supported the additional mission. Helping the foreign embassies would further undermine support for King Logan and, hopefully, limit his time on the throne.

Once the approval was received, Ryne asked Elisa to inform Albrun through the mental link. Part of the testing this morning included reconfirming the security of the team's various communication devices. The Aurarian comms earpieces were still deemed secure, but users had to speak to use them, making them less useful for stealth missions. The mana usage of the comms device was also higher than the mental link.

Albrun and Dreki-hratt gladly accepted the extra work. Albrun told Elisa to tease Ryne: *Yet another piece of your plan for world change falls into place.* Elisa relayed the message without understanding what it meant.

Ryne grinned. "I have a grand vision of how the world needs to change. I will tell you about it as we travel. Hopefully, I will convince you of how smart and charming I am. I need you to make the plan work."

Ryne was unlike most other noblemen. He was far more self-aware and willing to expose his vulnerabilities to Elisa. "William" shared those same traits, and Elisa found the attributes appealing in both her future husband and the elf.

Lily cleared her throat. Elisa found herself staring at Ryne. "Are you two finished flirting, or do you need a few more moments?" asked Lily with dry humor.

Elisa turned to Lily with a sheepish grin. Lily had caught her red-handed. Ryne did not look embarrassed at all.

The trio continued their planning without interruption. They would ride northwest to Auraria starting tomorrow morning. They would be supported by Conrad and his scouts, along with a small detachment of soldiers from Golden. Ryne's sudden appearance on dragon-back meant his normal escort had been left in Auraria. The party's escort contingent would switch halfway to Auraria, allowing the troops from Golden to return home in a week.

Aden's departure the following day meant that Princess Elisa would be without maids and a lady-in-waiting for the remainder of the trip. Ryne apologized for not having female servants available, but Elisa just laughed.

"I spent most of my teenage years with Aunt Sarai. She had little use for servants, so I'm used to taking care of myself. I took care of Aunt Sarai as well... That crafty woman—I was *her* servant!" Elisa reacted with false amazement. Lily and Ryne were both amused.

Ryne had an announcement that shocked Elisa for real.

"Your aunt was one of my mentors."

Elisa's eyes became large. "Seriously? She told me she knew you, but she never mentioned you were close!"

"We met each other when I was briefly living among the elves, back when I was a teenager. She clearly loved and trusted you, but she was also discreet. She was probably worried that acknowledging our friendship would harm my reputation. She was truly a remarkable woman."

"Thank you. When we have time, I would love to hear your stories of her," replied Elisa.

"Gladly," said Ryne.

Their discussions and planning ended midafternoon. The trio needed a break, so Ryne decided to formally introduce Elisa and Lily to the Aurarian communication network. This quickly degenerated into another round of bad jokes once Conrad realized a new person, Lily, had joined the group.

Prince Ryne's team members are so odd and so fun! Lily thought to Elisa.

I like them too. Ryne has assembled a great group. I hope we are a good fit.

The rest of the day passed without incident. Preparations were ready for Ryne, Elisa, and Lily to leave in the morning.

CHAPTER 12

In Llanos, Dreki-hratt dropped Albrun off near the city of Taronto and then left to feed. Albrun entered the city unnoticed and began to scout. Without her "William" form, she proceeded more cautiously, but the general unrest and confusion aided her stealth.

Albrun's plan was to infiltrate the city, use magic to locate Galene, and then extract her to safety. Dreki-hratt would protect Galene while the elf aided the embassies. Once the embassies' personnel were safe, Albrun would then inflict punishment on the people who had attacked the Water Gardens. Dreki-hratt would stand by outside the city, and he would not enter unless the situation was very dire. The massive creature would generate widespread panic and potentially expose himself to anti-siege weapons that were ineffective against human-sized targets.

The rescue-and-punishment mission would have been challenging by itself. Adding the escort mission increased the difficulty tremendously. Normally, a single person escorting multiple groups through a hostile city was simply impossible. However, Willow had sent legendary items to aid Albrun. Controlling the items—particularly Lahat Chereb—would push the young elf to her limits. Failure to control the sword could lead to widespread destruction. Albrun knew the gravity of the situation. Failure was not an option.

Under cover of darkness, Albrun made her way to the

devastated Water Gardens. Just days ago, the walled compound in the Merchants District had served as a calm and inviting retreat from the hustle and bustle of the city. The Gardens was the size of a large noble's compound, but its location allowed even commoners to enjoy its many pleasures. The outer area contained a series of small parks. Each park contained flora from a specific area of the continent. Magic allowed the plants to flourish while keeping the temperature and humidity comfortable for the guests. Each park had several areas where guests could picnic, talk, or just enjoy the scenery.

The inner areas were contained within a purpose-built mansion. Common and private baths, assorted spas, and a café were attached to a small inn. The master of the Water Gardens was Galene, one of the few widely respected non-human residents of the city. Galene was a half-elvish woman of great beauty. She treated all guests with respect, regardless of their social status or race, if they obeyed the rules. Unruly guests were removed quickly and efficiently. The Water Gardens did not offer brothel services—guests seeking those pleasures needed to search elsewhere. However, the inn, with its private baths, was a popular location for trysts between lovers. As in all things, Galene and her staff were discreet.

The gardens now lay in ruins, and the mansion was heavily damaged. Albrun felt her anger rising as she searched the compound. She quashed her anger for now—she would save it for the perpetrators. The inside of the mansion was in shambles. Looters had stolen anything of value, and fire had damaged the structure. The bodies of several workers were scattered throughout the building. All possessed defensive wounds. Their weapons were tools of their trade—gardeners with hoes and scythes, maids with brooms they had used as staves. The staff had been trained to deal with small numbers of drunken guests—this attack far exceeded their capabilities. Their attackers had been numerous, well-trained, and well-armed. A noble's private guards, perhaps?

Albrun continued her search further into the mansion. Just outside Galene's office, the fighting had been particularly fierce. Here the Garden's best fighters had assembled in a last-ditch effort to protect their master. Members of the attacking force had likely died during the battle, but no bodies remained. The attackers must have taken their fallen with them. Perhaps the villains had realized that the attack would lead to a response from the Elven nation.

Albrun searched Galene's ruined office. As elsewhere, the attackers had used fire to remove traces of their passage. Assuming Galene recognized her enemies, she would have taken steps to record that information. Something that would be obvious to her elvish brethren but hidden from all other eyes. Albrun continued to inspect the office. What could it be? She tried using magic, but the walls were resistant. She could increase the power of the magic, but doing so risked being noticed by magic-sensitive people nearby.

Albrun inspected the small closet on the west side of the room. It might have once held office supplies or clothing—it was difficult to tell now. Something felt odd about it. Ah, the water level. Throughout her search of the mansion, each room had held a few centimeters of sludgy water—the remains of the now-broken baths. This closet was different. There was only sludge—the water had drained. Where did it go? Ah, the closet had a false back. After several minutes of searching, Albrun found two release mechanisms. She activated them, then pushed on the wall. A door appeared and swung away from her, revealing another room beyond. She heard whimpering somewhere in the darkness.

Albrun's senses were on full alert. Two small figures—halflings or maybe children—were in the room. She increased her light spell to reveal two children in the dirty uniforms of the Water Gardens. They were both injured and weak.

Deciding that the children were victims rather than threats, Albrun began healing them and giving them food and drink. After a while, they were calm and recovered enough to speak. Their parents had been workers for the Water Gardens. The children had worked part-time as park assistants. They had been injured during the initial assault and fled to Galene to inform her of the attack. Galene had hidden them in this room, which also served as the Garden's main treasure room.

The children were able to identify the attackers—private soldiers from the Thornhill family. The children did not know all the details, but the eldest son was a nasty man who had been banished from the Water Gardens for abusing the staff.

Albrun relayed this information through the mental link. Elisa was currently on duty—since Albrun's operation would likely take all night, Elisa and Lily were taking shifts staying awake to communicate with Albrun. Elisa knew the family well. The patriarch of the family was a count and a well-known supporter of King Logan. Among Llanos nobles, the man was considered unpleasant but useful. He was willing to do unsavory things, and he had many retainers to carry out those duties.

Elisa speculated that Count Thornhill's men had been ordered to kill several of the old king's supporters during the Night of Forgotten Vows, as the incident was now being called. The attack on the Water Gardens had happened later in the night, so it may not have been a primary target. The eldest son's banishment supported the theory that it had been an act of revenge carried out during the chaos.

Galene's body had not been found inside the mansion, so there was a possibility she was still alive. However, a day had passed since the kidnapping, so Galene likely had suffered at the hands of her kidnappers.

Albrun turned her attention back to the children. Now that they were calm and their hunger was gone, exhaustion caught up with them. Albrun placed a small enchantment on them to guarantee good rest. She then opened her extra-dimensional space and placed them inside. The enchantment would ensure they remained asleep, and the pair was much safer inside the space than they were outside of it. They would be fine as long as Albrun removed them within a day. Albrun also took the remaining valuables from the treasure room. Galene would need the money to rebuild her business.

Albrun decided to change the order of her plans. Galene, if alive, would require an extraction. Punishment of her attackers would need to happen before the embassies' personnel were escorted from the city.

With the children now safe, Albrun left the Water Gardens and proceeded to the Nobles District. The Thornhill family compound lay midway between the Nobles Gate and the King's Palace. This district was more active than the last. All the inhabited houses and compounds had deployed their family guards. The city watch was absent, but the king's guards patrolled the streets. Albrun took extra precautions, as the patrols included wizards and war priests to guard against magically enhanced enemies.

Two hours before midnight, Albrun arrived at the Thornhill Estate. She scanned the property for guardians, both magical and mundane. The exterior wall had a proximity alarm—anyone crossing on or over it would set it off. Albrun used suppression magic to make herself invisible to the alarm. Between the wall and the mansion, packs of trained dogs patrolled. Albrun charmed the beasts to treat her as a friend.

Albrun now risked using search magic to look for Galene. Among the treasures in the secret room, the elf had found an item of personal significance to the kidnapped half-elf—a wreath of magically preserved elven flowers. Albrun used this item to strengthen her image of Galene.

Albrun found Galene with surprising ease. The half-elf was not a high-value prisoner hidden behind a magical barrier. Galene was being treated as a disposable spoil of war, a plaything for the soldiers of Count Thornhill. She was barely alive and in a truly wretched state.

Albrun relayed her findings back to Elisa. The elf was

switching the rescue to a hot extraction. The time for stealth was gone. She would use speed and surprise to carve a path to Galene. Prince Ryne relayed through Elisa that he understood and wished Albrun good hunting. Albrun asked for him to start notifying the embassies that had asked for help. She would be outside their compounds in less than an hour.

Albrun cast her personal enhancement magics and readied her bow. Her senses were magically enhanced to detect enemies. The shortest path to Galene was through the front door. Albrun began to run.

The guards were unprepared. Each fell before they could raise an alarm. Albrun was at the front door before the last body had fallen. She used earth magic to breach the door and wind magic to silence her passage. A dozen retainers were stationed inside the entrance hall. Twelve arrows stilled them forever. Albrun continued through the grand hallway to the dining room in the back. She burst through the doors, taking the spectators by surprise. Men stood around the edge of the room while Galene's unconscious form lay on the dining room table. Albrun leaped upon the table and spun, sending a steady stream of arrows into the men, hitting each of them. A few seconds later, the room was silent.

Albrun had to move fast. Reinforcements would be arriving soon. She confirmed that Galene was still breathing, then used a healing potion in each hand—one to resolve Galene's exterior wounds and one for the interior ones. The magic worked quickly.

Galene woke in Albrun's arms. "Queen Willow sent me. I am your vengeance. Rest now." Galene nodded, then closed her eyes. Albrun placed her into a healing trance, then put her inside the safety of the extra-dimensional space.

Albrun stored her bow and unsheathed Lahat Chereb. The blade burst into flame. Albrun calmly walked back through the entrance hall. Soldiers lined her path but quickly parted when they witnessed the fate of the first fighter to engage

Albrun. He had closed to melee range and swung his sword. Before he could connect, he had burst into flames. The fire had been intense, melting even his armor.

Albrun exited the mansion and stood in the entryway. She activated a property of her armor—Crowd Speech. She began to speak in a normal voice. The powerful magic broadcasted her voice across the city. Each person who heard it would think Albrun was speaking directly to them.

"Citizens, residents, and visitors of Taronto, I am Albrun, daughter of Queen Willow of the Elven nation. Last night, the Llanos Water Gardens, sovereign elven ground, was attacked. The enemies killed the employees, looted and destroyed the grounds and mansion, and kidnapped the elven proprietor. Queen Willow reached out to your new king for aid, but her request fell on deaf ears. Make no mistake, the chaos of your leadership's current crisis enabled these crimes. We will not involve ourselves in the internal affairs of Llanos, but we will defend our interests and those of our allies. I am here to deliver vengeance on those who attacked the Water Gardens and to escort our foreign allies out of this city. Do not interfere with me. Those who do will suffer the fate of the Thornhill family, whom I now name as enemies of the Elven nation."

During the speech, additional soldiers surrounded Albrun outside the mansion. A man in his forties, likely Count Thornhill, was standing on the balcony of the entry hall and screaming at his men to attack. The battle aura radiating from Albrun prevented them. She ignored the count until naming him an enemy. She looked directly at him as she spoke the last sentence. His screams of frustration were silenced by the light and heat of the sun itself.

Albrun activated the principal power of Lahat Chereb. A terrifying weapon that had only been used once before, Lahat Chereb allowed the wielder to control a massive summoning gate whose opposite end was the surface of the sun. Activating the gate and controlling it required a magician with immense mana and extreme skill. Willow had used this power to end the Catastrophe three hundred years ago, earning herself the title of the Witch Queen. Today, Albrun proved herself worthy of the title as well. All the magically sensitive people within the city felt the legendary power being unleashed.

Albrun carefully controlled the power of the sword, preventing the unimaginable heat from leaving the Thornhill Estate. Inside the estate, she let the power rage freely, keeping only a safe space directly around herself. Flora and fauna were obliterated within seconds. The buildings and stone features took longer, but they succumbed as well. The extreme heat shattered the ground and sent shock waves through the cities. Damage outside the estate was minimal, but it was felt by all.

Within minutes, the walls of the Thornhill Estate contained a molten pool of lava hotter than any volcano. Albrun exited the property and terminated the gate spell. Her energy, both physical and magical, was drained after fighting the sword for control. She shifted the sword to a single hand. She drank a recovery potion for a quick mana recovery and then ate a mana fruit for a full recovery. Her work for the night was not done, but she hoped she did not need to use that power again.

Thornhill destroyed. Headed to Embassy Row, Albrun thought to Elisa and Lily.

The reply on the other end was delayed. *Sweet Goddess...* was Elisa's eventual reply.

The mental link allowed Elisa and the now-awakened Lily to feel the titanic power firsthand. Elisa was a very skilled caster, but she felt like a novice compared to Albrun. The sword's magic had been incredibly chaotic and threatened to overwhelm the elf several times. Elisa had felt Albrun straining to contain the magic and channel it to do her will. Many hundreds of kilometers away, Elisa felt numb and exhausted just having been exposed to the sword. The ever-clever Elisa was speechless. She was in awe of her new friend.

Relying on her military training, Lily replied calmly, *Copy,*

Albrun. Embassy personnel are ready for escort. The female knight's nerves were just as strained as the princess's.

Back in Taronto, Albrun sprinted through the streets, the sword firmly in her grasp. The area around her was lit brightly as though by a midday sun. No one moved to stop her, but many watched her pass.

Several minutes later, Albrun arrived on Embassy Row, the street dedicated to foreign embassies. She paused in the middle of the street, lifted the sword above her head, and cast barrier magic. A canopy of bright light formed above the street and spread the full width of the street for two blocks in front of Albrun and two blocks behind. The canopy draped to the ground on all sides. Openings in the wall of light were made at each of the gates of the dozen foreign embassies. While only three had asked Ryne for help, Albrun offered her assistance to all of them.

She used the power of her armor to broadcast her voice to the nearby buildings. "A mutual friend told Queen Willow of your plight. Taronto is not safe for the foreign-born. My queen, through me, offers you safe passage out of the city. She asks no compensation in return. If you wish to join me, please do so now. I will hold here for five minutes, then proceed."

The gates of the first three countries opened immediately. They exited their compounds fully armed, armored, and ready to travel. Within a minute, two more countries joined. They hastened to prepare and were soon ready to travel. Three minutes into the wait, three more countries opened their gates to send their non-essential and non-combat personnel to safety.

At the end of the wait, Albrun spoke. "We are now going to walk through the city and into the countryside. We will go through the Nobles District and then head to the Merchants District. We will leave the city through the Merchants Gate. Stay well away from the wall of light. There will be no fighting amongst us. After we leave the city, I will release the barrier once we are out of range of the city's weapons. You will then be free to follow your own paths. Are there any questions?"

No one answered Albrun. The air was tense. Albrun began to walk forward, the center and the focus of a strange procession.

The wall of light provided gentle light inside the canopy but fierce light outside. The intensity difference was obvious to the marchers inside. Those outside had to shade their eyes to look at the wall.

After a few minutes, resistance appeared before the procession. A wall of debris two meters high blocked the street in front of them. Two lines of pikemen were stationed behind the debris. Archers were stationed on the roofs of the buildings. Spellcasters were mixed with the archers. A loud voice from behind the pikeman yelled, "In the name of King Logan of Llanos, I demand you to stop!"

Inside the light canopy, Albrun responded. "I've already given my warning. Move or be destroyed." To the members of the procession, Albrun said, "Shield your eyes."

When Albrun did not stop, the leader called on his troops to open fire. A torrent of arrows descended on the procession. Each one was incinerated when it hit the wall of light. On the inside, the arrows looked like stars that flared brightly, then faded away. A first volley of spells also hit the wall. The reflection of those spells back upon the casters was unexpected by all but Albrun. A second volley did not occur.

The front edge of the light canopy flared when it touched the debris. The debris burned to ash within seconds. The front row of pikemen was wedged in by the second row and could not move fast enough to escape. Most of the second row got out of the way in time.

Apparently, morale broke among the guards within the Nobles District. No additional attempts were made to stop Albrun and her companions. They passed through the gate into the Merchants District.

The atmosphere in this district was different than the last. The difference between King Logan's controlled area versus Prince Miller's area was striking. People lined the cross streets and alleyways, but they were spectators to the odd night parade. Hostility was missing here, and many of the people allowed their children to view.

"Does anyone know any good marching songs?" Albrun asked.

One of the older guards, a grizzly veteran, replied yes. He began to sing. His song was simple, but the tune was catchy, and by the third repetition, most of the procession was singing along with him. The mood of the outside crowd shifted further, with some cheering and others joining in the song themselves.

The guard was talented. He changed the song every ten minutes so that no one got bored. Midnight arrived as they passed through the Merchants Gate. They were singing a rather rowdy sea shanty.

Several minutes later, the procession was no longer in sight of the city walls.

Albrun said, "My friends, I am sorry we have to meet under such conditions, but I am glad we met." The others echoed her sentiment. "I need to take my leave, so please prepare yourselves before I drop the barrier. I don't sense any enemies, but they may be hidden."

A minute later, everyone was ready.

"Farewell, my friends, until we meet again." Albrun dropped the barrier, sheathed her sword, and vanished.

Dreki-hratt was a hundred kilometers northeast of Taronto when Albrun awakened Galene. They were headed for Leilani, the elven border town nearest Auraria. On their present course, they would arrive by midafternoon.

Albrun needed to discuss what to do with the children. She had waited this long to have enough distance to discourage pursuit but still be close enough to change plans if needed. Albrun cast several healing and calming spells on Galene before Albrun woke her. Galene's physical injuries were quickly treated, but the emotional and mental traumas she had suffered were severe. The town of Leilani contained several highly skilled healers, and Albrun hoped they would help Galene fully recover from her wounds.

Galene awoke with a start, her face twisted in fear. Seeing Albrun's elven form broke Galene's panic.

"You are safe now. I'm Albrun, daughter of Willow."

"Thank…you." Galene's voice was choked with emotion. Her tears flowed freely. Her people had rescued her.

After Galene grew calm, Albrun asked about the children.

Galene said, "Their parents worked as gardeners in the Gardens. Did any of the staff survive?"

"The children you hid were the only survivors. All others perished. Since Prince Miller controls the Merchants District, we will ask him to give the dead a proper burial," Albrun replied.

"Thank you. The children have no other family, so they are now orphans. Their parents were my friends. I'll take care of them."

"We are headed to Leilani. I want you and the children to stay there until you recover. After that, Prince Ryne and I will move you to wherever you wish to go," said Albrun.

"I've no desire to ever return to Llanos. Sarai has passed, and her last wish that I look out for Princess Elisa is now complete. The children are human, so an elven border town would be an odd place to raise them." Galene thought for a few moments. "I hear that Prince Ryne now controls Auraria. Would he permit me to rebuild my Water Gardens there?"

Albrun nodded. "Absolutely. When you are ready, Ryne will support you."

Galene breathed a sigh of relief. The loss she had just experienced was staggering, and the trauma the Thornhill family had inflicted was unimaginable. However, she had a purpose. She could not give up. The children needed a parent.

Albrun could sense that Galene was still in shock. Her road to recovery would be long, but the elves would guarantee that the half-elf received the help she needed.

Albrun reported the status back to Ryne through the link with Elisa.

CHAPTER 13

The next morning, Sir Aden and the surviving escort members left the retired captain's estate outside of Golden. A detachment of Prince Ryne's troops would accompany them to the Vorland-Llanos border. Sir Aden's father, with support from Prince Miller, would have loyal troops waiting for Sir Aden's group. Aden said his goodbyes to Prince Ryne, Princess Elisa, and Dame Lily. He then started the long trip home.

Ryne, Elisa, Lily, and Conrad thanked the retired captain for his hospitality, then left for Golden. Ryne planned to use this opportunity to check on his subordinates as he returned to Auraria. Conrad and his group of scouts resumed their defensive screen of the trio.

Ryne had offered to get Elisa another carriage, but she just laughed. "Aunt Sarai insisted I learn to ride. My skills and stamina need improving, but this trip should help both. A carriage-bound princess would seem a poor fit for you."

"My lands are rougher than those of my brothers and far more rugged than any in Llanos. I appreciate your understanding, Elisa."

"Actually, if you have a supply wagon, Elisa can handle it as well as any journeyman teamster. All of Sarai's little outings gave her plenty of experience," teased Lily.

"Please don't remind me!" Elisa facepalmed, then laughed. "Then again, the royal guards never identified us or caught us."

Ryne looked thoughtfully at Elisa. "Are you serious? Do

you have skills as a teamster?"

Elisa nodded. "I do. I drove the wagon after we left the ambush site. Could my skills be helpful to you?"

"Absolutely. We've only recently reestablished consistent supply runs to Auraria. We have a surplus of goods in Golden that need to make the trip. If you would be willing to drive, or even work as a relief driver, that would be a great help."

As Ryne spoke, Elisa started to grin. Lily saw the smile and knew the princess had just thought of a new plan.

"Ryne, I would be willing to help you with the delivery if you will help me with my introduction to your troops."

"What do you mean, Elisa?" asked the intrigued prince.

"Nothing much, just an entertaining way for people to get to know me." Elisa then explained her plan, and Ryne was completely supportive. Lily kept her groans on the inside.

Two hours later, the trio was in the quartermaster's office in Golden. Princess Elisa was dressed in common, sensible clothing. A cap covered her blonde hair. She wore no markings or insignias of her rank. The Master Wagoner returned to the office and notified Prince Ryne that the test was ready. Ryne had requested that his new recruit, the small woman at his side, be tested for her driving skills. Ryne requested the complete test, which meant he wanted the woman's knowledge and skills pushed to their limits. This was not the first time the prince had requested a skills test that bordered on hazing. Ryne must be trying to put the woman in her place.

Everyone stepped outside into the wagon yard. The area was not huge, and there were several wagons in various states of repair. The paddock for the horses was adjacent to the yard, with a small stable for tending to the horses. On the other end of the yard was a warehouse full of supplies. There was a four-horse team already stationed at the warehouse loading dock, ready to go. A set of six barrels were on the dock. There was an unusually large number of soldiers stationed about the yard. They were trying to look like they all had things to do, but they were doing a poor job. They were clearly spectators here to enjoy a show.

The Master Wagoner said, "All right, recruit. Your job is to load those barrels on a wagon and deliver them across town."

"Sir, yes, sir," replied the woman. She walked across the yard to the ready wagon and began to inspect it and the horses. After a couple of minutes, she returned to the middle of the yard. "May I ask a question, sir?"

"You may."

"Do I have to use this team and wagon, sir?"

"What's wrong, recruit?"

"Several things, sir. First, the horses are hooked up incorrectly. The stronger pair should be in the back, and the lighter and more alert pair in the front. Second, the left front collar is cracked. Third, the left back belly band has been nearly sliced in two. Fourth, the tack smells of garbage, so all of it was probably just retrieved from the junk heap where it belongs. Finally, the right back wheel on the wagon is loose. It will stay on so long as I only go straight. I request permission to set up my own team, sir!"

The Master Wagoner offered a thin smile. "Granted, recruit. Men, clear this sorry excuse of a wagon out of my sight." Several of the men standing around moved to obey the order. "Recruit, will you be keeping the horses?"

"I request permission to pick my own."

"You heard her, men. Put all the horses back in the paddock."

The area in front of the loading docks was quickly cleared. The woman then went over and inspected the wagons. She found one she liked, but it was behind two others that were being repaired.

"Do you need assistance, recruit?" asked the Master Wagoner.

"Sir, no, sir!"

Several of the men jeered at her response. It would take several people to move the defective wagons out of the way. To pass this part of the test, one only had to identify the correct wagon, which she had done.

The woman ignored the spectators. She dropped to one knee, placed both palms on the ground, then began to chant. The earth underneath her hands began to vibrate in response to the chant. After a moment, she was done. The crowd held its breath. They had not been expecting magic.

The woman went to the first damaged wagon, which was missing its two front wheels. With one hand, she lifted the wagon off the ground and used the other hand to push it back several feet. The crowd's jeers had turned to cheers.

The second wagon was in worse shape. None of the wheels were on it. It was resting on its axles. Sliding it back risked damaging the wagon further. She moved to midway on one side of the wagon where the frame was strongest. Pushing with one hand while pulling with the other, she cantilevered the massive wagon into the air above her head. She moved several feet to the side. She then used earth magic to make pillars upon which to rest the wagon so the wheels could be attached easily. She accomplished the task with ease, and the crowd's cheering grew louder.

She moved the wagon that she wanted into the center of the yard. She then went to the stables and retrieved the tack for setting up the wagon. Afterward, she headed to the paddock to identify her horses.

"Your Highness, do you see the problem?" the Master Wagoner asked Ryne.

"She left the wagon in the middle of the yard. She should have backed it up to the loading dock before attaching the horses."

"Correct, Your Highness. She has been perfect so far. We will see how she gets out of this problem."

While in the paddock, the tiny woman moved around the

horses with practiced ease. She whistled as she approached and patted the massive animals. After a couple of minutes, she began retrieving and attaching four horses to the wagon.

"How did she do with picking horses?" Ryne asked quietly.

"I could do no better, Your Highness." This was high praise, indeed.

The woman then gracefully climbed into the driver's seat. She took the reins, unlocked the brake, and looked at her wagon and then the loading dock. Rather than being surprised by her predicament, she calmly removed her cap and shook out her golden hair. The crowd had grown quiet again, sensing that something special was about to happen. There were several gasps when she removed her cap as the spectators realized how beautiful she was.

Holding the reins loosely in one hand, she turned to stare at Ryne. She had a slight smile on her face as she began to whistle commands to the horses. The horses came to attention on the first command. The following commands made them sidestep and back in unison, and the wagon began to turn. Over the next thirty seconds, the woman guided the horses into turning and backing the heavy wagon into the perfect place for loading. She only whistled commands, and she never broke eye contact with Ryne. The deed done, she applied the brake and secured the reins. The crowd roared with approval.

The woman jumped over the seat to begin loading the wagon when the Master Wagoner yelled, "Enough, recruit! You have shown us your skill. What is your name?"

The woman bowed to the Master Wagoner, thanking him for the compliment. "My name is Elisa, and I am pleased to meet you all."

The crowd was silent for a moment, and then scattered whispers began. A new story had begun making rounds in the taverns and mead halls. Two women from Llanos, a tiny blonde princess and her powerful guardian knight, had recently saved the village of Viverna from a horde of monsters. The noise got louder as the crowd realized the identity of the new recruit. Murmurs of "She must be the princess!" and "The tall one must be the Dragon Lily" were heard in the crowd.

Prince Ryne stepped forward and addressed the spectators. "My fiancée told me she had skills as a teamster. I sought to initiate her into the ways of the Vorlandish military, perhaps making a bit of fun of her if she failed. My friends, I fear I am the one who received the lesson today. Never doubt this princess. She may be small, but she is fierce."

The crowd cheered. Ryne was incredibly popular as a down-to-earth royal who cared about his people. Elisa had made a strong impression on the people today.

"Princess Elisa, the Dragon Lily, and I are going to enjoy a long lunch today in the mess hall. Stop by, say hello, and introduce yourselves."

As they were walking away, Elisa thanked Ryne for playing along with her introduction.

"I just had to get the test set up; you had to pass it. Your skills are the real deal!"

"Thank you, my prince. Oh, how did the tale of Viverna reach Golden so quickly?"

"Edmund maintains friendly relations with several bards across the country. We provide them with their own long-distance communication network, and they help us spread word of our latest achievements. We find controlling the public narrative of our various adventures to be quite helpful. Never fear; the legends of the Hero and the Guardian Angel of Viverna are growing even as we speak," replied Ryne with a smile.

Dreki-hratt landed outside Leilani on schedule. An elven border town was used to unusual comings and goings, but a full-size dragon was far beyond the ordinary. Fortunately, the local temple had been alerted, so the priests met the group far enough away from the town to not terrify the inhabitants. Albrun said her thanks and goodbyes to the dragon. While Willow had accumulated the debt of favor by asking Dreki-hratt for help, Albrun acknowledged her own willingness to aid the dragon if the need arose. Dreki-hratt departed.

Albrun and Galene accompanied the priests back to the temple. Albrun removed the two children from her extra-dimensional space. They were still in a deep, magically induced sleep. With the priests' help, Albrun slowly woke the children. They were still in shock from the attack on the Water Gardens, so the priests began to provide care for them. The two children had a tearful reunion with Galene.

Once the half-elf and two children were safely transferred into the care of the temple, Albrun left and made her way across town. She was well known in Leilani, so her trip took longer than expected due to the greetings and well-wishes from the town's residents.

It was nearly dinnertime before she arrived at her family's home. Due to Willow's extreme age and the long lives of the elves, Albrun's family was very large. Willow maintained several houses across the elven nation for the convenience of the family. Albrun entered the house and found it empty, but Willow had left a note saying that she would be returning later that night. Albrun went to the bathroom and cleaned herself, but she was too exhausted to enjoy soaking in the bath. Using Lahat Chereb to destroy the Thornhill Estate and then protect the procession through Taronto had pushed Albrun to her absolute limits. Her supply of mana recovery fruit was gone, and stamina-refreshing magic was no longer effective. Albrun needed sleep.

She returned to her room. It was clean and simple, with no personal touches. The bed looked warm and inviting. She used one last bit of magic to set wards on the room, and then she fell into a deep, dreamless sleep.

About four hundred kilometers away, Elisa and Lily felt

Albrun's utter exhaustion. They sent her pleasant thoughts, but they refrained from contacting her. They would talk with her after she had recovered.

Ryne, Elisa, and Lily were up late into the evening. Word had spread that the new princess was in town, so town leaders, business owners, and those who were simply curious flocked to meet her. Ryne and Elisa thrived on the attention, but Lily found dealing with so many new people quite tedious. Lily was rescued by a couple of Ryne's knights. The three went to a tavern favored by the Vorlandish military. These were Lily's kind of people, and they drank and told stories until late at night. None of the men, neither young nor old, made a move to ask Lily for a date. However, even Lily, who was often oblivious to the feelings of others, could tell she made many new admirers that night.

The next morning, Ryne, Elisa, Lily, and their escort left Golden. True to her word, Elisa was driving one of the five supply wagons. This time, the Master Wagoner had set her up with a strong team and a wagon in good repair, so Elisa did not need to make any last-minute changes. Elisa was driving the center wagon, with two other wagons in front of hers and two behind. Ryne rode on horseback on the left side of her, while Lily did the same on the right. Their escort party members were arrayed around them for protection, but they were far enough away not to bother the trio. Elisa increased the trio's privacy by using barrier magic so that they could talk freely.

Once they were underway, Ryne invited questions. "We have several days on the road. Time for many discussions. You must have many questions. What would you like to talk about first?"

Elisa chuckled. She had been waiting for the opportunity for days. "I want to know about your grand plan for the future. But first, Albrun is still asleep, so we are less likely to bother her through the mental link we share." Elisa gave Lily a sideways glance when she said this. Lily was gradually getting better at controlling her thoughts within the shared mental space. Lily blushed at Elisa's mild admonishment. "Please tell us about Albrun and William and how the two came to be. I asked her before, but she said it was your tale to tell."

Ryne nodded. "Okay, I will. I need to give you a bit of backstory for the tale to make sense. When I was fifteen and a freshly minted knight, I was sent with the Vorlandish army to fight in the south. That year, Llanos was our ally, and the Osman Empire was our foe. We spent much of our time skirmishing with the Osman army around Crater Lake. Since you are from Llanos, you may know that Crater Lake is the result of the termination of the Catastrophe." Ryne paused to look at Elisa and Lily. They both shook their heads. He laughed a bitter laugh. "If the education of two Llanos nobles is missing the details…well, I'll save that discussion for a later time. Back to Crater Lake—the lake is the site of a world-shaping battle that happened three hundred years ago. I spent many nights camping on the shore of the lake. At first, I had dreams of a long-ago battle. Before long, I had waking visions of warriors fighting beings I did not recognize. I could not interact with the visions; they merely played out in front of me. I quickly realized that no one else could see them. Rather than be called crazy, I hid my knowledge of these visions.

"The visions went on for months. I thought I was seeing history replay itself, so the visions were more interesting than they were frightening. One day, near the end of our season of battle and almost time to return home, I was found unconscious outside my tent. My comrades thought I had been attacked, and they were quick to render aid. My body was covered with odd burn marks, although there was no sign of fire, magical or normal, near me. The healers were able to cure all the burn marks except for a couple on my chest. What

I could not tell my comrades is that I experienced the instant that Crater Lake was formed. I saw an elven woman with silver hair and dressed in armor that flowed like silk swirling a large flaming sword around her head. Then the world grew stunningly bright, and I woke up later in the medical tent. The elven woman's magical power was so great three hundred years ago that a vision of her from that point in the past can cause damage in the present." Ryne paused for a moment.

Lily took the break to interject. "That woman seems very familiar…"

Ryne nodded in agreement. "I soon returned home to Vorland. I spent the fall and winter seasons looking for answers to my visions. I've never been a scholar, but I searched nonetheless. My search was fruitless. The event occurred three hundred years ago, and we have libraries full of documents that extend back a couple of thousand years. Why is there no documentation on the Catastrophe?"

He looked at Elisa and Lily. "What do you know about the Catastrophe?"

Lily answered. "The Catastrophe was an ancient evil defeated by the elven queen more than three hundred years ago."

"Okay, what else?"

"What do you mean, what else?"

"Where did the battles occur? Who was the enemy? Besides the queen, who fought the enemy? Where is all the common knowledge that you could learn about any other major battle?"

Lily blinked. She was unclear on how to answer. She now knew the where—Crater Lake—because Ryne had just told her. But the answers to the rest of the questions—nothing.

Elisa gasped. "The magic that William uses to make people forget him. Is knowledge of the Catastrophe guarded by a similar magic?"

Ryne gazed at Elisa with pride. "You are every bit as astute as William said you are."

Elisa briefly glowed in the prince's praise.

Ryne continued, "No human or human document could give me the answer. Since my dream was of an elf, I traveled to the nearest elven border town, Leilani."

Lily giggled. "Is that what you told your mother? I'm going to Leilani to seek 'knowledge'?"

"No, I told her I was going there to trade money for the tender affections of a lovely elven lover. I mean, that is why everyone goes to an elven border town, correct?"

Lily was surprised by Ryne's honest answer. Elisa just smiled.

"I made the trip to Leilani, hired the most expensive courtesan I could find, took her into a private room, and told her about the visions I had been having and described the elven woman I had seen in my dream. At first, she was wary. Perhaps a client desiring knowledge, rather than a physical transaction, put her ill at ease. By the end of my story, she had a thoughtful look. She asked me to wait in the room. Several minutes later, she returned with instructions. I was to wait in the town for a week. I would then be contacted for more information. I gave her the name of the inn where I was staying and left.

"Over the next week, I was carefully surveilled. My activities and behaviors were monitored. I traveled by myself, so I did not have companions with whom to pass the time. I did not engage in the principal activity for human males, as I feared it would undermine the seriousness of my request. Not that I wasn't tempted—elves, both female and male, seem universally gorgeous.

"When I arrived in the border town, I had chosen a quiet inn far from the entertainment district. At breakfast the next morning, much to my surprise, all the other guests were elves. They did not seem to mind my presence, and I was careful to not offend. Then again, I did not know what elves would consider acceptable or offensive. The innkeeper came to my aid. When I explained my predicament, he suggested that I hire a tutor for the week. He had a nephew who was both willing to teach and available, so I began my lessons later that morning.

"As I have mentioned, I am a warrior, not a scholar. But I do have strong determination. For the next seven days, I spent nearly all my waking hours studying with the tutor. I learned bits of history, the rules of etiquette, and how to speak and read Elvish a bit better than a toddler. Well, a dense toddler. The tutor was wonderful, even if he did occasionally laugh at my pronunciation.

"Each morning at breakfast, a couple of the guests would greet me in Elvish. I would reply the same. It was a different pair each day, so I guess I was a curiosity for the guests, or at least a source of entertainment. As the week progressed, the morning conversations became a bit longer, and I improved my skills.

"On the eighth day of my stay, the day when I would get more information, the atmosphere of the breakfast room was different. At a table for two by the window sat the most beautiful being I've ever seen. She was gorgeous. And you already know what she looks like—the woman was an older version of Albrun with green eyes." Ryne paused to take a drink from his waterskin.

"Her physical beauty was not her only trait. Her presence in the room, her social grace, all the experience she had gained in a millennium of life—I experienced it in that moment. I was starstruck and unable to move. The innkeeper was kind. He took pity on me and guided me to her table. I was able to regain my composure during the walk, so I greeted the woman with the best elvish manners I could muster.

"She instructed me to sit, and we enjoyed breakfast together. At the conclusion, we adjourned to the inn's private garden, where she asked me to tell my story. I started at the beginning and left nothing out. She quietly listened to me. After I was done, she asked me to stay seated. I did so, and she circled me, inspecting me. She cast magic with which I was unfamiliar.

"After a few minutes, she sat back down and faced me. 'Thank you for indulging me, Ryne. My name is Willow. I don't know why you are special, but you are the first human in a hundred years to experience the visions of the Catastrophe. You saw me in your visions, and you sought me. You have now found me. What do you want?'

"I told her that the visions did not feel like a history lesson. They felt like a warning. That whatever awful thing that had happened then was going to happen again. I must have said the correct thing, for Willow's expression relaxed. We engaged in a discussion that lasted until dinnertime.

"She told me the threat of a new attack was real, but it was not imminent. She gave me a means to contact her, and we agreed to talk every few months. She expected the new attack to be different since the previous one had failed. She would research from her end. I would contact her if I found new information when I traveled near Crater Lake. She told me many things about the enemy, but I will save them for a future discussion since our primary interest, here and now, is Albrun and I have not talked about her yet.

"We parted ways but kept in touch. The wars in the south took me near Crater Lake every year or two. I continued to experience the same visions and learned nothing new. I became the Liege Lord of Auraria, got married, and began a family. Twelve years passed. I was asked to lead the Vorlandish army to subjugate the Osman Empire that year. It had been three years since my last trip to Crater Lake, so I accepted.

"The visions changed. I began seeing new scenes in locations that were unfamiliar. The style of dress was contemporary, unlike the ones from three hundred years ago. One thing that was particularly terrifying was that huge hordes of monsters ravaged throughout the land. I did not recognize where. I contacted Willow and told her of the change. We agreed to meet in Leilani after I returned.

"During my trip home, my brother asked me to change

course for Taronto. His son was looking for a bride, and a princess of Llanos had just come of age. She was available, so my brother wanted me to interview her. I found her to be intelligent, clever, and very beautiful. My nephew's loss for not trying to win her heart and hand in marriage." Ryne smiled at Elisa.

Ryne continued with his story, his face turning solemn. "I was delayed in Taronto on additional business for Vorland, so the detour cost me ten weeks. I should have been in Auraria when the monster horde attacked. I should have died with my family and my followers when the horde invaded the city. Instead, I spent the fall, winter, and spring fighting alongside the Vorlandish troops to keep the horde contained within my duchy. We finally succeeded.

"I was a broken man. I had lost everything that mattered to me. I used my thirst for revenge to fuel my attacks against the horde, but the rest of me was hollow inside. Success in preventing the spread of the horde was bad for me, as it removed the one thing that kept me going.

"I met with Willow the summer after Auraria fell. She said that the attack on Auraria had been caused by our enemies. My visions made me dangerous to them, and they wanted me dead. Their influence was still small, so their attacks required months to get ready. They had sent the horde against my home and family.

"My despair lessened, but I still needed to find a purpose for living beyond just destroying my enemies. That was when Willow introduced me to the fourteen-year-old Albrun.

"Albrun is an adolescent twin of Willow. They are identical except for the eyes and, of course, their ages. Albrun has ice-blue-colored eyes that match mine. I knew that the girl was not my child. I had not mated with any of the elves during my stay in the border town. Willow saw my confusion and explained.

"Albrun is Willow's clone. Willow created Albrun after

meeting me, and she used my eyes as inspiration for the clone. Willow is not a prophet. She cannot see the future. However, after our meeting, she sensed I would play a pivotal role in the next conflict with the enemy. I would need powerful allies if I were to succeed. Thus, she created Albrun for me." Ryne paused to let the gravity of his words settle.

Lily was shocked, but Elisa was skeptical and said, "Clones are not children. They don't have free will. While the caster lives, clones can serve as puppets for the caster's will. When the caster dies, the caster's soul and memories move into a clone. The clone then becomes the new caster."

"What you say is true," replied Ryne, "but it is incomplete. A foreign soul can also be implanted into an inert clone body. The procedure seldom succeeds, as the body will reject the soul. But if you have a very powerful soul, insert it into a newborn clone body, and then allow the clone to grow to maturity naturally, a new individual results."

Now Elisa's eyes became big. The audacity of placing a powerful soul into an equally potent body was shocking. Willow was either amazingly potent or incredibly reckless, or perhaps both.

Lily homed in a particular word. "What do you mean by 'foreign'?"

"The soul that inhabits Albrun is not from this world. Willow summoned the soul from another world. The soul was not a pure spirit, free of memories of its past. This soul remembers its previous life. Albrun remembers that former life."

Elisa said, "I saw glimpses of that world when William and I first bonded. He promised to explain those glimpses to me once Willow gives her permission."

The trio was silent for several minutes. Ryne's story was interesting and tragic, but the last minute of his story had contained several revelations that were hard to comprehend.

Elisa restarted the conversation with a question. "What do you mean that Willow created Albrun for you?"

"Albrun was trained from birth to be capable of handling any situation she might encounter. Weapon training, magic spells, skills of all kinds—Albrun was given the best tutors the elves could muster. Willow created the 'William' form with its powerful, obscuring barrier magic so that Albrun could accomplish tasks in the human world yet remain unremembered. I met her when she was fourteen. She trained for two more years before she joined my service. She does whatever I ask, whenever I ask, no matter how insane. Albrun has dedicated her entire young life to helping me achieve my goals. She does all this while remaining the primary agent of the elves in the human world. If that is not enough, the elves will recognize Albrun as an adult when she turns twenty. If I have not remarried, then Willow has promised Albrun as my wife." Ryne's voice started to break. He was very upset, but he continued speaking.

"No one should have to bear such burdens. I ask too much of her, and so does her mother. 'William' takes away her identity for the sake of her mission. The recapture of Auraria did not gain traction until she joined the team. We were asking an elf, a nearly immortal being, to put her life on the line several times per day to recover human territory. For humans that would shun her if they learned of her true nature.

"I want her to have a normal life. I want her to have friends who care for her and don't use her for her abilities. I want her to have the life that my children should have had."

The women bore witness to the deep pain and sorrow that Ryne carried inside him. He did not try to hide it. He let his emotions run their course. When he finally regained composure, he began to speak again. "I want you to know who and what I am. The things that drive me and the things that haunt me. I don't want you to be blindsided by unexpected dangers. I want your eyes wide open before you decide to follow me, be it in friendship or in marriage."

Lily answered, "I thank you for your honesty and openness." She turned to Elisa and asked, "Has he scared you away yet, Your Highness?"

"Not a chance," announced Elisa with a fearless grin.

"Yeah, me neither."

"Thank you. You are both wonderful," Ryne replied. "Oh, I should mention before we continue that only a selective group of people know about William and his other form. We are very careful to control this knowledge. If it were to spread through accident or malice, then the magic that protects William could unravel. We are careful to refer to William when he is in his form and by the other name when they are in that form. Treat them as two separate people. Yes, I know how harsh that sounds.

"The group of people that knows about William is easy to recognize. If we trust you enough to give you a communicator for the Aurarian communication network, then we trust you with William's secrets."

The trio turned to discussing lighter issues for the rest of the day's trip. This included a play-by-play description of Lily's battle with the Valkyries back in Folsom. Ryne asked several questions focused on how Elisa, Lily, and William had used their mental bond to control and direct the battle.

"Enhancing a dozen fighters at a time is quite a feat, Elisa," said Ryne. "Such magic could be very useful for our next monster subjugation...hmm, do you think you could do it without William present?"

"Your Highness! Are you suggesting that we go on a monster hunt right now? I do not want to expose the princess to that much danger!" exclaimed Lily.

"Fear not, guardian of my beloved, I propose nothing so bold." Ryne turned a dazzling smile on Lily, and her heart skipped a beat. "I was just thinking we could stage another exhibition fight at our next stop. We will be staying in a good-sized village this evening, and I believe the villagers might appreciate some entertainment before the long, cold winter begins."

Lily felt herself being swayed by the prince's words, at least until Elisa's laughter brought the knight back to her senses. The princess said, "Do it for the poor villagers, huh? Who do you think you are fooling? You are just envious that Lily and I had an interesting battle, and you want in on the fun."

"Perhaps you are correct," said the prince with a smirk. "But then, sweet princess, you are the one who has gathered hordes of new admirers as you travel across Vorland. I'm just giving you a chance to showcase your skills in my duchy."

"Oh, tell me more, my prince," replied Elisa. The expression on the princess's face was well-known to Lily. Elisa was hungry for more attention, and Ryne was willing and able to feed that need.

Albrun had asked Lily to be the adult supervision for Ryne and Elisa—to keep them from planning anything too outlandish while the elf was away. Lily heard glee in both royals' voices as they planned for this evening. With a sinking feeling, the lady knight realized just how hard controlling the pair would be.

Chapter 14

Albrun woke just before noon. The feel of clean sheets on a warm, comfortable bed in a cold room was a trap that could snare even the hardiest of adventurers. This was also the first time she had slept in her true elven form in several months. She missed just being herself. Her happiness was strong enough to reach to reach Elisa and Lily hundreds of kilometers away.

Ah! You caught me being lazy, admitted Albrun.

The shared mental space filled with laughter.

I think you have earned sleeping late, Albrun, replied Elisa. *We are headed to Auraria, and Ryne is telling us all kinds of interesting things. You were the first topic of conversation.*

How did the talk go? Are you still willing to associate with me?

Did you seriously doubt us? asked Elisa with surprise.

I wanted to give you options. My heritage is questionable, at best.

Sweet Goddess, girl. Your dedication to Ryne brought him to tears during the story. The more I learn of both of you, the stronger my desire to join your cause grows. Although we do need to discuss my marriage to Ryne. I am reluctant to overtake your claim to him. He loves you dearly.

Elisa, you must marry Ryne, please! He needs you! The panic in Albrun's mind was obvious. It was the first time either Elisa or Lily had felt Albrun get so emotional.

Elisa said in the shared mental space, *Don't get upset, Albrun. Marrying Ryne is still my intention. We are just going to have a conversation before it happens.*

Talking is fine, Elisa, but the marriage needs to happen. Elisa's sudden declaration had upset Albrun, so the elf needed a few minutes to calm herself. However, once her emotions were under control, Albrun could sense that Lily was anxious. *Lily, are you okay?*

Lily replied, *I'm fine, Albrun, I just...actually, I'm not fine. The prince and princess are planning a new exhibition fight for this afternoon, and their plans keep getting wilder and more extreme. Please help me.*

Even across the vast distance, both Elisa and Lily felt the elf's facepalm of exasperation. Albrun asked, *Princess, what are you planning...no, scratch that, I don't want to know. Why don't you do something simple, like have Ryne spar with Lily? That is guaranteed to be a crowd-pleaser, and perhaps the collateral damage won't be too high.*

Elisa's pout was clear through the mental link. *A fight between them relegates me to being just a support character. Why can't we redo the Folsom fight? That was fun!*

The elf was glad the princess could not hear stray thoughts at this distance. Elisa's ego required her to be a star. Albrun thought for a few moments before replying, *To safely reenact a Valkyrie-style fight, I would need to coordinate the attacks between you and Lily. I'm too far away to make that happen. However, I have a proposal for you. Will you hear me out?*

The princess was pouty, but she replied, *Sure, whatever.*

Thank you. Why don't you let Ryne and Lily fight to gather the villagers' attention, and then you steal the show with your own brilliant performance?

Oh, I like the sound of this. Tell me more! replied the princess.

Albrun spent the next few minutes detailing her ideas. By the end, both Elisa and Lily agreed with the plan. Albrun concluded the conversation, saying, *I need to go. My mother is waiting for me here in Leilani. Just promise me one last thing: if Conrad tries to change or alter the plan, don't let him. Under absolutely no circumstances should you let him suggest a game of "Hold My Mead." Do you understand me?*

Ah, now I want to hear the backstory, said the princess.

Is Ryne next to you? If so, ask him to explain the game.

The mental link was quiet for a minute. Lily was the first to break the mental silence by broadcasting her thoughts, projecting a sense of awe through the link. *When Elisa asked Ryne about "Hold My Mead," he got really embarrassed and now refuses to look at us. What happened?*

Ask Conrad at dinner tonight, Alburn replied with a mischievous tone. *Talk to you later.*

Albrun rose from the bed and clothed herself. She pulled her favorite dress from her storage. The dress was plain, but it made her happy. She had made it years ago while studying with a master tailor. She stopped by the restroom to refresh herself and then headed for the kitchen. Willow was cooking, and it smelled delicious.

Albrun said hello to Willow, received a welcome in return, surveyed the kitchen, donned an apron, and joined her mother in cooking the meal. This had been a ritual for the two women since Albrun had grown tall enough to reach the countertops. They cooked in silence, their movements as well-coordinated as a dance. Given the time of day, lunch was on the menu.

Once ready, they moved the food to the table and enjoyed their meal. Since Willow had started the cooking, Albrun performed the cleanup. When she was done, Albrun prepared tea for them.

The women retired to the study. They had not seen each other since the end of winter, and it was now late into the fall. They drank their first cup of tea while reviewing the events up to Princess Elisa entering Vorland. The second cup was consumed while covering all the events since. Willow had expected their enemies to make moves against the princess, but the shared mental link was quite a surprise. Willow and Albrun tried the same ritual to see if a bond with Willow could be forged, but they were unsuccessful. Willow suspected that Elisa's Aunt Sarai played a role in the link, but Willow would not be able to confirm that until she met Elisa and Lily in person. In any event, the link represented powerful magic with a lot of promise. Even if it could not be expanded to include others, allowing Elisa and Lily to use elf-restricted magic items could massively expand the capabilities of Ryne's team. Willow and Albrun made tentative plans to bring Elisa and Lily to Leilani.

The next topic the two discussed was Albrun's use of Lahat Chereb to destroy the Thornhill family compound and lead the foreign diplomats and their staff out of Taronto. As they talked, Albrun transferred Willow's legendary sword and armor back to her.

Willow said, "I monitored your progress through the city. Externally, you appeared calm and in control throughout the mission. What did it feel like on the inside?"

"I was terrified. I was barely able to control the sword when I leveled the compound. It fought me—it wanted to consume the entire city," explained Albrun.

"It was the same for me when I ended the Catastrophe. However, I needed to destroy an entire army. I was able to give the sword what it wanted. Still, it is not a weapon to use lightly. Now, the armor Orvar-Oddr is wonderful, is it not?"

"It truly is! It pains me to give it back," stated Albrun with a false pout.

"Orvar-Oddr is mine and mine alone, you brat!" teased Willow. "However, it was not the only set of armor that was made in ancient times. It has some lesser siblings. If you remain a good and honest child, perhaps I will find you a set when you come of age."

Albrun leaped from her chair and hugged Willow. "You always have the best taste in gifts, Mom."

"I know what you like since I am such a kind and wonderful mother."

"Am I your favorite child?" asked Albrun with her arms in a loose hug around Willow.

"Of course not. I love all my children equally. Now, I do love myself most of all, and you are my physical clone, so…"

The two women laughed. Their time together was short, but they planned to see each other again soon. The mystery of the mental link was too important to leave alone.

With their tea finished, Albrun began the ritual to assume her "William" disguise. She needed to return to human lands, and traveling as Albrun would gain the wrong kind of attention. With Willow's help, the ritual went smoothly. Willow promised to check on Galene before she left town. William remembered that he had the contents of Galene's treasury, so he transferred the items to Willow, gave Willow one last hug, and then set out on his way.

Far to the south, Lily sighed. She would have expected Elisa to be more sensitive, but Lily had just felt Albrun's emotions with Willow, whereas Elisa had not. The pure love and comfort that Albrun experienced with her mother, followed by the stoic resignation as she became William, tore at Lily's heart. Lily tempered her own emotions lest William feel them in return.

News of the prince's arrival spread through the village of Sonora like wildfire. Lily had already seen proof of Ryne's popularity in the town of Golden, but here, the villagers' affection was even more evident. Within fifteen minutes of entering the village, the prince and his party were standing on the village common, facing nearly every resident.

Ryne gave a short speech thanking the villagers for their support. "I know your lives are busy getting ready for the winter, but I have two people that I want you to meet." The prince leaned forward toward the crowd and said in a stage whisper, "Have you heard of the rumors of the Guardian Angel of Viverna and her trusted companion, the Dragon Lily?" As he spoke, the prince turned and made eye contact with various members of the crowd. There was excitement in Ryne's voice, and his mood was infectious. The villagers leaned in toward the prince, nodding or replying "yes" with barely suppressed enthusiasm.

Working the crowd with the skill of a master bard, Ryne continued his stage whisper. "Princess Elisa and Dame Lily have just arrived in the duchy, and I want to make sure they feel welcome. Will you help me?" A sea of heads nodding was the response. "Then let us give a warm welcome to..." Ryne's voice suddenly grew loud and deep. "Princess Elisa..." Thunderous cheering was the villagers' response. Ryne paused for a few moments, then said, "And the Dragon Lily."

The reaction to Elisa's introduction was louder and more enthusiastic than Lily's. The princess was quite pleased. What Elisa could not see, but the villagers could, was Conrad standing behind the princess. The centaur was pantomiming to the crowd how loud and long to cheer.

The prince spoke to the crowd, "The rumors of these two women's exploits have traveled far and wide. Would you like to see if the rumors are true?"

The villagers shouted, "Yes!"

"Then Dame Lily and I will spar for your entertainment. As for the princess...she has promised a sight to amaze the young and old alike," teased the prince.

The crowd moved back, providing space for the fight to occur. Ryne and Lily took positions several paces apart from each other as they began their preparations. The prince removed his travel cloak and handed it to an aide while Lily bent down and placed her hand on the ground. In a smooth motion, the knight stood up and formed a stone sword from the earth beneath her feet.

"Dame Lily, this is my first time seeing one of your stone practice swords. Would you kindly make me one as well?"

"My pleasure, Your Highness." Lily formed a second sword in her free hand, then tossed it to the prince.

"Hoho, this has some serious heft!" Ryne's actions belied

his words as he flourished the massive blade as though it were a rapier. "Dame Lily, would you be so kind as to make one more sword? I would like to present my current one to the crowd so that they may examine it." After Lily's agreement, the prince moved near the crowd and drove the massive blade into the ground. "You are welcome to try this sword, but be careful; it is heavy."

Several of the village teenagers surged forward to draw the stone blade, but one after another they failed to even budge it. A line of adults formed next, but they failed as well. Finally, the village's blacksmith, a stout and powerful man, succeeded in pulling the sword out of the ground. As his neighbors cheered him, the blacksmith attempted to swing the sword through a set of maneuvers. However, the extreme weight of the blade proved his undoing, pulling him off balance and causing him to stumble.

The weight of the stone blades now proven to all, the villagers turned back to Prince Ryne and Dame Lily with a renewed sense of awe. With Conrad acting as referee, the sparring match began. The two fighters started slowly, each using feints and small attacks to test each other's abilities. They gradually began to accelerate, and the impact of their blows strengthened as well. Soon, the ferocity of the fight resembled a duel more than a sparring match.

The prince and the knight were a study in contrasts. While each was a powerful fighter, their techniques differed greatly. Ryne was an elegant swordsman, even while wielding the stone blade. His parries were perfect, with just enough angle on his blade to deflect the incoming attacks. When he dodged, he used small, careful movements, moving just out of reach of Lily's swings. When attacking, Ryne employed the sword like a rapier, lunging and slashing with great precision. In contrast, Lily was less graceful, instead using fast and powerful swings to keep the prince at bay. She used far more energy with her style, but her endurance was so great that she did not seem to tire.

Both fighters had elected to spar without helmets, so their faces were visible throughout the fight. The prince wore a happy smile, and he seemed to be enjoying himself immensely. Lily had started with a serious and focused expression, but soon her eyes were shining, and her smile was genuine.

The sound of stone on stone was nearly constant, but the clang of stone on metal, signaling a hit on armor, happened occasionally. The volume of noise grew to be overwhelming.

After ten minutes, Conrad halted the match. Both fighters stopped instantly, then turned in confusion toward the centaur, who said, "I'm calling this match a draw. The spectators appear a bit too stunned." Surveying the crowd, the prince and knight saw that a number of the villagers looked slack-jawed. Conrad continued, "I was afraid if I didn't stop you, y'all would keep going at each other all night long." He spoke the last part of the sentence in a deep, masculine voice full of innuendo.

Ryne raised an eyebrow at Conrad to show his annoyance. Lily blinked several times in confusion, then finally realized what the centaur was implying. Her face turned bright red, and she quickly retreated back to the princess. The crowd's laughter chased the Dragon Lily as she moved.

Elisa handed Lily a mug full of mana restoration potion, and the knight chugged it. The princess's performance for the villagers was going to require an inhuman level of mana, and Lily was her reservoir. Elisa walked next to Ryne while Lily left the village common and entered a small building. One of Conrad's scouts had already arranged the room with a table next to a comfortable chair. A dozen mana restoration potions were lined up on the table. Lily sat in the chair, and the scout handed her the first bottle. Lily took a deep breath, then signaled to Elisa through the link, *Ready*.

Meanwhile, on the village common, the princess began her act. "Thank you for the kind welcome. We have just witnessed Prince Ryne and Dame Lily fight an exciting battle, the kind that stirs the blood and warms the body. With winter so close, the opportunities to find warmth can be fleeting. The ability to gather with friends is hard when the snow is deep. Unless, of course, people have a place to congregate. I wonder if I can make such a place... Gentlemen, if you please."

At the princess's command, four of Ryne's guards directed the crowd to move apart. Soon, an area was cleared on the south end of the common. The guards remained at the four corners of the large rectangular area. Elisa then walked to the center of the area, crouched, placed her hands on the ground, and cast a spell of major creation. Unlike the ritual casting she had used back in Viverna, this spell demanded a constant and staggering flow of mana. Elisa reached out through the mental link to siphon the power that she needed.

Back in the building, Lily felt a massive drain as her mana was sucked out of her through the mental bond. Her field of vision began to black out as the princess consumed the last of the knight's mana stores. Struggling to remain conscious, Lily chugged the potion in her hand and motioned for the scout to give her the next bottle. She repeated the feat until all the vials were empty, whispered *Done* through the link, and then surrendered to the darkness of sleep.

On the village common, the surface of the ground within the rectangular area became fluid. Elisa gracefully swept her arms about her, and waves of earth formed and dissolved in response to her motions. As her gestures became grander, the waves began to freeze in place, forming the stone walls of a building. With a wink and smile to the crowd, the princess disappeared from view as the building continued to grow around her.

A minute after Elisa began, the structure was finished. The building was solid stone and two stories high, with multiple openings for doors and windows. Chimneys had sprouted on opposite sides of the building. The princess appeared at the opening closest to the Ryne. "My prince, does this community great hall meet your approval?"

"The outside looks sturdy and attractive," Ryne replied. He gestured at the villagers. "May we all come inside?"

Elisa replied yes, and the prince led his subjects inside the building. The crowd was quiet at first, in awe of the magic that had generated a building from nothing but bare earth. However, curiosity and excitement grew among the villagers as they realized the building was both real and made for them.

At the prompting of the village elder, the villagers grew quiet and knelt before the princess. The elder said, "Your Highness, your gift is wonderful. You are amazing."

The princess smiled and spoke to the crowd. "I am merely a vessel of the Earth Goddess. We honor her through the protection of community and family. Please thank her instead of me," Elisa said humbly.

Ryne almost laughed at the princess's modest behavior. He knew how much she was enjoying all the attention.

"Your Highness, we wish to honor you both," replied the mayor.

"Thank you kindly," replied Elisa. "Oh, I do need to tell you about the building. I required plenty of material for the spell, so you will find two levels of basement carved below the building. Please use them for storing supplies when times are plentiful. As for the doors, shutters, and furnishings, I will leave those items to you. I wish we could have met sooner so that you would have more time to prepare for winter."

The elder said, "Your Highness, please return to Sonora in the spring. Part of our winter work will be finishing this great hall, and we would like you to see our results."

"I look forward to next spring then. Now, if you will excuse me. For some reason, I'm feeling tired." The yawning princess exited the building.

The prince's party stayed an extra day in Sonora to allow Lily to rest. Her mana exhaustion was extreme enough that even the elven mana fruit could not help. Upon realizing Lily's condition, William berated Elisa through the link and forbade her from using mana-sharing for the rest of the trip. Unused to such a scolding, Elisa began to fight back, but William shut her down immediately. The elf explained that the princess, by using Lily's mana without limit, had put the knight's life in danger. The chastised princess promised to behave.

William planned to spend the next four days running southwest to Auraria, while Ryne's party would take seven days heading northwest. William used the road where convenient, but he avoided interactions with the merchants and travelers who were trying to make a final trip before the snows of winter prohibited travel for all but the foolhardiest. The nature of the journey by Ryne's group was the opposite of William's. They engaged travelers at every opportunity and stopped in every village along their path.

The stretch of road three days past Sonora was long and desolate. Continuing their discussions gave Ryne, Elisa, and Lily a way to pass the time. Today's topic was why changes were needed in the world.

Ryne said, "Before we get started, please remember the reason that I believe changes are needed. Sometime in the future, we will experience an invasion. I did not previously name our enemies, so I will do so now. The cause of the Catastrophe was a demon invasion.

"Willow was able to stop the last one, but the human memories and records of that event have been suppressed. The demons take indirect actions for now, but my visions indicate that a direct mass conquest will take place. A single elven queen, no matter how powerful, will be unable to stop it. If humanity is to be ready, then we must prepare.

"First, the human nations have engaged in seasonal warfare for generations. This has led to highly skilled soldiers but no unifying leadership capable of directing humanity's forces. Without such leadership, individual nations will fall before the strength of the demon horde. You may think such a collective effort is impossible, but I submit that the Trade Hub of Taronto is an example of such cooperation. Even nations actively engaged in warfare do not risk attacking each other within the borders of Llanos. Such hostility would exclude them from the Taronto markets and place them at a disadvantage with respect to their neighbors. At least, this was the case until a few days ago when Prince Logan committed regicide to succeed his father on the throne. We shall soon see if the rash actions of one man will undermine hundreds of years of tradition."

Ryne continued, "Elisa, you worked your way into a position of leadership within the Trade Hub. Do you know the history of how it was formed?"

"No, the history of the formation is…murky," replied Elisa.

"It was one of Willow's sons. Apparently, he was annoyed that the supply of one of his favorite vegetables, which was grown far to the south, was inconsistent from year to year. He spent the next fifty years setting up the markets. Do not underestimate the strategic thinking of the elves. Their plans can span many human generations.

"But, back to my original point, humans will need cooperative leadership if we are to survive the next demon onslaught.

"Second, soldiers will not be enough. We need to cultivate new heroes—individuals capable of attacking and defeating the demons who will invade this world. However, such heroes are a conundrum. Beings capable of defeating demons could easily turn their abilities against an established nation, destroy the current leadership, and establish themselves as new warlords. We need powerful individuals, but we also need a way to control them.

"Third, we need to convince the leaders of each country that the threat we face is real. This is where the demons' indirect influence is already at work. How can we prevent future tragedies if the past tragedies are not remembered?

"Fourth, humans may not be enough. Our world is filled with many other races—elves, dwarves, centaurs, and halflings, among many others. These other races lack the numbers of the humans, but they have knowledge and skills that will be essential to defeat the enemy. However, the average human sees the other races as lesser beings. We need to find a way for the races to work together.

"Fifth, we need the weapons, armor, and supplies necessary to fight the demons. We need to plan for a series of massive, protracted battles. Small equipment shops cannot produce enough to accomplish our goals. We need to manufacture and stockpile equipment on a totally new scale of production. Oh, we also need to ensure these supplies are not simply used by one nation to attack its neighbors.

"These are not all of our needs, but they are the most immediate," Ryne finished.

Elisa and Lily spent the next few hours questioning and challenging Ryne on his assumptions and conclusions. He had laid out a series of impossible tasks. It had taken fifty years to convince the rulers of the world that common trade among all countries was in their best interests. Ryne's plans were far more daring. He needed to convince the current national leaders that an unknown foe threatened the continent and that the best course of action was a level of cooperation that no single human nation, much less several, had ever achieved with another.

Ryne, Elisa, and Lily continued their discussions the next day. They switched from discussing what changes were needed to a new topic: how to accomplish these goals.

"For the last couple of years, in the downtime between clearing monsters out of the city, my team has tried to determine what changes we will need to be ready for the next demon horde. In all fairness, many of these ideas came from William and his previous life's memories. We've refined them as a group, but the core concepts are from him."

"What kind of world did he live in?" asked Lily.

"You will need to ask him for details, but it was a place very different from our own. His memories are not very clear. He says he does not even remember his own form—whether he was male or female. So, the recollections might not even be his own. But the memories do show a world far more advanced than ours. Cities with buildings that reached into the sky and were filled not with thousands of people but with millions.

"Ask Albrun to share her stories with you. Her emotions and expressiveness make her a wonderful storyteller. Much better than William's emotionless and matter-of-fact delivery..." Ryne's voice trailed off. Elisa could tell he was angry at himself for accidentally comparing William and Albrun.

Shaking himself out of his funk, Ryne continued, "So what are the changes we plan to make? First, we are going to create a new organization that spans all countries. Based on the Merchants Guild model that was created hundreds of years ago, we will create an Adventurers Guild. Need medicinal herbs picked or a nest of goblins destroyed? Then offer a contract for the mission through the Adventurers Guild. Have talent as a warrior or a mage and want a safe way to find jobs in your area? Join the Adventurers Guild. The Guild will benefit its members by ranking both the members and the quests and then matching them for the best fit. A novice party will not be sent to eliminate wyverns, and a mission to parley with a dragon will not be given to a party of trigger-happy sorcerers.

"Towns and cities will want to host Adventurers Guild branches. The Guild will offer quick, efficient ways to deal with wandering monsters and gathering items in dangerous areas. The Merchants Guild will enjoy a supply of reliable, trustworthy guardians for their caravans beyond the Llanos borders. The leadership of each country will benefit by having a pool of exceptional individuals to help with extraordinary missions. The Adventurers Guild will hold its members to a strict set of rules, providing deterrents for those individuals who engage in bad behaviors.

"The Adventurers Guild will not get involved in wars between countries nor civil wars inside them. The Guild is not a mercenary group, selling its skills to the highest bidder. The Guild will, however, deploy its members to secure peace and prosperity in the areas where it resides. Is your town facing a monstrous horde? Your local Adventurers Guild will call upon its members to protect the town and its residents." Ryne's voice filled with passion as he spoke. The full force of his powerful charisma was directed at the women.

"The Adventurers Guild will allow us to cultivate the next generation of heroes in a way that benefits all of us."

Ryne thought Elisa and Lily had been stunned into silence with his vision of the future. The truth was somewhat different. The power of the speaker, rather than the subject, had deeply affected them.

Lily thought at Elisa, *Princess, please forgive me for my impure thoughts about your future husband! It just, oh my, I can't help myself...*

Elisa replied, *Huh? Did you say something, Lily? Whatever; I'm sure it is fine. I just need to drown myself in his gorgeous blue eyes...*

...

...

A faint voice could be heard through the mental link. *Elisa...Lily...can you hear me...please respond...*

Neither of the women responded.

A few moments later, the trio's comms devices activated. William's annoyance came through loud and clear. ‹Ryne, you used the voice again, didn't you? How many times have I told you? Do not use the voice unless I am there to supervise!›

Ryne's response was soft and apologetic. ‹Wait, what? I'm sorry, I just got excited talking about the Guild. I didn't realize...›

‹What am I going to do with you?› William asked. ‹Oh my. Well, please look at Elisa and Lily. What are they doing?›

Ryne said, ‹We are all just standing still. The horses aren't moving. Elisa and Lily are staring at me. Their eyes seem... kind of distant.›

‹Okay, so they are just stunned. This is not a repeat of Golden last year, correct?›

‹Yes, just stunned. Not like Golden. They have not started taking their clothes off...› Ryne was embarrassed at the memory of last year's town hall event.

‹Okay, I'm very far away, but I'll try to help them from my end.›

Hundreds of kilometers away, William found a safe spot to hide and then began casting magic. He needed to break the women out of their stupor. Ryne's ability was not directly harmful, but it was incredibly strong. Left unattended, the women would wake up from their very vivid daydreams in a few hours. Unlike those involved in the incident at Golden last year, Elisa and Lily were strong-willed enough not to start immediately acting out their deepest desires. William screamed a little inside. Ryne clearly did not understand his effect on people.

Ryne's ability was not a magic spell, so dispelling magic through the mental link would not work. Elisa and Lily were in a magically induced dream state, so he would need to enter their minds to recover them. If such interference proved too dangerous, he would let the state run its course and let them wake naturally. The problem was their shared mental space. William was already experiencing each of the women's secret desires. The dream states were spilling into the shared space and were influencing and merging with each other. William cast his strongest mental barrier magic, then poured magic into his link with Lily. Her mental defenses were not as strong as Elisa's, so he felt he had a better chance to recover her first.

Entering another person's mind is a weird experience. The way people perceive color, the way they hear sounds, and the way they experience the world is different for each person. Lily's dream was a new version of "Save the Princess" but now included events that followed the rescue. Lily's lack of worldly experience showed, as parts of the dream were very abstract. In this daydream, both Ryne and Elisa needed to be rescued. The way that each showed their appreciation to Lily would make a teenager giggle. Still, William could feel the deep love and admiration that Lily held for Elisa and the strong romantic attraction she felt toward Ryne. The dream cycle repeated itself a couple of times, and William was able to determine a suitable stopping point. By casting recovery magic through the link, William returned Lily to consciousness. His timing was fortunate, as the next loop started with William as the rescuee. He was not curious about how that loop would end.

After confirming that Lily was okay, William began to work on Elisa. Her dream was much more vivid and detailed. The emotions within felt exaggerated, so William guessed that Elisa was a fan of romance novels. There was also a hint of naïvety within the dream, likely indicating Elisa's lack of actual experience. William laughed a bit at himself—his firsthand knowledge was literally from his previous life. All that said, Elisa's dream was quite erotic. Ryne and Lily played starring roles, which William did not find surprising. Finding Albrun there, however, was shocking.

As before, William rode through a couple of loops of the dream to find a suitable stopping point. On the second loop, William noticed more ominous signs than he had the first time through. While the themes of love and affection were still present, there was an overarching tone of dominance. Elisa's need for power and control was always in the background, guiding her actions even in her daydreams. William put his concerns aside for now and used recovery magic to bring Elisa back to consciousness.

Elisa and Lily recovered, but that did not mean they were okay. These were not the normal dreams that fade when a person wakes. Because of the shared mental space, both women remembered each other's dreams as well. They each had strong romantic feelings for the other, which neither woman had wanted to reveal.

They were both embarrassed, and neither wanted to talk. William knew they needed time to recover, but they did need to talk to each other soon. He made them promise to talk with each other this evening before bed. Their next stop was scheduled for a large town with a good inn. They could find privacy there. William teased that if they did not talk this evening, he would facilitate it tomorrow. Neither woman wanted the added embarrassment of involving another person.

Through a private comms link, William suggested that Ryne suspend discussion of the future until they all reunited in Auraria. Ryne asked what was wrong. William was discreet, saying Elisa and Lily had just learned some new truths about themselves, and they would need time to process them. Ryne admitted he did not understand but said he would nevertheless be supportive.

William was able to monitor Elisa and Lily for the next three days, then the mental link dissolved. He did not pry, but he could feel the two women had become more comfortable with their newly discovered feelings for each other. William was pretty sure their friendship had survived the experience, and perhaps it was about to evolve.

William spent the next few days awaiting the arrival of Ryne and his party. William was not bored. The city was still recovering from years of neglect at the hands of the monster horde.

Edmund, majordomo for Prince Ryne, kept William busy with task after task.

Through the comms link, Commander Owen, Ryne's field commander, announced success in capturing and ransoming the mercenaries who had tried to attack Princess Elisa several days earlier. The capture had taken place in Prince Nevan's duchy, so Captain Refren was going to handle the final disposition of the enemy soldiers. They would be repatriated to their city-state back in Polis. Commander Owen admitted he was impressed with the professionalism of the enemy leaders and troops. They were talented enough to consider employing if a need for such a troop arose in the future.

In addition to Commander Owen, Runera, the halfling magician, would arrive home within the next ten-day. William was looking forward to having almost all his companions at home. Mizu was not able to return yet. She was still supporting Elisa's father, Prince Miller, in the standoff between the factions in Llanos. The trading season was coming to a close, and winter was fast approaching, but the danger to the Taronto Trade Hub would be real if the standoff was not resolved before spring.

A few days later, Ryne, Elisa, Lily, Conrad, and their escort entered Auraria. The group's supply train contained the five wagons from Golden. Auraria had worked hard over the last few months to become self-sufficient, and given the still-limited population, food production was adequate. The wagons contained items the residents of Auraria would need for the coming winter that they could not produce locally. That was the last run of the season before the snow fell in earnest. Fortunately, the local smithy had resumed production, so the wagons would not return to Golden empty. They would contain well-made suits of armor, weapons, tools, and other metal goods.

Princess Elisa caused quite a stir with the population. Her teamster skills, along with her beauty, made her an instant hit with the rough-and-tumble population of Auraria. The city and the lands around it were still very dangerous. The citizens did not see the need for a useless noble ruler. Elisa seemed like a good fit for both Ryne and the city.

William escorted Elisa and Lily to their new accommodations within Ryne's home. Rather than a mansion, Ryne and his team had rebuilt his previous home into a small fortress that could withstand a significant invasion force. The insides were currently spartan, but thought had gone into making the living quarters spacious and inviting. William gave the women a small suite with a living room and two adjoining bedrooms.

Lily timidly asked, "Do you have a room with a larger bed?"

Each of the bedrooms had beds that would easily fit Lily's stature. She had something else in mind.

William led the women to a single large bedroom meant for couples. "Will this do?" he asked innocently.

Lily mumbled, "Yes, it will be fine," and then proceeded inside with their belongings.

Elisa was giggling in the doorframe. "The trip was good for us. We've had several long discussions, and we are taking this new change in our relationship slowly. For now, I'm happy just to snuggle in bed with her."

"How can your tiny, adorable feet be so cold?" complained a red-faced Lily.

William laughed. "The toilets are down the hall, and we have men's and women's baths as well. A nice warm bath might help with the feet."

"That sounds wonderful! Lily, I'm headed there now. Please come join me!" Elisa said as she walked happily down the hall.

"On my way, Princess. Just need to handle some items." Lily grabbed a bag and a sheathed sword and then walked over to William. "You will be wanting this." Lily thrust the bag containing the elven armor at William, but she was unwilling to make eye contact. She and Elisa could no longer wear the armor since the mental link with William had expired. Lily also handed over the magic sword she had borrowed in Viverna.

"Lily, look at me," William said quietly.

The female knight slowly turned to face William. The embarrassment was gone, replaced with a mild sadness.

"Lily, how are you doing?"

"I'm fine."

"Are things really okay since Elisa's daydream?"

Lily flinched, but she repeated her line. "I'm fine."

"Elisa—"

"She's not a bad person. I know that she cares for me," interrupted Lily.

"Yes, she does, but she does so only on her terms. We both felt her craving for power. She wraps it in her quest for justice— her need to right the wrongs done to her. Her absolute certainty that she is right makes her blind to the feelings of those around her, especially you. And after what she did to you in Sonora, risking your life for her exhibition..." William was angry.

Lily stood quietly, not denying the truth in William's words.

"Do you want me to speak with her?" asked William.

"No! Please don't. I'm okay for now. I'm just worried about some of the plans she is considering. They make me uncomfortable. However, now is not the time to confront her."

"Will you tell me what she is planning?"

"I cannot violate her trust."

"All right, I will hold my tongue for now. Let me know if I can help you." William reached out his arms for a hug, giving her the option of accepting or refusing.

Reluctant at first, the female knight moved in to hug William. His embrace was surprisingly comforting. She took care not to squeeze him too hard.

After a few moments, William gently extracted himself and left.

Ryne's breakfast table was lively the next morning. Ryne and Lily had just finished refreshing themselves after an early morning workout in the home's interior courtyard. The two were crazy, as the temperatures had plummeted overnight, but they only referred to the weather as "brisk." Petras, a male dwarf and lead engineer for the Aurarian redevelopment effort, was in a detailed discussion with William about the construction of the Viverna village wall. Elisa was discussing the state of the city's winter supplies with the majordomo, Edmund. Though the table was long enough for twice as many people, all of them had congregated at one end. Food was served buffet-style—it was warm, tasty, and plentiful.

After a few minutes, Elisa stopped and looked around.

"Everything okay?" asked Ryne.

Elisa's eyes were misty. "I've been dreaming of friends like you in a place like this for a long time. Thank you for having us."

Ryne smiled. "You are now part of our large, crazy, extended family. Welcome home!"

In unison, everyone except Elisa and Lily, including the kitchen staff, repeated the greeting. "Welcome home!"

CHAPTER 15

After breakfast, Edmund took Elisa and Lily on a tour of the city. He proved to be an amazing guide, answering military-oriented questions from Lily as well as addressing Elisa's logistical supply concerns. The current population was about ten percent of what the city could hold, assuming all the buildings were repaired. The plan was to reach forty percent by the end of the next year, eighty the year after, and full capacity by three years hence. Families with small children had not yet arrived. If the winter construction went well, and the safety of the duchy continued to improve, then some of those families would join the next wave of settlers. Ryne's team, particularly Petras, was excited to explore what Elisa, Lily, and William could do to accelerate the repairs to the city.

The tour took most of the day. The residents of Auraria included the people who had helped Ryne clear the city of monsters, as well as the first wave of settlers. They were hearty folk, used to living on the edge of dangerous lands. They like to know their neighbors, and Edmund taking time to escort the two women piqued the interest of the citizens. There were frequent stops and introductions.

The women were also surprised by the diversity of races within the city. As the major trading hub for the continent, Taronto in Llanos had hosted virtually every known civilized race. However, non-humans in Taronto were considered a necessary evil, and comingling with humans was actively discouraged. Auraria was the opposite.

"Prince Ryne believes the rebuilt city will be stronger if we put aside the divisions of the past." The pride in Edmund's voice was obvious.

Lily looked exhausted when they finished the tour.

"Are you doing okay, Lily?" Elisa asked as they traveled home.

"My head hurts. Too many names to remember," complained Lily.

"Well, they all know you. The dwarves at the weaponsmith shop were calling you 'the Dragon.' Your fame has spread far enough for your new title to become a name. Pretty cool, won't you admit?"

"I admit nothing," grumbled Lily. She acted annoyed, but Elisa could tell that Lily was secretly enjoying her new reputation.

"At least none of your nicknames end in *-itch*," teased Elisa.

"I think you will find our people more accommodating, Princess. The humor can get rough, but we support each other," said Edmund.

"My life improved the moment I set foot in Vorland. I've only had three attempts on my life in the last month."

Edmund paused for a moment, not knowing how to respond.

"That was a joke, Edmund, but it was also the truth," the expressionless Elisa explained.

A wide smile spread across Edmund's face. "Oh dear, you have a dry sense of humor. You are going to be so much fun at our parties."

Elisa's response was a Mona Lisa smile.

Dinner was done, and Ryne, Elisa, Lily, and William retired to a large room in the basement of Ryne's fortress. Ryne called it his office, but it was the size of the fortress's formal dining hall. The left wall was covered with bookshelves. Perhaps a third of the shelves were filled. The right wall was honeycombed with holes for storing maps and scrolls. The wall from which they had entered held shelves and cabinets. A section was used for refreshments, while the rest displayed mementos and pictures from Ryne's travels. The opposite wall was the most stunning. A series of extremely detailed maps covered its surface. Elisa, who had once entered the secret rooms of Llanos royalty, had never seen such accurate information.

Ryne had a large desk and chair in the room, as did Edmund. A long table ran parallel to the entry wall. It could easily hold two dozen people. A series of comfortable chairs and sofas ringed the center of the room. At that time, four chairs faced each other in the center. The corner of the room between the map wall and the scroll storage was covered in magical darkness. Lily looked questioningly at William.

"Ryne likes an air of suspense when he tells stories," replied William.

The four took their seats. William was on Ryne's right, and Lily was on his left. Elisa sat in the seat opposite Ryne.

Ryne began to speak. "A few days ago, we were talking about changes we need to make in the world if we are to defeat the demon horde. I described the Adventurers Guild, and perhaps I was a bit too passionate—"

William cleared his throat loudly.

"Correction, way too passionate. Sorry." Ryne seemed genuinely apologetic for his actions.

Elisa giggled. "Lily and I saw the value of your proposed guild even without your impassioned speech. We would appreciate calmer discussions going forward. Direct exposure to your...powerful personality...is very pleasantly distracting." Elisa's cheeks were slightly red, while Lily's were hot enough to boil water.

"How about I serve us some tea?" asked William, presenting a distraction to allow the women to recover. A few minutes later, everyone was calm again and ready to proceed.

Ryne picked up where he had left off. "I mentioned how the Adventurers Guild was based on the Merchants Guild. The next change we wish to make has a similar connection. We want to revolutionize how children are educated. Currently, human commoners learn basic knowledge from their parents and special skills from a master through the apprentice system. Human nobles have the money to hire private tutors, and their children can pursue any field that strikes their interest. There is no uniform system for teaching human children, with the result being that knowledge resides with the privileged few. The churches and knights' academies are the rare exception, allowing truly exceptional commoners to better themselves through their own hard work." Ryne acknowledged Lily as he said the last sentence.

He continued, "Did you know that by the age of eight, every halfling child knows how to read and write their own language as well as the common language, can perform basic math, and has learned history and geography? If they have the magical aptitude, they learn spells for basic healing, poison removal, and disease elimination, as well as common household spells for cleaning, fire starting, and water collection. All halfling children are trained in self-defense.

"All this education occurs before they decide which specialty to pursue. Halflings can do this because they have dedicated, knowledgeable teachers who instruct every child in their village. Wealth level and status do not matter. Every child gets the same basic, wonderful educa—"

"Ryne, stop. Bad prince. Down boy!" interrupted William. "Elisa and Lily understand. Please continue."

Ryne continued in a calmer fashion. "So, as I was saying, the halflings have a wonderful model for education. I'll defer talking about the elves, as discussing their system would just get me in trouble again. Suffice it to say, elven education is the pinnacle for which we should strive.

"Changing human education will not be easy. Nobles benefit by limiting the education of commoners. Education takes time, money, and a safe environment. Rural communities need their children to work to gather and raise food. Just placing a school in such a community without changing the behaviors and expectations of the residents is destined for failure.

"What can we do? Where do we start? We will establish a school on neutral ground, like the sovereign territory that the Merchants Guild Trade Hub uses in Taronto. All countries will be welcome to send their nobility and exceptional commoners to the school. Like the Adventurers Guild, the school will remain independent of inter- and intra-country warfare and disputes.

"William called it the Switzerland effect—armed neutrality to protect the people within its region while not taking sides in the world outside. Our working name for the school is Turicum, again a nod to William's past life memories." Ryne paused to allow the others to comment and ask questions.

"How will you get nobles to send their children to your school?" asked Lily.

Ryne was about to answer when Elisa raised her hand. "In addition to the education, the students will forge relationships with each other, learn leadership skills when their mistakes can be minimized, and learn and practice social skills before their lives depend on them. Anyone who does not send their child puts their child at a disadvantage with their peers."

"I could not say it better myself," Ryne said to Elisa. "Now, where do we put the school? It needs to be convenient, so Auraria is off the list. We were considering near Taronto, but that idiot Logan has messed up the plan. So where now?"

Elisa got out of her seat and walked over to the wall of maps. The continental map had sufficient details for her needs. "Llanos is still a good choice, because the Trade Hub is there. But given the recent events, moving the Trade Hub would be a good idea. Building a city on an endless plain is kind of boring. You are a foothill-and-mountain kind of people. I can respect that. Hmm." After a few minutes of consideration, she pointed to the edge of the Triangle Mountains in southeastern Llanos. "Here; you are planning to place it here."

Ryne turned to William. "You told her, didn't you?" scolded Ryne.

William snorted. "No, that's just how smart she is. It took her five minutes to decide. How long did it take you?" taunted William.

"Never mind," Ryne deflected.

"Elisa, I know there is a major road nearby, but isn't that area filled with monsters?" asked Lily.

Elisa explained, "It is, which means that even my father, who rules the land, has little use for it. As for monsters, Auraria was once full as well. Plus, an early version of the Adventurers Guild could recruit members and train them."

Ryne was looking at Elisa with shock on his face. William was trying not to laugh and failing.

She said, "Prince Ryne, please don't feel bad. They are really good ideas, and you did have them first." Elisa was trying to comfort Ryne, but it just made him feel worse. "I'll hush now. Please continue," she requested with a smile.

Ryne had everyone walk to the corner of the room that was covered in darkness. He snapped his fingers, and the darkness turned to light. An illusion of a miniature city built in the foothills of a chain of mountains was displayed before them. The women gasped at the sight. It was magnificent.

"This is Turicum. The Adventurers Guild occupies this hill, while people live around these hills. We will divert a portion of this river to supply fresh water to all the buildings, and we will have underground sewerage to handle the waste. The school will be built into the side of the mountain."

The illusion of the city was controlled by a magic item. Ryne moved it to the center of the four chairs, then explained how to change the illusion—zoom in and out on areas and changing perspective. The user could also change the time index and show how development was scheduled to occur over the next few years.

Ryne handed Elisa a ledger that estimated the number and kinds of supplies that would be needed for each phase of the build. It was also linked to the illusion so that each building could be examined in detail.

"Who built these magical items?" asked Lily.

Ryne replied, "Runera, whom you will meet in a few days, made them with substantial help from William."

The women were impressed. These tools offered views and insights that drawings could not convey. Ryne put away the tea service and switched to alcohol. Elisa and William favored wine, while Lily tried a rum from the Osman Empire that Ryne liked. The four spent the next couple of hours discussing the city and the school.

William left first, and Lily soon followed. Once they were alone, Elisa asked Ryne a very direct question. "You are building this city for Albrun, aren't you?"

"What makes you say that?" asked Ryne.

"You are in love with Willow, but you can never have her. She made you a twin of herself, but you cannot see Albrun as a lover. You see her as your child. You are very conflicted. You want to protect and spoil Albrun, but you need her to enforce your will. To be your right hand, she has denied being herself and instead became a person who leaves no trace in the world. You see the discomfort that being William causes Albrun, and you hate yourself for it. For now, you need William. But later, when Turicum is finished, someone will need to rule it. Someone with the strength, foresight, and longevity to make Turicum the shining city on the hill. A beacon of hope for all mankind.

"You and Willow have already started her legend. The Witch Queen Albrun defied the evil tyrant to bring justice for her people, then went out of her way to save the foreign diplomats from the clutches of that same tyrant. One day, William will be cast aside, and Albrun will be the ruler that

Turicum needs." Elisa paused for a sip of wine before asking, "How did I do?"

"Closer than I would like to admit," admitted Ryne. "You are incorrect—I don't see Albrun as my child. She is a child, according to the elves, and children cannot consent. In terms of her age, she will become an adult in eighteen months. In her case, she just wielded Lahat Chereb in combat. That should be proof enough of her maturity if the Elven Council of Elders agrees.

"Marrying her is not an option, regardless of how I feel. Only the children of a human female will be acceptable heirs in Vorland. While my feelings for her are strong, my goals are far stronger. I need my royal position to prepare for the next demon assault.

"You are a different story. You are a perfect match for me. Your Merchants Guild contacts will be invaluable in accomplishing my goals. Why are you trying so hard to avoid marrying me?"

"Does it seem that I'm trying to avoid you? Well, I told you what I thought of your intentions with Albrun. Why don't you tell me what you think my intentions are?"

"If you insist, Princess. This is going to be a long list of my impressions of you." Ryne took a deep breath and began. "You reluctantly accepted my invitation to come to Auraria, not because you feared the journey but because you yearn to punish the people that killed your Aunt Sarai. You decided to accept the invitation because you don't mind serving a cold revenge. You are concerned that our marriage will limit you, but you trust your own powers of persuasion enough to keep the marriage as an option. However, you will try to negotiate a better deal for yourself, one where you can get access to my power and resources without accepting limitations. You see me marrying your devoted servant Lily as your best current option. I'll talk more about that in a moment.

"Your gender frustrates you. With your ability to ferret

out the truth, had you been born male, you would have been lauded as the incorruptible knight who saved his country from the evils of the tyrant Prince Logan. Instead, you share Sarai's reputation as a witch—an uncontrollable woman to be feared. You think the William ritual may be your answer, if you could learn it. A way to strike your enemies while protecting yourself from retaliation.

"I'm not sure of your opinion on having children, but you don't seem eager for motherhood. Again, children would limit you, and you have too many plans to accept those limits. You know that children are a must-have for me, so we have a clear conflict.

"Lily is your source of guilt. You must use her for protection. Even though it gives her great pleasure to be your guardian, she sees herself as your servant rather than as your equal. You have thought of making her your lover and running away together, but your need for revenge is too strong. Now, you are exploring how to include her in your plans for dealing with me.

"You are already working to elevate Lily in rank and build her self-confidence. At each turn, you have amplified her legend, starting with the trial by combat. If you raise her status enough, then Lily will make me a perfect wife. You will give your best friend what she desires most—the man of her dreams. She can give me the children, the heirs, that I need.

"With my help now secured, you can pursue your newest goal, the person you now desire, Albrun. She represents the power and knowledge that you crave." Ryne paused for a sip of rum, then asked, "How did I do?"

Elisa was gobsmacked. She finished her wine in a single gulp and took a few moments to compose herself, then said, "I'm used to being the smartest in the room. I apologize. I underestimated you." Elisa sighed. "Your assessment of me is not flattering, even if it is accurate."

"Elisa, every leader seeks to gain and retain power so that they can shape the world in their own image. Your pursuit of power is natural. Your problem is you haven't sought allies. This does not surprise me, as Sarai spurned those who would help her."

"No one would help Sarai. She stood alone against her brother Logan."

"That is untrue. A year after my family perished, I reached out to her, asking her to join me. Your father tried to persuade her, but she turned me down."

"What? That was only two years ago. No one ever told me!" exclaimed the princess.

"You and Lily made places for yourselves in Taronto, so she was unwilling to ask you to leave. At the same time, Sarai knew the threat of Logan was growing, so she was unwilling to leave you."

Elisa was silent for a couple of minutes as Ryne's words sank in. "What are you asking me to do?"

"Talk with me. Let's see if we can help each other. Perhaps I can offer you a path you have not considered."

"I'm listening."

"As I have mentioned, my goal is to house the Adventurers Guild and the school in Turicum." Ryne paused for a moment, deep in thought. "What if...we move the Merchants Guild there also? We take the Trade Hub away from Taronto, depriving King Logan of all its prestige and revenue?"

"I think I would prefer a blade in his guts, but crushing his ego? That idea has merit," said Elisa with a wicked smile.

"You recognized that the ideal location for Turicum is southeastern Llanos in an area controlled by your father. The civil war in Taronto has shut down the Trade Hub. Let's take advantage of the disruption and relocate the Trade Hub to Turicum."

The audacity of Ryne's suggestion overwhelmed Elisa. She searched his face, but he was serious. The look in his eyes was intense, and it sent a shiver down her spine. "You would do this for me?" she asked.

"I would do this for us. We would do it together, with the help of every ally we can find. Logan has made a grave mistake, and even if your father defeats him, the damage is done. The Llanos king will need time to rebuild trust with the Merchants Guild before the Trade Hub can open. If we accelerate our timelines, we could be ready to open the spring after next—five seasons from now. That should be quick enough to outmaneuver the Llanos king."

Elisa's mind was on fire. She had never met anyone, Sarai included, who fueled her imagination like Ryne did. She had finally found someone who recognized her brilliance and complemented hers with his own. Looking at the excitement in his eyes, his feelings mirrored hers.

The next hour was spent drinking and making plans. The timeline was insane, but Logan had made a mistake, and they were going to make him pay dearly for it.

Eventually, exhaustion and inebriation took their toll, and the pair turned to lighter topics. Somewhere in their conversation, Ryne and Elisa moved seats, and they now sat together. The tiny princess wanted to snuggle against the massive prince, but she refrained. Business came first.

"So, have you decided if I'm an acceptable groom?" asked Ryne.

"You are starting to convince me, but what do I do with Lily? She is madly in love with you. I'm not sure I want to have my best friend drooling over my husband."

Ryne's laugh was deep and wonderful, and it struck a chord with Elisa. Despite her best efforts, she felt herself falling for the prince.

"No worries, as we can always follow William's suggestion. He recommended that I pursue both you and Lily. Noble polygamy is common in both Llanos and Vorland. Of course, Lily would need a noble rank, so William's plan is to have Lily be rewarded for her defense of Viverna. She would be raised to the level of Viscountess or Countess by my brother, Prince

Nevan. You would be my first wife and my bond to Llanos. Lily would become my Vorlandish wife."

"We could add Albrun to the marriage—your elvish wife. Since we would be leaving Vorland behind, Albrun is now acceptable. Then again, you might want to collect a wife from each country lest you offend someone," teased Elisa.

"I am but a mortal man and an older one at that. Are you trying to kill me under an avalanche of brides?"

Elisa laughed. "Many men would welcome such a death, but you see the horror of it. Yet another reason you are so attractive. Having all three of us marry you would solve another problem. The mind link is powerful, long-term magic. It is too useful not to use. But using it exposes the participants to the emotions of the others. Add the joys of marriage for some of the participants but not the others? That sounds like the complete opposite of fun for those on the outside." Elisa proceeded to tell Ryne about Lily's recurring "Save the Princess" dream and the effect it had on William and herself.

Ryne warned, "Be careful making long-term plans based on the mind link magic. Willow has already expressed her concerns. She wants to examine the three of you as soon as possible. I'm sure she is worried about the vulnerabilities that the mind link creates."

"What do you mean?"

"A disabling attack on one person in the link could disable the others as well. Willow is a strong proponent of threat mitigation. You will need to convince her that the mental link is worth it. And just so we are clear, if she tells her daughter to quit using the magic, Albrun will obey."

"Thank you for the warning. I'll need to be convincing." Elisa yawned. "Well, that's enough planning for me tonight. Shall we tell the others in the morning?"

"Yes. Harsh morning light is best for exposing the flaws of plans made while drinking," replied Ryne.

Ryne asked the kitchen staff to arrange breakfast in his office the next morning. The change surprised Lily. "Why are we moving downstairs?"

Petras was walking beside her. "The boss does this every few weeks. An office meal is meant for serious thinking. He has likely come up with some crazy plan, and he wants us to talk him out of it or make it better. Lass, you should eat food that is easy on your stomach. Some of the boss's plans have been known to give us tummy aches," advised the dwarf. His laughter made her more uneasy.

Ryne, Elisa, Lily, William, Edmund, and Petras were soon eating breakfast at the office table. The group ate in silence, but there was a sense of anticipation. Ryne was in a very good mood, while the princess was positively beaming and kept glancing at her knight. Lily stopped eating halfway through the meal. She wished she had taken Petras's advice. Elisa clearly had a plan that would upset Lily.

With the meal concluded, the group moved over to comfortable chairs. There was a couch with four chairs arrayed in front of it. Ryne and Elisa took seats on the couch together. They were not touching, but they seemed comfortable next to each other. The remaining four sat in the chairs.

"Did you engage in…negotiations…after I left last night?" asked William. Petras laughed at his choice of words.

Ryne answered, "Lots of drinking, lots of discussion—it was a productive evening. I'm still in the process of wooing the princess, but as you can see, we are now closer to a solution."

William rolled his eyes at the bad joke. Elisa giggled.

The prince continued speaking. "This morning, I have three topics. The first topic is the latest report from Mizu. The second is personal and concerns my marriage. The third topic is about the timeline of our plans for Turicum."

"There is news from Llanos?" asked Elisa.

"Yes. Mizu reports that a muffled explosion was heard within the royal palace. No reports of deaths, but there is significant chaos."

"Lily, when was the thief-deterrent magic set to expire on that magical bag that Logan confiscated?" asked Elisa.

"Should have happened...last night!" exclaimed the female knight.

Gales of laughter erupted from both women. A couple of minutes had passed before they calmed enough to explain the fertilizer trap they had set for Llanos's new king.

"Apparently, it was set off in his office. I'm surprised he fell for your ruse," said Edmund.

"The magic I used would not show as dangerous. It is a simple spell used by Earth priests when we help farmers," replied Elisa.

"Well played, ladies. Well played. Now, for the remaining two topics—" said Ryne.

"Let's get the marriage discussion over with first," interrupted William. His tone was very matter-of-fact, bordering on aggressive. Lily felt like she was the only one to notice his sudden change. The others seemed to ignore it.

Ryne said, "As you wish. Elisa and I are working on establishing common ground where we can support each other to achieve our individual goals. If we are successful, then we will get married. Do you agree, Elisa?"

"I do, Your Highness. Hehe, I do...see what I did there?" The princess's attempt at humor fell flat.

A few moments of silence paused the conversation. William broke it. "We are waiting for the big surprise." His tone was now clearly irritated.

"Why do you think there is a surprise?" asked the princess.

"There would be no need for a discussion if you just accepted Ryne as your husband. You are planning something," accused William.

"Well, William, we wanted to discuss the idea that you suggested. That Ryne should marry both Lily and myself, and perhaps you as well." Elisa searched William's face, looking for a clue as to why he was angry.

"Wondering why I'm not happy? Don't look at me; look at Lily," commanded William.

Elisa's focus had been fully on William. Shifting her gaze to Lily, she was shocked. Tears were flowing down her knight's face. "Lily, what's wrong?" said the princess with sudden concern.

Lily lowered her head and refused to face Elisa. The princess was at a loss for what was happening, and she turned back to William.

William rose from his seat and moved to stand behind Lily. Her quiet sobs became louder as he comforted her by rubbing her back. He said, "Princess, what I am about to say will likely make you angry. Would you like to dismiss Edmund and Petras before I proceed?"

Elisa was still bewildered, but she had grown wary. "This is a place where thoughts can be expressed safely. They are my new teammates. I would prefer not to hide things from them."

"Understood. Elisa, you are a royal, and your word is law for your servants, including Lily. However, you also profess that she is your best and truest friend. If you want to make her decisions for her, then do so. If you want to treat her as your friend, then talk to her and *listen* to her before you make plans. You are placing her in an awkward position where she cannot refuse you. She does not want to be in your harem."

"My harem? I'm suggesting this for Ryne's sake."

"No, you are trying to consolidate your influence. Having Ryne marry Lily and me is a convenient excuse for you to control the shared mental link and the power it represents. This is all about you, Princess."

Elisa felt the anger rising inside of her. "You are the one who suggested polygamy, William," she accused.

William sighed. "Ryne's memory is rather selective. Sometimes he only remembers what he wants to hear. I suggested that he pursue Lily if you spurned him, not that he marries both of you. You are the better match for his goals, and he will help you achieve yours. To do that, you will need to become part of this team and learn to assist others besides yourself. Above all, you will have to quit taking advantage of Lily's caring nature.

"However, if you want to continue down your aunt's path of the solo hero against her multitude of enemies, then step aside and let Lily be the woman who can give Ryne the happiness he deserves."

The room was quiet once William stopped speaking.

Through a Herculean effort, Elisa kept her anger in check. "Why did you say I take advantage of Lily?"

"You use her skills and abilities to make yourself look good without caring about the impact on her. In some cases, like fighting the Valkyries, that is fine. She enjoyed the battle. But did you feel the strain she was under while building the Viverna wall? Your vanity project caused her sleepless nights and physical illness. She hid it from you so you would not worry."

"Lily, is that true?"

The lady knight would not meet Elisa's stare, but she did nod her head.

"Then it is her fault for not letting me know!" shouted Elisa. Lily flinched at the angry words.

"Did Lily's near-death mana exhaustion in Sonora get your attention? Let me guess; after I scolded you, Lily made light of the incident. Or did she take the blame so that you would not feel bad about yourself?" William's voice was filled with cold, biting anger. "Lily suffered for you in silence so that you could get your way, and now you blame her. That is an okay reaction for a princess or a master, but it is a horrible reaction for a friend."

"What do you want me to do, William?"

"If Lily is your friend, then treat her as an equal, not as your servant. Lily wears her heart on her sleeve. It is not hard to read her emotions. Pay attention to her before you order her to do your bidding."

"Your accusations are unfounded. I always treat her like a friend, and we've been getting along great, especially since the trip from Golden."

"No, you've been happier since the trip, and you've needed her constant attention. What I've seen is Lily's exhaustion. She does not want to sleep with you, not because she does not love you, but because she cannot adequately guard you. Now you suggest she serve as Ryne's second wife, second to you. You think that is a great solution, but she sees it as a punishment. Do you understand why?"

"I do not. I thought marriage to Ryne would make her happy."

"The guilt and anxiety of being with her master's husband will eliminate any joy she might feel. Lily deserves better than being the substitute wife."

"Hurting Lily was not my intention."

"She knows that. Even I know that, but your intentions do not match your actions." William paused for a moment in thought. "Princess, for the first time in your life, you have a chance to have true allies at your side. Everyone in this room, and several people who are not, will be willing to fight and die for your cause. But first, you must accept us and learn to work with us. The first person you must accept is Lily. If you cannot learn to treat her as a friend, then the rest of us are a lost cause."

The room lapsed into silence after William finished speaking.

After a while, Ryne spoke. "Why don't the rest of you take a break? The princess and I need to talk for a while. William and Lily, why don't you two go spar for a bit? Some exercise will do you good. Lily, I'll send a runner for you in about an hour. You and the princess should take a midday bath—it makes the stress go away. Everyone, we will reconvene at midafternoon to discuss the Turicum timeline change."

Chapter 16

A magical alarm sounded just before noon, indicating that Ryne's fortress was under attack. This particular alarm indicated a spatial disturbance—likely a planar rift, a spatial gate, or teleportation. The fortress contained wards against such intrusions, and in fact, Runera had engineered magical traps to counterattack would-be invaders. However, any attacker who had access to such powerful magic was a clear and present danger to Ryne's team and their servants.

The Aurarian communication network immediately became active. Lily snapped out a quick set of details. ‹Women's bath; Princess under attack; Need help.› Her comms link went silent.

Prince Ryne took decisive control. Countless battles to reclaim Auraria had honed Ryne's situational awareness and leadership skills. He knew he had to assess the attack, determine the proper responses, and deliver clear tactical commands to his followers. ‹Edmund, secure the perimeter. William, reinforce the wards room and disable the spatial attack. Petras, retrieve the panacea solutions, then run to the women's bath. Conrad and I will head to the bath now.› The prince knew the strengths of his team and deployed each person with efficiency. The team responded with a chorus of ‹Roger, wilco.›

Thirty seconds had passed since Lily's request, and Ryne was now a few steps from the door leading into the women's bath. The thundering sound of hooves on stone indicated that Conrad was close behind. The prince smashed through the door, and with three long strides, he cleared the dressing room and entered the bath at a run.

Ryne surveyed the room in an instant—several items caught his attention. A heavily injured Lily was facing multiple attackers. A new foe was entering the bath through a gray, shimmering spatial distortion. There were a number of dead attackers, but they were of no consequence for now. However, among the bodies, the princess's crossbow-bolt-riddled body was lying face down in the water.

The sight of the unmoving Elisa shocked Ryne, bringing him to a standstill. With great mental effort, he forced himself to recover. For Elisa to have a chance at life, he had to move swiftly and buy time for her resuscitation.

The prince continued to give commands. ‹Conrad, relieve Lily when you arrive.› "Lily, prepare to withdraw and heal Elisa." Both centaur and knight agreed.

Next, Ryne aided Lily and Elisa while working to block access from the spatial distortion. Water was his preferred element, and the bath had an abundance. He animated the water to flip Elisa over and push her away from the battle, temporarily creating a wall of water in front of the spatial distortion. Then, using the water as a medium, Ryne cast healing magic on both women, freely pouring his mana into them through the connection. The water allowed him to check their conditions. Even with Ryne's healing magic, Lily was in poor shape, as a strong poison diffused through her body. Elisa was worse—Ryne felt only a faint sign of life from the princess. She was fading fast.

Ryne continued to pour mana into the water, sustaining Lily and Elisa until more help arrived. His focus now turned toward securing the bath. He did not know how many more enemy reinforcements might be ready on the other side of the distortion.

Ryne's experience kept his mind focused as he dropped his temporary wall of water. He lunged at the man coming through the spatial distortion, driving his sword through the man's chest. The prince used his momentum to slam the man's body back through the gate. The foe disappeared beyond the shimmering gray portal, but Ryne's body hit its unyielding surface as if it were a stone wall. He barely noticed the pain. ‹William, I need the wards up now!›

‹Ten more seconds› was William's reply.

Ryne kept his eyes on the portal, watching for new foes to appear. Ten seconds was an eternity. Behind him, he heard the centaur arrive. "Conrad, help Lily!"

"On it, boss!"

The prince tossed a pair of daggers at the magical distortion, but they ricocheted off its gray surface. The portal was shielded against intruders on this side. The prince racked his brain for a solution. The empty scabbard at his side provided his clue. His sword had passed through while embedded in the chest of the foe he had engaged earlier. The distortion was a controlled gate that allowed only the enemy to pass. Perhaps a dead enemy could pass as well.

Wasting no time, Ryne formed a picture in his mind of the item he needed as he plunged his hand into the magical pouch at his waist. He pulled out a metallic object the size of a lemon—one of the flash-bang grenades that Runera had created for stunning rooms of monsters. The prince grabbed a dead foe floating in the bath near him, jammed the flash-bang into the dead man's mouth, and then hurled the body through the gate. The body passed through easily, taking the grenade along as well. Ryne quickly recast the water-wall spell to seal this side of the gate against the imminent explosion.

A moment later, the spatial gate popped like a bubble. The water wall collapsed, having absorbed the residual energy of the gate.

Ryne spun around to face the remaining attackers. Conrad had smashed his way between Lily and her three attackers— make that two remaining attackers, as Conrad used his hind legs to slam a foe into the bathroom wall with a chest-caving impact.

‹Wards restored and reinforced. Heading to you now,› stated William.

Ryne saw Lily, relieved of opponents, working on Elisa. The prince turned his attention to the remaining foes.

The attackers were well-trained, and their teamwork was superb. Conrad kept them corralled away from Elisa and Lily, but the attackers were pushing him to his limits. The fact that Lily had already defeated several foes was a testament to her skill and her grace under pressure.

Ryne drew a deep breath and stepped forward into the attackers' line of sight. With his magically enhanced Voice, he commanded the foes, "*Sleep!*"

One dropped immediately, face forward into the bath. The other blinked and appeared to be stunned, but he did not stay that way for long. Conrad's sword parted the man's head from his shoulders. With a smooth follow-through action, the centaur grabbed and restrained the last living, unconscious opponent. "I'll secure him, boss!" stated Conrad.

With the scene secure and the opponents defeated, Ryne was finally able to turn his full attention to Elisa and Lily. Lily was desperately trying to heal the princess, even though the knight was on death's door herself. The prince moved to assist Lily. He stopped feeding his mana into the water—this form of healing was not precise enough to further aid the women.

Several crossbow bolts were embedded in Elisa's body. As the prince watched, Lily used magic to extract the quarrel lodged in Elisa's chest, precisely where the princess's heart was. The wickedly barbed bolt was designed to shred flesh, then shatter upon hitting bone, leaving multiple fragments within a gruesome wound. Fortunately, Lily was a combat medic and experienced in dealing with aggravated wounds beyond the capabilities of most healers. The knight removed the bolt along with its detached pieces, then separately cast healing magic to stabilize the wound even as she began removing the next quarrel.

The prince did not dare interrupt the carefully balanced surgery and healing that Lily was performing. Ryne instead examined the discarded bolt. It was an instrument of assassination for unarmored targets. Even moderate armor would have prevented penetration. The attackers were tracking Elisa precisely enough to know that she was highly vulnerable, and they had used weapons created to exploit that knowledge.

The design of the bolt seemed familiar to Ryne, but he was unable to recall the correct memory. He would explore further when he had time. The prince carefully stored the quarrel, then turned his attention back to Lily. She had finished removing the final bolt and amplified her magic to focus on healing Elisa. The knight was struggling as her own wounds took a toll on her.

Ryne knelt next to Lily, who was cradling Elisa's limp body. He reached out to take the princess, but Lily refused him. "Lily, hand her to me. I'll help Elisa." The knight's response was to hold the princess's body even more tightly, silently rejecting the prince's request.

The prince grew desperate. Lily's healing had removed all the exterior wounds on Elisa's body, but the continued healing was no longer effective. Using his magically enhanced Voice, Ryne commanded, *"Healer, heal thyself!"* The compulsion was strong, and Lily no longer had the stamina to oppose Ryne. With tears streaming down her face, the knight began to focus her healing magic on herself.

Ryne carefully extracted the princess's body from Lily's arms, then stood and moved swiftly back to the changing room. He laid Elisa gently on the floor and took a few moments to slow his heart rate and calm his breathing. The magic he prepared to attempt required extreme focus. Unlike the brute-force healing that humans used, this elvish-taught magic required subtlety and finesse.

The prince began the spell. Combining gentle amounts of the four main elements, the magic began to move air in and out of the princess's lungs and forced blood to circulate through her body. Seconds passed, but the princess remained unresponsive. Ryne heard Lily enter the room and sit across from him, but he did not have any concentration to spare on her.

After several more seconds, Ryne reached out and placed his palm on Elisa's chest. An electrical charge left his body and entered hers. Her body spasmed in response. Lily gasped but did not intervene.

Petras arrived in the changing room, his labored breathing announcing his entrance. He passed a crystal vial into Ryne's outstretched hand. The dwarf then dropped to the floor next to Lily. He pulled the knight's upper body onto his lap, supporting her head and back with one strong arm. Lily began to pass out, but Petras successfully administered the potion. The golden liquid of the panacea touched her lips and tongue. The cure-all magic, worth a king's ransom, began to work immediately. The dwarf ensured that she drank every drop.

As the panacea spread through Lily's body, both current wounds and old scars faded. Her pain abated, and her exhaustion was dispelled. The angry, discolored patches of skin near her wounds vanished as the poisons were eliminated. Her breathing calmed, and her eyes closed in gentle sleep.

Across the floor, Ryne mirrored Petras's actions by similarly pulling Elisa's body into his lap. He used his magic to continue circulating both air and blood. He opened the vial with one hand, then brought it to her lips. The princess's inert body was incapable of swallowing, so Ryne used the magic to flow the golden liquid down her throat and into her stomach.

Seconds turned into minutes, but Ryne's magic only gave Elisa the appearance of life. At some point, William entered the room, but the prince scarcely noticed. Ryne continued giving shocks to Elisa's heart every minute, but nothing changed.

"Ryne," said a familiar voice at the edge of the prince's awareness.

"Prince Ryne!" the voice repeated.

Ignoring all else but the princess, Ryne pulled her tiny body to his chest as his tears began to flow. His skills and magics had failed him. The panacea only worked on the living, and Ryne's elven-taught magic only worked on people who were not too far gone. He had lost his soon-to-be bride to an unseen enemy, perhaps the same vile being who had killed his first family.

William sat nose-to-nose with Ryne as he tried to break the prince's stupor. The elf's voice was having no effect, so he resorted to violence. William slapped the prince hard across the face.

Ryne blinked, but his eyes did not focus.

William repeated the slap, yelling, "RYNE, COME BACK TO ME!"

This time, the prince caught his breath, blinked a few times, and then gave William a puzzled look.

Seeing that he had Ryne's attention, William continued speaking in a loud, clear voice. "Ryne, you need to look at her back. Hand her to me. Look at her back!"

Ryne did as William commanded. The prince handed the princess's body to William, and then he focused on the princess's bare back. His mind struggled to understand what he was seeing.

Two sets of magical inscriptions were visible on Elisa's back, one set layered upon the other. The top layer was large and crude, whereas the bottom layer was small, precise, and dense. The magic from the underlayer was providing illumination, thereby causing both sets to be visible.

The small, precise writing of the underlayer seemed familiar to Ryne. His memory was muddled, but he soon placed the writing. "Sarai?" the prince asked.

"Yes, I think so," replied William with barely contained excitement. "Elisa's aunt gave her one final gift—single-use resurrection magic. Can you read the innermost inscription?"

With his hope renewed, Ryne read the first line of the inscription aloud. "Don't let me die here. There must be something more. Bring me back to LIFE." At the center of the inscription, there was a pentacle—a five-pointed star within a circle.

Ryne looked at the inscription with a sense of awe. Resurrection magic was the stuff of myth and legend. There were magical ways to postpone dying and escape Death, but returning directly from his realm was exceedingly rare. That Sarai had gone to such lengths to protect the princess proved both the unsurpassed skill of the Witch of Taronto and her deep love for her niece, Elisa.

"The inscription gathers mana from the environment to auto-initiate the resurrection. However, that will take a while. If we feed it our own mana, we may start the process now," said William.

"I'll do it. I want her return to life to be in my arms," said the prince confidently.

As Edmund entered the room, he commented, "How very romantic, but the princess might not appreciate waking up naked in front of so many people." He took clean robes from a cabinet—one for Elisa and the other for Lily—and handed them to Ryne and Petras respectively.

"Good point!" replied Ryne. "Team, until we know our enemy, we're moving into the bunker next to my office. Petras, you and Edmund move Lily to the bunkroom. William and I will be there soon with Elisa."

"I'll recall Owen and Runera posthaste. What about Mizu?" asked Edmund.

The prince thought for a moment. "I need Mizu to stay with Prince Miller for now. Please let all three know what has transpired."

"Will do," answered Edmund as he left the dressing room. Petras and Edmund soon followed, using a bench as a makeshift stretcher to carry the sleeping Lily.

"Conrad, how are you doing in there?" asked the prince.

"One secured prisoner and eight dead attackers. All male humans, dressed in black clothing and high-quality, flexible armor. Their weapons are very well made with no maker marks. No distinguishing tattoos on the men, at least none that I can see without magic."

William gave the next set of orders. "Move the prisoner to the dungeon and keep him under watch with at least two squads of soldiers. The mage who formed the spatial gate had a way to track the princess's location even through our wards. He may try to retrieve the prisoner. Also, please have our soldiers remove the dead from the bath and burn the remains outside the city."

"Roger, Will-i-am," replied the centaur.

"I'll be along shortly to conduct the interrogation personally. Please ensure that none of the guards are squeamish." The cold, hard look in William's eyes contained no mercy.

"Understood," said Conrad as he left the room.

Now that they were alone, Ryne and William turned their attention back to the princess. William dressed her in the robe, but he put it on her backwards with the opening in the back. Ryne would need to touch the pentacle to transfer his mana.

William had a mildly startled look on his face when he completed dressing the body. In answer to Ryne's questioning gaze, the elf replied, "Just triggered a past life memory. Thin gowns used on patients in places of healing. The gowns protected the patient's modesty but did nothing against the cold of the building. Oh well, to the task at hand. Are you ready to begin?"

"I am," replied the prince.

"Place your fingertips on the pentacle and start transferring your mana. Begin with just a trickle," explained William.

Ryne did as he was instructed while using his other arm to hold the body. As seconds passed, he grew more impatient, but he fought the urge to rush the process.

William was seated on the floor, holding Elisa's wrists in his hands. He was monitoring the flow of mana as it filled the resurrection inscription. "You are doing great, Ryne. I know you are anxious, but keep the flow slow and steady. The ritual could take at least an hour, and we may be in for some surprises. Regardless of what happens, keep the mana flow just like it is right now."

"What kind of surprises?" asked the prince.

William explained, "The bolts the assassins used bore a very toxic poison. Whoever ordered Elisa's assassination wanted her to die quickly and without hope of revival. That is why your resuscitation magic was unsuccessful. However, our foe is unaware of Sarai's inscriptions. Sarai's magic is more powerful, and even more importantly, the resurrection magic existed before the princess was injured.

"As for the surprises, your resuscitation magic spread the poison throughout Elisa. But it also spread the panacea. The princess's body is going to be a battleground between a human-made poison and an elf-made cure-all. My money is on elven magic, every time."

"Well, you are kind of biased," taunted the prince.

"For good reason, and you know it," responded William.

The two men became quiet, focusing their attention solely on the ritual magic, speaking only when necessary. As William had guessed, the princess's resurrection was not a peaceful event. Twenty minutes into the ritual, the princess began to move on her own. While not conscious, her struggles showed her desire to live. Three times, Elisa's body almost succumbed, but her willpower was strong, and she fought through the pain and trauma.

Just shy of an hour after the ritual began, Elisa opened her eyes and gazed at the prince's face above her. Even with his eyes bloodshot from tears and his face covered with dried blood, Ryne was the most beautiful sight that Elisa had ever seen.

"Welcome home," the prince said in a voice filled with emotion.

"I'm back," replied the princess.

Within three hours of the attack, William had traced the other end of the magical gate to a mountain cabin an hour outside Auraria. Finding the location had been difficult, as the unknown mage hid his magical signatures well. However, the combination of the prisoner's interrogation and some tracking magic on Ryne's missing sword provided the clues the elf needed.

William arrived at the cabin to find it deserted except for the corpses of two black-clad attackers. Ryne's sword was still buried in one man's chest. The other man was missing his head, having carried the flash-bang grenade through the portal. The flash-bang must have had a direct effect on the mage, as scraps of burnt cloth were scattered across the floor. William gathered the clothing scraps but left the sword, fearing it might now be booby-trapped.

While Elisa and Lily continued to recover, the rest of Ryne's team was very busy over the next two days. Edmund and Petras coordinated improvements to the fortress and city defenses, while Conrad led increased patrols around Auraria. Ryne and William's activities were more secretive, but they were clearly consulting with a wide range of people, including Mizu, Willow, Ryne's brother Nevan, and Ryne's father, King Balder of Vorland.

Elisa and Lily were allowed to move between the bunkroom and Ryne's office, but two of the other team members were guarding them at all times. Elisa chafed under the constant attention, but Lily was thankful for it. The knight was not ready to resume her guard duties.

Owen and Runera arrived in Auraria late at night on the second day following the attack. They had taken only a small escort to make their travel time shorter.

The next morning, all available members of Ryne's team met in his office. The mood in the room was very different than the last meeting before the attack. The normally jovial prince was thoughtful and focused, and the air was tense with anticipation. Ryne sat with Elisa close beside him, one of his arms protectively surrounding her.

Of course, with Conrad present, a joke was never far away. "Feeling a little overly protective, Your Highness?" taunted the centaur.

"No, just the right amount of protective. Got a problem with it, horse-boy?" asked the prince.

"Not at all. Heck, I was just thinking the princess looked pretty good for having been recently deceased," replied Conrad.

Elisa sneered at the centaur. "Sweetie, I always look good." She held her smile for a moment, then started to laugh. "I love being among the living, even if I have to put up with you," she teased Conrad.

The others joined with mild laughter, and the mood in the room lightened. The meeting was ready to begin.

The prince began to speak. "Before we get started, I need to dispel some rumors. We're not immediately marching on Taronto to demand King Logan's head. I know this may disappoint some of you, but Llanos faces enemies on every border. Whether Logan dies from a single cut or a thousand, it matters not to me. His eventual destruction is assured.

"Our more immediate problem is the unknown mage who is responsible for the recent attack on the princess. This mage has a way to track Elisa that pierces all our obfuscation magic and defensive wards. Furthermore, I recognize the design of the crossbow bolts used during the attack. Whether we have a mole within our ranks or merely some planted evidence to sow dissension, I cannot say for now.

"Tomorrow, Elisa and I are headed to Leilani to solicit Willow's help. Lily and William will accompany us. We believe this mage is responsible for the attack on Viverna and that he or she supplied the human bombs that General Johnson detonated on Elisa's escort on the way to Golden." The prince's voice grew angrier as he spoke. "Given the nature of the monster horde at Viverna, I now believe this unknown mage also summoned the horde that destroyed Auraria and my family. We are going to find this mage and end them."

Ryne's voice was raw with pain and fury, and he took a moment to calm himself. "We have freed Auraria of the monsters' grip, and yet this city remains unsafe for us. We are going to make some major changes. I had planned to accelerate Turicum's timeline, with the founding of the city to occur the spring of the year after next, five seasons from now. With these recent events, my new plan is to open Turicum during the spring of this next year, twenty weeks from now."

The room was quiet as the team members absorbed the information. Elisa and William knew the change ahead of time, so they kept their thoughts to themselves. The audacity of the prince's plan was beyond crazy. Ryne was asking for the impossible.

Edmund, as majordomo for Ryne, was used to impossible requests. "Let's put aside for a moment whether we can accomplish this new goal. Why do we need to accomplish it? Why do we need Turicum so soon?"

The prince responded, "King Logan of Llanos is our enemy. He is opposed by Prince Miller, Elisa's father. If Vorland openly supports Miller, then we risk backlash from Logan if he wins the stalemate. However, if we were to buy from Miller a particularly nice piece of land in southeast Llanos, well, that would just be a business transaction. If Miller decides to use the payment to finance his war against Logan, that is his choice."

Runera asked, "If Logan wins, won't he move against us as we are building Turicum?"

Owen, Ryne's field commander, addressed this concern. "Whoever wins the stalemate will be busy for a while. We expect the surviving Llanos government to be significantly weakened. Llanos is a nation of riches with many neighbors. We are expecting many, if not all, of its neighbors to attack Llanos beginning in the spring. Llanos is still powerful, but it cannot fight so many fronts at the same time. By next winter, I would expect Taronto to still be standing, but the borders of Llanos will have receded significantly."

"Vorland neighbors Llanos on the east. Will Vorland consume its share?" asked Lily.

The prince said, "In a word, yes. Father and my brothers are already planning their move. However, I think we have developed a plan that will stay their hand. In exchange for a stand-down with Prince Miller's forces, I will renounce my position as a Prince of Vorland, and I will cede Auraria."

"Are you daft, Ryne? We've just spent the last three years reclaiming your home from the monsters and rebuilding the place!" shouted Petras.

William laughed. "You are right, my friend. Our leader is crazy...crazy like a fox. We've built up the equipment and personnel that we need to create the city of Turicum. We've been training the skills we need for the last three years..."

Petras said, "I understand what you are saying, lad, but you are asking a dwarf to abandon a project to start another one. I hate leaving things unfinished."

William responded in a teasing manner, "True, Petras, but the new project is not about rebuilding broken structures. It's about starting something completely new. You get to design from scratch..."

Petras's eyes were starting to defocus as he began to think.

"Make things the way you want them to be..." He began to smile. "Make them the right way—okay, I'm in," announced the dwarf.

Lily's eyes grew big at Petras's abrupt change of mind.

Petras stated, "The boy knows my weaknesses. I'll be the first dwarf in a hundred years to construct a city from scratch. That makes me...happy."

Lily thought the dwarf was more than just a little happy.

Ryne continued, "Turning back to the question—why do we need Turicum now? I want to take advantage of Logan's mistake. His actions forced the Trade Hub to shut down in Taronto. I want to move the Trade Hub and the Merchants Guild headquarters to Turicum. We need to make this happen now, while Llanos is still divided."

Edmund thought for a moment before speaking. "The nations of this continent have lost faith in Taronto as a secure, neutral site for the Trade Hub. You are suggesting we provide an alternative site before someone else can. Hence, the reason for the urgency of Turicum."

"Well said, Edmund," replied Elisa. "There is also the possible complication of my father winning the stalemate. He will not take kindly to losing a major source of income for his country. But as things stand now, he is in no position to oppose us."

"How goes the stalemate? Are there indications of which faction will win?" asked Runera.

William answered these questions. "The ongoing stalemate in Llanos between the self-appointed King Logan and his brother Prince Miller has locked down the city of Taronto. The Merchants Guild's Trade Hub closed early for the season, as the security of the participants cannot be guaranteed. This early closing is particularly harsh, as there is a late-season rush of negotiations between traders that always occurs before the Hub formally closes for winter.

"The general consensus is that Prince Miller would be a better leader for Trade Hub's reopening, but who will win the stalemate remains uncertain. Miller has more popular support, but Logan's recent pruning of opposing nobles has left his faction in better shape—"

"Pruning? That is quite the euphemism," interrupted Elisa.

"Compared to Albrun's annihilation of the Thornhill family, *pruning* sounds reasonable," commented Ryne.

"Touché," acknowledged Elisa.

William resumed his overview. "The royal guard supports the crown, which is currently held by Logan. The army of Llanos has not taken sides yet, despite the manipulations of the recently appointed General Johnson. Whoever gets the support of the army will be the clear favorite. If the army splits along factional lines, which is expected if the situation continues, then Llanos will descend into civil war."

"So, Miller needs our support, but it comes at a price. Why would he negotiate?" asked Petras.

Ryne answered, "If Prince Miller makes a deal with us, it will secure the southern and eastern borders of his duchy. Granted, his land will shrink, but what remains will be easier for his personal troops to maintain. If he becomes king, he can focus on the other borders of Llanos. As for what we will trade—he needs portable wealth. King Logan controls the Llanos treasury and can outlast Miller. If we give Miller a strong monetary infusion, he will stand a better chance against his brother."

"Buying part of a kingdom sounds expensive. How will you afford it?" asked Lily.

Edmund said, "I can answer this one. Monster subjugation is very, very lucrative. Ryne's team has been quite successful over the last three years."

"How lucrative?" asked Elisa.

"Before you get an answer, the team needs to know your views on your father and your loyalty to him," stated Ryne.

"I wish him, my mother, and my brothers well, but let's be honest. They did not save me when Logan tried to kill me. They did not raise me. My loyalty is reserved for those who help me: once, just Lily and Sarai, and now, the rest of you. My father is in a tough spot. I'll happily negotiate with him." Elisa's smile did not reach her eyes.

Edmund wrote a number on a slip of paper. "This is the amount we can comfortably offer." The majordomo passed the slip to the princess.

Elisa looked at the number, then passed it back. She approached the map of Llanos on the wall, gesturing as she spoke. "With that much money, we could get a swath of land a hundred kilometers wide from the border at Viverna southwest to the Osman Empire. If I push, I can go for less cost or more land. What would you prefer?"

"Less expense. That tract of land is plenty big for our needs," answered Ryne. "This land will be our new nation, independent of Llanos, Vorland, and everyone else. It will be our 'Switzerland,' as Albrun calls it."

"Do you have a name for your new country?" asked Owen.

"Saman," said Ryne.

Princess Elisa smiled. "That means 'together' in Elvish. I like it."

"All right, we understand the urgency. Let us assume we make a deal with Miller. What happens next?" asked William.

Elisa answered, "Our first priority is establishing the Trade Hub. If it does not open in the spring, it would severely impact the free-flowing trade that has existed for centuries. The Trade Hub operates despite disagreements and wars between countries. If the tradition of the independent Trade Hub was broken, restarting it might be impossible."

"So, by the beginning of spring, we need a secure location, free of monsters and bandits, and the infrastructure needed to host the traveling merchants from the Merchants Guild. We cannot form a city in time, but we might use Elisa's wall-forming magic to create defensive barriers and some of the buildings. At least enough to show the Merchants Guild that we have a serious plan for rebuilding the Trade Hub on neutral ground," commented William.

Ryne's team continued to plan and debate for the rest of the day, breaking only for meals. Edmund's role was to document the actionable items on a large chalkboard. Fortunately, his handwriting was immaculate, as the board soon filled with dates, priorities, and resources.

Surveying the board after several hours' discussion, William spoke. "Ryne, I'll be the bad guy and speak up for everyone. You are asking us to do the impossible with the resources we have."

The prince replied, "You are correct, William. Here is where some major changes come into play." Ryne turned to face the centaur. "Conrad, are you ready to fight for leadership of the herds?"

The centaur smirked. "I'm no longer the weakling troublemaker that got thrown out years ago. I'll fight for supremacy over the winter and deliver the centaur herds to your land by the beginning of spring." Conrad brimmed with confidence.

"Well, don't you look manly?" teased Runera.

Conrad puffed out his chest and struck a heroic pose. "I like being the centaur of attention."

A chorus of groans filled the room. Elisa was kind enough to giggle.

Ryne cleared his throat to bring the meeting back to order. "Runera, Petras, are you willing to call your tribes? We make a home for them in Turicum."

Runera replied, "There are plenty of humans who do not want to live beside demihumans."

The prince laughed, "Those humans aren't invited. Their loss."

"Then expect a few dozen halflings before spring."

Petras replied, "As for the dwarves, once I tell them our plan, we can expect them before year's end."

The prince answered, "Thank you, my friends. Now, for the last major and most important change. I'm going to renegotiate my agreement with Willow."

Lily did not understand what Ryne meant, but there were several sharp intakes of breath in the room.

Edmund asked, "Ryne, are you sure that is wise?"

The prince exhaled loudly and said, "I'm sure that it is not. However, we need to take advantage of our enemy's weakness. We cannot succeed without help from the elves."

Owen looked at William. "Do you know what concessions Willow will demand?"

William stayed quiet and motionless, unwilling to answer the question.

Ryne said, "I'll deal with Willow's demands, same as I did the first time. We will know the price of her help in just a few days. If we secure elven assistance, we will begin our plans in earnest."

The mood had grown somber. The team took a break for a snack, then returned to work. As they began to wind down sometime after midnight, Ryne poured drinks for everyone and then spoke.

"Team, I know I am asking the impossible, but we have a once-in-a-lifetime chance to move our goals forward and far more quickly than planned. This plan puts us at incredible risk, as many things must occur for us to succeed. We're casting aside the lives we made here in Auraria for a dream that may go unfulfilled. Please know I would not attempt such a crazy plan if I did not have friends like you. So, I toast to you, the enablers of my dreams. Cheers!" shouted the prince.

"Cheers!" the others replied, then drank.

"To Saman, the nation we will forge. Cheers!"

"Cheers!" More drinking.

"To Turicum, the city of dreams. Cheers!"

"Cheers!" More drinking.

"To bed, which is where I am headed. May the harsh morning light expose the flaws of our plans."

Laughter filled the room as they all headed for slumber.

THE END OF BOOK 1

TO BE CONTINUED IN BOOK 2

Acknowledgments

(It takes a village ...)

Map and interior artwork: Sarah Kay Stephens

Developmental editing and proofreading: BE Allatt

Atmosphere Press and its staff, particularly Art Director Ronaldo Alves, Erin Larson for her proofreading, and Managing Editor Alex Kale.

About Atmosphere Press

Founded in 2015, Atmosphere Press was built on the principles of Honesty, Transparency, Professionalism, Kindness, and Making Your Book Awesome. As an ethical and author-friendly hybrid press, we stay true to that founding mission today.

If you're a reader, enter our giveaway for a free book here:

SCAN TO ENTER
BOOK GIVEAWAY

If you're a writer, submit your manuscript for consideration here:

SCAN TO SUBMIT
MANUSCRIPT

And always feel free to visit Atmosphere Press and our authors online at atmospherepress.com. See you there soon!

About the Author

Tab Stephens is a first-time novelist who lives in central Texas with his wife, Keri, a professor at the University of Texas–Austin. While his Ph.D. in Materials Science from Caltech is quite useful for his day job, he now wishes he had taken writing classes back in college. Thank goodness for editors!

Combining their love of breakfast tacos with a desire to write together, Tab and Keri started frequenting the covered porch of a local BBQ restaurant. While she worked on her academic papers, he explored his creative side. Tab found the process to be both challenging and rewarding.

Tab enjoys cats, anime, fantasy, science fiction, and stand-up personal watercraft.

He is the second person in his family to purchase a retired metal railroad caboose.

For more information, please visit:
tabstephens.com